"Ms. Beryl, will you  deep voice was all of a su now that I had time to thi enough in company m conferences.

It would be my luck that the one drone having issues would be my boss doing an impromptu screen check of the services and how his drones were performing. Such an overachiever, and much too sexy of a voice to have to listen to him firing me when he made it up the elevator.

"Of course, sir. I'll just finish up this diagnostic screening and transfer my overlays." I tried to sound all official, like nothing was wrong, because there was still a chance. Even if it was a small one, that maybe he was too preoccupied. That was a big maybe and, given his attention to detail, highly unlikely.

"No need. I've already finished transferring your data."

Shit. That was not promising.

"Please head straight there. I won't be long." The calming chime noises of the door closing on the drone signaled the conversation was over. And just like he said, all of my drones in my sector blinked, disappearing from my overlay viewer.

Game over.

I was no longer the one in charge of monitoring them.

# Kingdom of Acatalec

by

## S.M. McCoy

*The Acatalec Series, Book 1*

**Kingdom of Acatalec**

Cover Art by *Lisa Dawn MacDonald*

The Wild Rose Press, Inc.
PO Box 708
Adams Basin, NY 14410-0708
Visit us at www.thewildrosepress.com

Publishing History
First Edition, 2022
Trade Paperback ISBN 978-1-5092-4271-9
Digital ISBN 978-1-5092-4272-6


Published in the United States of America

## Dedication

We find freedom in our pursuit of desires,
While our desires take control of our freedom.
To my fellow beings that strive to find the balance.

# Acknowledgments

It is with the support, tenacity, kindness, love, and accountability of:

my husband, and our motivational squad of tiny human progenies;

my mother for wrangling the offspring and always reading every version of my books from first draft to abandoned product; my mother-in-law for supporting my dreams by watching the kids during my writing time; my sisters for keeping my writing spirits high; my papa for bragging about my writing accomplishments before I even felt accomplished;

my friend, Tom, for helping maintain my website, keeping me accountable to my goals, and listening to me ramble about my dreams;

my editor, Ally Robertson, for believing in my work and helping me take my writing to the next level.

and to all the readers who have joined me on this fantastic journey, without you, I'd be alone talking to the characters in my head.

Thank you for reading.

Chapter One

*Drone Pilot*

How was it possible that all the local drones were with passengers already, or still returning from a drop off? It wasn't. Any attempts at hailing one within the next five minutes would be near impossible, and the only reasonable explanation was… Jessi, the bane of my work life, thought it would be hilarious to make sure every drone nearby was redirected to other locations. Rushing out the door with a bagel hanging from my teeth, I had minutes before being late to work. I didn't have those precious minutes to spare.

Typical.

It wasn't like she wasn't on the boss's good side. Second best drone pilot in our sector, she always rubbed her customer ratings in my face every chance she got.

She wasn't a complete monster.

I knew she'd only delay my request by the few minutes I needed to avoid being tardy. To keep her off my back I resorted to desperate measures, or risk losing my job, which wasn't necessarily illegal, but it wasn't *not* illegal either. Though, if Mr. Azel knew what I was doing, I'd probably have lost my job long before now.

And that was exactly what Jesse wanted to have happen.

Quickly, I tapped into my NeuralGo, which was second nature and as easy as blinking since I'd had mine installed at the time of my accident. Most don't get theirs so early, considering brains weren't fully matured until twenty-five, but I was a special case, and it was probably why it was so easy to use. Because my brain grew-up with it.

Pulling up my work's designated drone airspace, D.D.A., I found the closest drone was only one minute away heading right past my home. The NeuralGo connected to my contacts through RedTech, and I haven't needed the keyboard on an overlay display to enter data since I was sixteen. This was easier than deciding whether I should or shouldn't eat the last cookie in the box. No one wants only one cookie later, so it's better to let it mingle with its friends in my stomach.

Intercepting the destination, I plugged in the new coordinates. My contacts flashed red, letting me know the authorization protocols had triggered. Entering in my password, I logged in my credentials: *Pilot officer class A*. Link to on-route drone connected, and rerouting to my location.

Guilt made me cringe and to ease that little demon I made sure to setup the programming so that as soon as I was dropped off it would go back to its original pickup. Adding a few upgrades to their service, and a small credit as compensation for their extra wait time. Who would complain about that? They probably wouldn't even notice the few minutes delay, with how glued most people were to their social media. Every time I ever went out, they all looked like zombies staring off into space, but really just surfing the linked-up interface in their contacts.

The drone landed in front of my apartment building and the wind drafted through my hair. If it weren't already messy, it would've been then. I would have had a slower descent for a normal passenger, but I was in a hurry, and there was no time to waste. Kelly, my best friend ever since I temporarily borrowed her family's drone without permission, would probably be clucking her tongue at me right now in disappointment with how I left the house in what she would consider rags.

Tossing out of bed last minute did have its advantages. I smirked thinking about my best friend Kelly's reaction if she saw me disheveled like this. I'll let her act appalled later in our video chat, when I describe what I deigned appropriate to wear to work today. Wrinkles were my new best friend today. I'd have to tell Kelly she'd been replaced.

I didn't wait for the ramp to assist me. Before the elevating hatch even finished lifting on the transport, I popped a wheelie, which was the first thing I tried to learn how to do when I was eight, and then used the handlebar assist to pull me and my extra weighted equipment into the drone. Rapid-fire pressing the close-door function as soon as I was in helped soothe my anxiety. I knew it did nothing to really speed it up, but it was something to occupy the seconds, so it wasn't a complete waste. Letting my fingers pound out some nervous energy was the least I could do.

Once inside, I connected to the panel in front of me and bypassed the auto function, pulling out my manual joysticks. Now these suckers were off market; I had to spend a diamond worth of credits on these, all in the spirit of illegally hacking commercial passenger drones for manual flight.

Not that the joysticks themselves were what controlled the drones. It was the chip inside that held manual function code and security breaches. The joysticks housing the chip just made it easier for the link in the NeuralGo to process my intentions, plus made the whole experience a little more tactile. I never understood why everything had to be so hands off these days, but in a pinch knowing I could do it without the joysticks was comforting, even if a little less enjoyable.

Lifted back in the air, I connected my overlay to my contacts with the current drone airfields, so I could track where I was in relation to other drones, and off we went. Bypassing the speed restrictions and maneuvering around other air traffic was no picnic, when traveling at these speeds. At least, for a normal person it would be terrifying.

For me, this was heaven, and it was over all too soon. Zipping up, through, around, and into the parking lot. In minutes I arrived at work, and the clock read: 7:58 a.m. My fastest time yet. I might actually clock in for work on time for once. I was really pushing my luck on having my pilot record outweigh my work ethic, but I did my job, and I'm pretty sure that's what counted.

Pushing the door open to speed up its slow ascent, I yanked out my joysticks shoving them into the hidden compartment under the legs of my chair, that should never see the light of day unless I had a wish to see the inside of a jail cell and snapped the panel back into place.

Preprogrammed to go back to its original destination before I commandeered it, I didn't have to worry about things as I turned off my speed restrictions on my chair to supercharge this baby out of the drone and through the automatic doors of this over-sized office tower. I took a moment to peek over my shoulder and confirmed that the transport was already lifting off and forgetting all about our short adventure together.

As I entered work, a green light flashed over me reading my authorizations to enter the building through my NeuralGo. Before I could even wheel up to my desk, the screeching voice of my prissy co-worker could be heard behind me, probably coming from the break room already.

"Are you ever on time?" Jessi groaned. "You know the rest of us have to pick up the slack when you're late. Eight a.m. is when the drones are supposed to be active, not when you're supposed to be at your desk. Here," she waved her hand at my cube with disgust, and a notification popped up on my interface, "These are the results from your sector's drone tests this morning... Or didn't you remember that we had an update last night."

"Thanks," I said reluctantly. I supposed I should have been more grateful that she came in early to run the tests on my sector, but it was hard to even smile at her. This was honestly the nicest she had ever been to me.

"These should be good to go," she said arrogantly. "Maybe next time you should come in earlier for software updates." It was only a matter of time before that girl got me fired, but really who was I kidding. I would be the reason why I got fired. Being on time wasn't my strong suit, but I was the best drone pilot in the business. My boss valued my skills more than my timeliness, and even Jessi knew that, though against her nature to admit it.

Most employees at Zeiten Drone Transportation had to be here earlier, but I tended to take advantage of the disability leeway that was given to me. Extra time to get to work didn't seem to help me much. Sleeping in seemed like a better use of that time.

The green light on my monitor scanned me before my computer turned on. A notification popped up showing that the software updates had been downloaded just like Jessi said. I really should've come in earlier to do the testing before the drones were swapped out and live. But, thanks to Jessi, I didn't have to. My computer then prompted me to confirm software testing was complete. I only had to think the word, cleared. My sectors drones were now live.

Jessi sauntered back to her seat, and I could see a clear gleam in her eyes. She smiled briefly before her eyes met mine and it turned into a scowl.

If it weren't for me, she'd be considered the best drone pilot in this sector. Her resentment was clear on her face. It wasn't her fault that her reaction times weren't as fast as mine. She didn't have the history I had. Maybe if she was forced to plug into the neural networking at a young age, she'd be well past where I was in terms of integrating with the software. My brain had more time to create more pathways, it was as simply as that, and one of the reasons why I was so highly ranked within the company without actually having a title to show for it.

I brought up the traffic on my interface. Drone airspace always reminded me of the old school arcade game Frogger. All the many little dots representing the drones leaping in and out and zooming across the screens.

Being a drone pilot was pretty boring for commercial passenger drones, but the true skill and fun was in manual operation. That's when I truly felt alive behind the manual interfacing that linked you directly to the controls. Avoiding other drones, controlling the speed, and getting to your destination faster than any flight service could ever do. There were restrictions on how fast a drone could fly, because after a certain speed it's hard to control the airspace. But not for me. Instinct took over, and that's all that mattered. Those extra neural pathways made me feel like I was the drone. Like lifting a finger, chewing your food, or smiling.

It was all natural to me.

My screen lit up red.

One of the passenger drones was sending a distress signal. It was rare for there to be an issue on the job. This would be the most exciting my glorified observation appointment had been since I started working here five years ago.

Quickly, I manually entered the programming and discovered that the flight simulation that controlled the sensors did not download the new software appropriately. It wasn't reading the location signals of the other drones in the airspace, and it already picked up a passenger. It would collide with another drone if it didn't start communicating with the other drones in the sector.

But, more likely, it would collide with a building, because it's on-flight location was malfunctioning, and other drones still had collision avoidance. This shouldn't be happening, the new updates were only supposed to update valid air traffic locations, and any adjusted flight courses to different destinations. It was solely used to better the passenger's experience and make the service faster. The only way this could have happened was if there was an error in the download of new information. Maybe even a loose bit of hardware, that should have been caught during the… test run this morning.

The test run done by Jessi before I arrived. She would have seen that there was an issue with this drone before I sent it out for pickups. She may have hated me, but did she hate me enough to put a passenger in danger? There was no way. This would get me more than fired. It would put the whole company at risk. Zeiten Drone Transportation had a spotless record, and one incident like this due to human error, would defeat the whole slogan that the company was built on—safety guaranteed. No other drone service had been able to provide this level of security, and I wasn't about to ruin that reputation because of Jessi. I may have been ethically in the gray zone, but I had my pride.

Protocol would be to ground the flight and comp the passenger as another drone comes to finish the transport, but then the passenger would know there was a problem, and one review like that would be the end of my super boring, but well-paid career. I wouldn't get another drone pilot job anywhere, not even in the private sector, why would they hire someone with a reputation for not double checking the test flights after a download.

I wouldn't let her have the satisfaction.

Already mapping the flight course into my contact screen, I took a quick look around to make sure no one was paying any particular attention to me. They had their own screens to focus on, but it was still a risk. I pulled out my manual override joystick from the hidden compartment in my wheelchair's seat. This would have been considered the best part of my day, to manually drive the drones on the clock, but the whole thrill of it was short lived considering the drone wasn't empty, my cube mate Kline could see my illegal accessory at any moment, and I had to seamlessly transition to make sure it followed its path as if it were being automated.

"Good morning, this is Tyler from Zeiten Drone Transportation. I'd like to offer you the opportunity to earn a complimentary five-minute transport by filling out one of our surveys. Do you accept?" I tapped into the passenger's microphone feed to distract them from my manual adjustment. It would be slight, barely noticeable, since all I was doing was making small adjustments to the straight away, before the turnoff up ahead.

"Continue," the man's voice said in approval. It was an odd response, but I was too busy maneuvering for upcoming drones, and the pathway ahead to think too much on it. I mean, most people would say something more along the lines of a typical sure, yes, no, or something.

I eased over to adjust for an incoming drone passing by with upgraded speed, giving them the right of way on the airspace. This was normally an automated process, with all the drones communicating with one another about their locations, but not this drone, and not today. That's why the company had pilots on staff as puffed-up watch dogs, for the very, very rare occasion that we actually had to fly one ourselves. But that was rare, if at all, hence how depressingly boring and soul sucking being a pilot for a commercial passenger service was.

"Thank you. The survey will appear on your screen before the end of your trip, and the credits will show up on your account once completed. May the spirit of travel take you safely to your destination." I tried to be pleasant enough, saying the mandatory closing phrase after any communication with a passenger. I exited the communication before I could even hear if the person had a response, it didn't really matter, the likelihood of the person having said anything that required my involvement was too low of a probability to warrant keeping the line open, plus it's our policy to not eavesdrop. Privacy and all, less I'm connected to their comms the less likely I'll have to overhear anything I can't unhear, like that time Passenger Handy accidentally pressed the pilot assistance button while indecently indisposed. I can never unhear those noises, and I'll never be able to even hope to have that much fun in a passenger drone. Except maybe during a manual drone race. Those always did get me a little hot under the collar, but not quite the same way.

Lucky for me, the ride for the passenger was a fairly short one. Only five minutes, and at regular passenger speed, not upgraded which would have made my manual piloting a lot more obvious at those speeds. Finally, I put the drone on descent, and sent the survey to the drone.

The man decided to complete the survey, which was also not very common, since most people decided to say screw it and exit the drone immediately. I'd look at it later to see how much I'd fooled them into thinking I'm a perfect machine of transportation piloting safety, which would undoubtedly make this whole ordeal feel worth it. If anything, maybe I should be thanking Jessi for the impromptu opportunity to log some manual piloting hours.

Before exiting the drone, the passenger pressed the pilot communication button, also a rare occurrence.

"Thank you for completing the survey. Your credits will appear on your account shortly," I informed him, because I couldn't think of any other reason why the comm button would be initiated, since he'd already landed at his destination.

Speaking of destinations, I was too distracted with following the on-screen flight directions and drone location overlay on my contacts. The whole thing felt like an arcade game with higher stakes distracting me from noticing the final coordinates until it was flashing in front of my sight lines. In big green bold lettering: Zeiten Drone Transportation…

They were coming here. I'd just manually transported someone who worked here. Meaning that there was a higher probability that if they were a pilot like I was… then they could, if they were good at their job and paying attention, tell the difference between automated and manual. Though, I was hoping the short duration, and the distraction of the survey was enough to make sure the later didn't happen.

I mean, most pilots weren't really into manual operation like I was. They wanted the paycheck, and most of the time even in instances like this they could just push the code into the drone to have it descend and send another drone out. Their piloting education was mostly just a piece of paper that meant in a pinch they could, in theory, pilot a drone.

"Ms. Beryl, will you see me in my office?" The deep voice was all of a sudden much more recognizable now that I had time to think about it. I'd heard it often enough in company memos and quarterly video conferences.

It would be my luck that the one drone having issues would be my boss doing an impromptu screen check of the services and how his drones were performing. Such an overachiever, and much too sexy of a voice to have to listen to him firing me when he made it up the elevator.

"Of course, sir. I'll just finish up this diagnostic screening and transfer my overlays." I tried to sound all official, like nothing was wrong, because there was still a chance. Even if it was a small one, that maybe he was too preoccupied. That was a big maybe and, given his attention to detail, highly unlikely.

"No need. I've already finished transferring your data."

*Shit.* That was not promising.

"Please head straight there. I won't be long." The calming chime noises of the door closing on the drone signaled the conversation was over. And just like he said, all of my drones in my sector blinked, disappearing from my overlay viewer.

Game over.

I was no longer the one in charge of monitoring them.

My heart skipped, and the pit of my stomach churned that quickly eaten bagel in my belly like a day-old burrito. Lucky for me I didn't have to worry about keeping steady on my legs, I'm not sure they would have held me even if I had full use of them to begin with. The manual magnetized brake on my wheels clicked off, my NeuralGo seamlessly connecting.

Wheeling back and away from my desk, for me it was as simple as other people walking, but it didn't change the stares people gave me as I passed. I could see Jessi peek out from her cube, and the way she smiled made my blood chill. If I didn't suspect it already, that look confirmed it. She knew the testing had a drone with an invalid upload and made sure that I thought she'd already cleared the drones before I arrived.

I glared over my shoulder at her as the elevator came to greet me, and she merely shrugged as if to say, *I'm not the one who didn't check the report, I just ran it.* And she was right, which made me even more infuriated. I shouldn't have taken her word for anything. I should have scanned the report she gave me before initiating all the drones out for transport. I would have caught the error in the drone and sent it in for engineering to make sure everything was fine with the hardware. Even though she was a sneaking, conniving skank it *was* my fault that protocols weren't followed, and it was also my choice not to immediately ground the drone. I didn't have to like it though.

The doors closing behind me, I heard Jessi say, "It's about time."

Chapter Two

*Top Floor*

I opened my mouth for a retort, only to have the elevator doors shut. I didn't even know what I would have said, only that I would have liked the chance to see how witty I could have been. I'm sure I would have said something epic. I mean why not, considering I was probably being fired anyway.

Careful what you wish for, was what I should have said, because she knew deep down, I could ruin her career along with mine. She was after all just as responsible. They were her reports that I keyed in for approval to send out the drones on their runs. Her signature was all over that data. I could play innocent, I mean this was supposed to be a collaborative environment, I trusted her, I would say all too sweetly. If I could trust anyone in the company it should be the second-best drone pilot in all of Seattle. I grinned to myself evilly. Both at the thought that I would probably get away with it and secretly jab at her position simultaneously. I felt my heart sink, knowing full well I wouldn't do it. No matter how evil she was, I couldn't blacklist her whole career like that.

I mean I wouldn't... would I?

The elevator opened up to the top floor, and it wasn't anything like I expected. I didn't really know what I expected, possibly a receptionist, some corporate artwork, and some glass offices for the big honchos of the company.

That was not what I was walking into. The light between the elevator and the floor blinked green as I rolled over it and a female voice that sounded like a famous actress on that strange college humor TV series that I couldn't remember the name of said, "Would you like a beverage while you wait?"

"Uh, sure," I stammered. I mean, why not enjoy the high life while I was still here. And it certainly was grand. The top floor was huge, a penthouse for the rich and fabulous. It had a luxurious sitting area with a large wall screen surrounding it to make it seem like you were watching the waves at a secluded beach, but one I'd never seen before. Did he send out a drone to an unoccupied beach somewhere warm and tropical that'd never been touched by human feet just so he could 3D record the location and download it to his office? I mean, sure, if you're rich, bored, and entitled that sounded like it could have happened.

In the middle of the sandy serene scene, a pop up projected out and prompted me to connect with my contacts listing off the beverage options. My eyes grew wide at the selection. The most prominent of the options being an expensive glass of dessert wine, and why not have a sweet glass of liquid courage before being kicked in the ass out the door? At the very least I'd get a nice, delicious buzz to dull the reaction time, maybe coming out of this meeting with some of my dignity intact. Let myself wallow in misery of self-loathing when I got home.

A spout came out of a sliding compartment in the

wall above the beverage counter. Wine on tap, and automatic... now that was fancy. In the distance I could hear the faint sound of a cork being popped from a bottle, giving you the impression of freshly opened wine even though every glass was probably just as fresh with it being contained in an airtight spout system, but the ambiance was not wasted on me. I let out a sigh and wheeled up to the counter and picked one of the crystal glasses. Once I placed my glass under the nozzle it sloshed out like a tasty waterfall that I imagined sticking my face under like a wild animal. I didn't of course, but the image was enjoyable to think about, I even shook my head in the air in reverence to it, with a stupid grin plastered on my face before I heard a gruff voice clear its throat behind me.

I paused, took a deep gulp from my glass before setting it down. I spun my wheels around to face him, and gave him a big smile, hoping it hid my embarrassment. But who was I kidding, it was him, and those brown chocolate eyes were always so analytical. They saw everything. I'm pretty sure he had X-ray vision, like Superman's evil twin.

"A *Trockenbeerenauslese* shouldn't be wasted. Grab your glass and join me in my office." Even his voice was as smooth as the aftertaste still lingering on my lips. He didn't have to tell me twice. I grabbed that glass and held it in both my hands like a precious goblet made of the most expensive jewels that even a dragon would be envious of, because it was the last expensive thing I would probably ever touch. I had to savor every last drop, and every smooth, chill-filled touch of the glass. While his back was turned, I even lifted it to my lips and let my tongue play with the little drone shaped ice that floated in the liquid. I mean, even his ice cubes were special.

I didn't really know which part of this massive floor was his office since it appeared to be a living space, until I saw a chair lift up from the floor in front of us. The glass windows around us became opaque and a folder with my name on it appeared on the screen. I could imagine this file taking up more data storage than the average employee with all of my late clock ins, and even bigger file if they knew about my after-hours activities.

Good Lord, not being able to stand had my eyes straight drinking in the full view of his finely tailored pants, and that wasn't even the after-hours activities I was thinking about previously, but now it most certainly was.

I cleared my throat to change the spiral I was heading into. I took another swig of the wine, staring into the crimson liquid when I was done. When I finally lifted my gaze slowly, determined to enjoy my glass of last-ho-rah, he was seated in the chair, his eyes intently examining me. I shifted uncomfortably in my chair and smoothed out a wrinkle on my pants. The whole wardrobe was full of wrinkles, even the one I smoothed out clung back into its original crease when I lifted my fingers.

If I'd known I was going to be coming up to the top floor with Mr. Perfect, I might have decided to at least throw my stuff into the dryer for a few minutes to dampen the whole washed-up-to-shore look I was gunning for.

But if I'd done that I would have been late, and honestly, that might have been better since Jessi would have been forced to finish the update acceptance on her own, and the drone would have gone to engineering. A late marker would have been preferable to what I assumed was coming.

I lifted my free hand, about to pull on my hair to try to tame some of my unruly mane but thought better of it. I mean, it was what it was at this point. The more I tried to make myself presentable, the more I would bring unwanted attention, and I decided I'd just own up to it. I was a mess, and shrugging I thought to myself, I preferred it that way.

Who was he, in his designer clothes, to change that? Oh yah... my boss for the next couple minutes anyways.

He finally motioned to the screen and my file opened up like it was real printed paper, but with all the papers inside having unreadable, blurry writing.

"Ms. Beryl, what do you think I'd find in this file?" he asked, but his eyes never wavered from me. Switching my attention from the screen back to him, I shouldn't have strayed back to him, his expression was much too similar to the file... unreadable.

Was I in trouble? Did he know I manually flew his transport drone, or that I should have grounded it as soon as I found out it had a malfunction? Did he think I was just joyriding on the company credit?

They all varied in degrees of consequence, none great, but some better than the truth.

I opened my mouth, then closed it. I was about to confess everything, because that's what being around him made me want to do. Every bone in my body ached to just unleash all of my problems to him, unburden myself.

I blinked several times to stop that stupid train of thought, how dumb did he think I was? That would be tantamount to quitting, and as much as I hated how boring this job was, I only needed to work here long enough to qualify for a private piloting license. As soon as I had that, I could leave, and actually feel the speed of a drone, fly in private airspace, do tricks, and utterly enjoy all the possibilities without as much restrictions as passenger drones.

Convincing my boss that I'm worth the risk of keeping on, despite my poor choices on which company policies I followed, seemed impossible. But I could perform in the Skylark Drone Parade or even be the star in the Seattle Technology Fair to show off new features, anything, to keep my job.

"Glowing reviews?" I joked, knowing I may not be the best at customer service interactions. I could almost see a smile at the corner of his mouth before it disappeared. At the very least, if he fired me, I might be able to convince him not to say *why* I was fired to future employers.

Maybe I could get a job in packaging delivery services for a while? An even shittier job, for the worst of the drone pilots in the business. I mean those things pretty much ran themselves, and the companies made the drones so cheap that they could care less about one breaking down and crashing into a fiery pit of disaster. Really, all the pilots were there for was to make sure that, if they did fail, they landed somewhere it caused the least amount of damages to surrounding things, avoiding a building, or a person walking on the street. Bonus, if the package the drone was carrying landed safely enough not to be damaged, so that another drone could go pick it up and complete the delivery. Please, don't fire me. Might as well fall to my death now.

The awkward silence building between us was making me more nervous. Like a bandage I wanted him to rip it off and tell me what I needed to explain myself out of to keep this job.

"It's a good thing we have preprogrammed A.I. for most customer needs, though you weren't all that unpleasant earlier today." His silky voice made even my shortcomings seem like a compliment. I wasn't *unpleasant*, and the way he said it, I found myself blushing at my almost, but not quite, pleasant nature. Tell me how not unpleasant I am again, was what I wanted to say, but of course bit the inside of my lip instead to prevent any more embarrassment.

I doubted any of that talk would help me keep my job, but if it did then I'd be screwed, because I didn't think I could bring myself to act like a smitten dum-dum in front of someone so annoyingly perfect, too much of a power grab. And not even one I could pull off successfully. Got to keep the little dignity I had to be able to wheel myself out of here after it was all said and done.

"I'll try to keep that in mind next time I offer a survey. On the bright side, one less survey to give out to meet my quota." If there was even a next time. I tried to keep my best poker face on, the same one I used when I wanted to fool my mom into thinking our communication was broken. I had enough listening to her complain about when I'd get out of the house, and meet 'people'. If only she knew what I did when I *got* out of the house to make some extra credits.

"When not responding to my personal drone, feel

free to utilize the automated A.I. for your survey quotas." He paused to let that sink in. I had future surveys to complete, meaning I still had my job. He didn't check the reports in my sector yet, I still had some time. "What are your goals at Zeiten, Ms. Beryl?"

Relieved, I turned my attention away from those chocolatey eyes of his to gulp down an obscene amount of wine to steady my nerves. I didn't even get to enjoy the flavor, but I couldn't keep holding the glass in my hands anymore. My hands were sweating, and I feared I'd either let the expensive crystal slip and shattered on the floor any second, or even worse, crush it between my fingers with a single nervous twitch when trying not to let it slide out of my grasp. Coughing on the sudden intake of wine, I wiped my lips, and as gently as I could set the glass down on the small table holding a house plant. I nearly shoved the thing into the plant itself, just to hide it, but he was watching me.

"Well, I would like to advance to a position that can utilize my piloting skills more regularly. Eventually, that is," I didn't want to sound greedy for a promotion when moments before I thought I was going to be fired, "It's just that you know, I know those positions don't open up regularly. So, I can wait, that is, it would be nice eventually to transition to the adventure side of the business. You know, like a maybe help out as an event pilot for tourists and thrill seekers when someone goes on vacation?" I quickly add, "No rush or anything. I don't dislike my job," I tried to clarify that this wasn't a dissatisfaction of my current job, because I really couldn't afford to lose it, but really… who would be satisfied with this job? But he didn't need to know that, right?

I can't believe I even told him about my dream of being an event pilot. Seconds ago, I thought I was being fired, and I had the nerve to pretty much say I wanted to be promoted. What was I thinking?

Those damned eyes kept sucking out my secrets, if he didn't stop staring at me, I'd probably start blabbing about how attractive I found him, especially in those fitted slacks. Why couldn't there be a desk in front of him so I didn't just let my eyes wander all over his sleek muscles?

I mean, he wasn't like ripped or anything, but definitely toned. Who was I kidding, he had to work out for that, I just really wanted to say something about him that wasn't absolutely everything a girl could ask for. All I had was, maybe he could have been taller, but even that didn't matter considering I sat in a wheelchair. He would always be way too damn tall for me.

That's it, he was too tall.

Take that Mr. Perfect.

He merely nodded at me before letting me see one of the documents in my employee file. It had my piloting scores… and I would have felt smug about it, until he pulled up Jessi's scores right next to mine. So, she wasn't bad at her job, so what? I could have done better on that performance drill, but Jessi always found a way to get into my head, even during training.

"We do have a part-time opening for something a little more hands-on than your current position, though—" He then pulled up another document on the screen which showed my customer reviews, my tardiness, and all the rest of my dedicated work history statistics. And just like I feared, he also pulled up

Jessi's stats next to mine. She was much more pleasant than I was and got a lot better scores than me in her work ethic, and customer satisfaction ratings. "As you can see, you are not the only candidate for the position."

"So, then," feeling much too bold for my britches I responded with a sour, "What did you call me up here for then?" To rub it in my face that the only thing going for me was my piloting skills, and I was a less than pleasant person to work with?

"You've demonstrated much higher piloting capability than your previous scores indicate, as if you've been getting more manual hours logged than what your charts have recorded." He flourished to the screen showing my pilot hours awarded, and the stats of those hours. My cheeks burned, and that heat sank deep into my belly making that glass of wine in my stomach create waves through my nerves. Was he saying what I thought he was saying?

He knew.

I was getting fired.

With my mouth ajar I stared at him, unable to confirm or deny this statement. He was right, I was getting in a lot of extra piloting hours through illegal drone races, and those events were known for extreme circumstances that required a lot more maneuverability and practically a Hail Mary prayer to your intuition to remain under the radar, and in one piece. Or in my case, skill, and a lot of manual unlogged overrides every time I went to work. I mean the only life I was putting at risk was my own, and that risk went way down with all my practice.

"It was nearly seamless," he praised, "you would

have got away with it, no one the wiser if it were anyone else."

Nearly? I pressed my lips together tight to stop myself from asking the only thing that mattered to me in that sentence, where did I go wrong? What could I have done to make sure he never knew?

He grinned at me, an amused quirk of his brow at my crossed arms and poorly masked agitation. "I've only seen this level of piloting where I grew up, but," like answering my prayer I eagerly anticipated him telling me what tipped him off, I leaned in, "You could use some more practice, so I'm going to increase your allowed manual training time."

"You're what?" I choked, realizing what he was giving me was way better than a promotion, because a job was still a job that dictated what kind of things I could do with the drone, and this... this was free range skill training. I couldn't be happier, unless he folded that offer into different words that didn't include, you could use more practice. I needed to know how he noticed? And almost as important, why I wasn't fired?

"And I'll be changing your pass codes to only work during training hours," he added as if he didn't just stab me in the gut, "When you come into work, you'll have to come grab me so I can log you into your terminal with restricted access codes."

He might as well have fired me. This was like chopping off my left tit and feeding it to a grinder. I wouldn't be able to manually redirect a drone or fly my own transport on the way to work. My login credentials wouldn't work outside these walls, and even if I wanted to manually take over a passenger craft again, I wouldn't have the access to do it even during work hours. He was suspending my access, and if anything were to happen like today again, I would be forced to get an infraction and ground the drone no matter what.

I'd have to find an upgraded chip to even think about link fixing a drone to manually fly again. That would mean more credits, that I didn't have.

"You can't be serious?" I said deadpan.

I checked my interface, and scrolled through my work credential settings, and they were still intact. A second later it refreshed, and an icon with a red circle and white dash appeared. I activated it and a pop up appeared saying: Restricted access to training drones during the hours of four a.m. to six a.m. and eight p.m. to nine p.m. only.

"That's insane!" I huffed out after I read it. No sane person was going to come into work before work hours and stay after work hours to login to training.

"I'm very serious, Ms. Beryl. I can't very well have you training during peak customer hours. These are our lowest trafficked times."

"But how am I supposed to work?"

"Your job is the same. I'll log you in when you come in, and I'll log you out when you leave. Should you require an emergency need for further access, you can transfer the drone to me by activating the call button in your interface."

"But—"

"The updated credentials shouldn't interfere with your typical duties. I'm actually very surprised you had this much access to begin with, but it makes sense considering you were one of the original hires for this sector when it expanded." He pushed up from his seat, like the conversation was over, and the chair receded back into the floor.

He walked towards me, and my breath hitched up as he stopped beside me. His strong hand reached out, making me nearly choke on my own spit, thinking he was going to push my hair behind my ear. My cheeks flushed like I'd just applied fresh makeup powder before his hand passed my face and picked up the empty wine glass. "I'll log you in after you've had some time to let this settle." He took the glass to the counter, and it slid out to reveal a dish washing rack. It closed, and I couldn't bring myself to leave this spot in his office. The screens with my records and Jessi's records blew off and faded back into a serene oasis on the glass walls.

"You're welcome to stay up here until you're ready," he added while he motioned to the couches.

I dumbly brought attention to my wheelchair like he was the government expecting me to reveal my alien nature by uplifting myself from my contraption to lie all vulnerable on his couch with no way to escape. My chair wasn't obnoxious like some peoples, it was sleek, and had see-through silicone padding with clear plastic in the most tapered down design so it was as close as possible to disappearing. I preferred to be as much like a floating magician as possible, even my wheels were actually omni-directional treads, and as unobtrusive as my budget could afford.

If it were up to me, I'd upgrade to the magnetic field chairs, or if I were getting into the crazy expensive category, I'd swing for the new AmbularGo upgrade. But, with my paralysis not being a recent accident it made the whole process of rebuilding neutrons and nerve-endings to attach to the device a pretty intense process. Hence the expensive and the crazy part, but so worth it to have my legs be connected to my own will again. Who cares if I couldn't feel them, as long as I could make them do what I wanted with just a neural connection from my NeuralGo to my AmbularGo. Even that was still a maybe, in terms of rebuilding the neural pathway that's deteriorated already, but a chance is a chance, and I'd take it faster than my NeuralGo could connect to a drone. And I've disabled my delay sequencing, so that's faster than even my brain could interpret.

Lost in my own thoughts about walking, which was why I wanted one of the highest paying drone piloting jobs available… and why I even entered illegal races to begin with, besides the excitement of manual flying. To be able to walk again, I mean, I can't even remember how it felt anymore. I was eight at the time. It was like he teleported in front of my eyes when I saw him again, he was kneeling in front of me.

He had misinterpreted my far-off gaze for drunkenness.

"You are a lightweight, Ms. Beryl. If I'd known this, I would have insisted you indulge in a different beverage." Before I could protest, he bypassed my wheelchair's security system measures and disengaged the straps that kept me secured so I didn't have to actively adjust myself all the time. I'd never really considered myself a lightweight, and I'd never let anyone, not even my mother, help me transition anywhere.

I preferred to handle it myself, and yet for some reason I couldn't bring myself to get angry at the fact that his toned muscles were cradling me, and I was forced to wrap my arm around his neck. My fingers grazed his soft hair, and I resisted the urge to stay there and pet it, or grab it. Partially because he was my boss, and also because yanking his head back for thinking I couldn't do this myself if I wanted to would be detrimental should he drop me. He gently placed me on the couch, and the lights dimmed.

I found myself unable to prevent the words from coming out of my mouth, "Just because you're handsome, doesn't mean you can get away with pretending to be some strange prince charming swooping me up like some cave man. I'm perfectly capable of moving myself to wherever I want to go." I knew then that the wine really had gone to my head, because I couldn't excuse my lack of filter otherwise. "This is like slapping HR in the tit, and flexing your man muscles around like it's okay to demoralize little old pathetic me, who had my accident before AmbularGo was invented, so I need someone tall, dark, and handsome to come rescue me…" I stammered, and realized I was talking out loud, and not in my head before adding, "Well, I don't. You know… need your help, that is. I could've done it, and…"

"You don't need me," he finished for me. His eyes grew dark, and I didn't think that was possible given how dark brown they were to begin with, but I rationalized he did turn down the lights. He gave a short nod before adding, "You are more than capable of doing anything yourself, but the point I'll make is that you don't have to. I assisted not because I slap HR's 'tit' as you say." My face burned as the reflection of my words came back to haunt me in his own voice, "but because your eyes are clearly dilated with the effects of the wine, and I value the safety of my employees, and that of the passengers of our drones, more than decorum to remain distanced." He stood then and gave a small head bow to me as his silent way of saying goodbye before he gracefully left me there, and the elevator doors chimed closed behind him.

What was the next step below getting all my credentials being controlled by my boss? I almost wished I was fired, just so I didn't have to face him again. How was I supposed to look him in the eye after this?

Chapter Three

*Above Company Policy*

I smacked my forehead with the palm of my hand.
Stupid, stupid.

I went from thinking I was getting fired, to
brazenly asking for a promotion, all the way to staying
long enough for the wine to let my tongue flop around
like a dead fish and accuse my boss of harassment for
trying to be gentlemanly. This was probably why no
one shows any old-world chivalry anymore. Doesn't
help that most things considered chivalrous were taken
over by automated systems. I mean every girl in this
company, even the married ones, would sacrifice a little
dignity to be held in his arms gladly.

He flustered me so much I completely missed the
most important part. How did he bypass my locks on
my wheelchair? That stuff used the whole quantum
encryption codes used for all medical devices... it
shouldn't have been possible, unless he knew my
password? I didn't even know my password. It was
saved in my NeuralGo.

My metabolism was fast enough to be back to my
normal self in under an hour, but not fast enough to
prevent my mind from lingering on the way it felt to be
held in my boss' arms. Most would have just shut the
hell up and enjoyed the ride, but not me. Oh no, can't

enjoy the only man to touch you in in years holding you like you were a precious extinct baby panda. That would just be too much for macho me to endure.

I groaned. It was for the best that I made a fool of myself anyways. Pushing him away was for the best. He was my boss for one, and secondly even if I were fired later today that would just make me a washout that wouldn't come close to being good enough for someone like him. But it wouldn't hurt to brush my hair next time I had to come up to his office.

If there was a next time.

Not that I should ever want a next time. It was never a good thing to be called to the top floor. Most business was done by memo, or video conference anyway.

I pushed myself up and lugged my useless legs over the side of the couch. Thanking the NeuralGo deities that it didn't matter if I was physically on my wheelchair or not to move it. It just meant I had to use different neurons to activate it, I mean basically instead of thinking of it like I was moving, I had to think of it as if it were a drone. Not difficult to do, considering it's what I did for a living.

I chuckled, realizing that maybe my skills as a drone pilot weren't just natural skill after all. It was finely tuned practice every day since I was eight years old using my wheelchair. That stupid thing actually did something awesome for a change. It rolled over to me, and I grabbed the handles to pull myself over. Re-locking the belt across my hips, I checked the beverage bar one more time to find a custom blend coffee from India and said, yes please in my mind.

The back splash tile rotated on a wheel that

dispensed a coffee mug in place, and above it a steaming dark liquid poured out, along with a frothed milk. I grabbed it and moaned as it slid down my throat. It even had a spicy hot kick to it, and I didn't even know how they were able to splice a coffee bean to include that, or maybe I just didn't notice a separate dispenser that added the flavor punch? It didn't matter. It was heaven.

I vowed never to drink wine in the morning again, even if I did think I was getting fired in the minutes to come.

Making my way back to reality, where the walls were just walls, and I could smell the B.O. of my very sweaty cube mate Kline close by, I rolled up to my station. Linked up to my screen, I got the notification pop up in my contact that my credentials were denied. Breathing deep, I tried to calm myself from freaking out. This was just as embarrassing as everything leading up to this point. No... it was more, so much more.

I cracked my knuckles and rolled my head from side to side to ease up the kink forming in my neck. Everything was tensing up. I had to find my boss, like a child, and ask for permission to do my job. Not just right now, not just today, but for who knew how long? The rest of my career? If I had a mirror, I'd see that my neck was covered in hives, because I felt like scratching my skin so bad.

Jessi looked over from her screen to see me backing away from my desk, yet again today. Confusion was plastered all over her face. She was just as shocked as I was that I still had a job, but the day wasn't over yet. For all I knew, he'd review the reports later, and decide my handicap wasn't enough punishment, and it was best to let me go.

"What is she doing here?" Jessi didn't try to whisper, or keep her disgust hidden. She'd obviously had a field day letting everyone know I'd been summoned to the boss' office, and probably wasn't returning. Now, in front of everyone, I'm going to have someone several ranks above everyone on this floor come log me into my interface like an invalid.

Ignoring Jessi, I checked the company intranet, restricted office network, for the calendar feature. I knew he wasn't in his office, and I didn't see him on this floor, so the next best thing was to check where he was supposed to be right now. Zeiten was pretty transparent with employees about executives' schedules, with an available when you need us policy. For once I was thankful for the transparency, though I always wondered when I would ever utilize it.

Today was the day.

According to the calendar, Executive Azel was currently in the server room, since that's where his ID scan was last pulsed. Down to the basement then. I rolled off to the elevators and felt pins and needles as if Jessi were staring at me like I was a dart target. She probably was, because in her eyes I was the biggest slacker there was. Not sure how it was my fault the job was easy, and I worked my links so well I could monitor from anywhere. Not that I could do that anymore, with my reduced authorizations. I have to be directly linked in, within the building, to access my interface now.

"Looks like someone was in denial about being fired, or maybe she just wanted to give me the pleasure of watching her do her walk of shame," she paused dramatically, "Oh right... roll of shame."

My ears became hot and it took everything I had not to turn around, turn off my speed regulator and run her over. I'd show her a roll of shame and roll over her shameful face until it was as flat as her skinny ass. My shoulders shook in fury.

"Aw look, I think she's crying. I would too, knowing being fired from the biggest transportation company this side of the states is basically career suicide."

"Come on, Jessi." The especially fragrant cube mate, Kline, even came to my defense despite his crush on my arch nemesis. He rarely ever spoke, "She has enough to deal with..."

"What... because she can't walk?" Jessi retorted.

"Well..." Kline stammered, and whatever credit I had given him on growing a pair quickly dissipated realizing he was giving me pity, and not actual human courtesy.

"Does that automatically make her above company policy, and to ignore—" she stopped herself.

I opened my eyes to see the elevator was finally open, for how long I didn't know, because I was still shaking, and blinded by the red in my vision.

"No, Ms. Felmon. It is her exceptional flight record, zero infractions, and near flawless safety measures that have given her the top pilot score in the sector next to yours. Those reasons alone, are why she works here," Mr. Azel's voice boomed throughout the floor stopping every employee in their tracks. If a drone were to flash for an emergency in that moment, I wasn't sure anyone would have been in the right mind to act.

He commanded the room, and all eyes were on him... including mine, as he exited the elevator.

Chapter Four

*Life Savings*

Towering in the elevator was Mr. Azel, and I pressed my fists into my thighs as I diverted away from him… still much too embarrassed about this morning. I could still hear him repeating my comment about HR's tits.

I bit my lip.

"I'm sorry if I kept you waiting, I didn't realize you'd be feeling better so soon. I personally locked your computer myself." He walked over to my station, and it scanned him with a green light. The interface activated, and he gave me a curt nod before saying, "It should be ready for you now." He left as quickly as he came.

Whispers hummed through the floor pretty much along the lines of: she isn't fired, did you see the way he looked at her, did she blackmail him, Jessi must be furious, how did she manage that, he even opened her interface for her, I could eat him that's how delicious he is, I want him to open my interface, and then I muted my white noise so anything below a certain decimal would be filtered out, so I didn't have to listen to it anymore.

This was what my life came down to, being an extra in a pathetic office drama. Without turning up my white noise I watched people's mouths like a silent film deciding I'd already become the center of attention as it was, what did it hurt to give them a taste of their own shit.

"Unless you want your pores to smell like last night's burrito dinner, I'd get all of your noses out of my ass and start paying attention to your interfaces for once," I snapped.

Most of the chatty coworkers' mouths hung open in disgust for a while before they mumbled in resignation to get back to what they were paid to do, which was be glorified babysitters for finely tuned machinery. I really hoped at least a few of them, particularly Jessi, got a call activation during that whole distraction, so their numbers would be dinged due to poor customer reviews, and or infractions for failing to update someone's destination. I smiled before focusing on my interface, imagining Jessi's satisfaction score dropping below mine.

My eyes had trouble not glazing over with how boring my job was without the extra authorizations I regularly abused to busy myself throughout the day. The only call button I got was because a toddler thought it would be fun to press it over and over again. I was so bored that I welcomed the short game, and even decided to keep the comm open and ramp up the entertainment value by making animal noises. Bark, bark goes the dog. Meow, Meow goes the cat. Apparently, the kid had a cat at home because it sounded like she said some version of kitty after I did that one. Afterward, I thanked the mom for her business, and the fun game. She filled out a survey without being prompted, and I saw my employee score jump up, as well as made sure she got the typical credit refund for taking the time. Finally, a notification popped up on my screen letting me know the work hours were over, and my interface would be utilized for the next shift.

It was officially five p.m. and two hours away from actually being able to utilize my manual training hour. I sent a request to my best friend Kelly asking what she was up to. Without any hesitation a link request for video chat popped up for me to accept. A screen popped up on my contact lens and it interfaced her scan in front of me like she was actually standing there.

Black perfectly groomed curls with auburn highlights fanned out from her head in a naturally sculpted flounce. Her deep ebony skin was so smooth she could have been a highly sought-after model because she didn't need any touch ups to look that good. Kelly was wearing her usual geek fanfare with a slogan T-shirt (Today's said: The Past Met up with the Future for a Present, it was Tense), and a miniskirt that highlighted her envy-instilling legs. I never allowed my own video to capture anything more than my upper torso, there was nothing to really show off, so it was easier that way.

"Tell me you've read your email," she practically screamed with excitement.

The elevator door opened, and I saw an augmented reality version of Kelly standing with her hand on her hip right next to a very serious Mr. Azel, my boss.

"If I didn't know better, it would appear you were leaving before being dismissed." He stepped to the side for me to enter the elevator.

"Who is that sultry voice I hear in the background?

Tell me how yummy he is?" Kelly chimed in. Luckily, she couldn't see him, as he isn't linked to the video call. I mentally placed my microphone on mute and added an overlay message letting her know I'm temporarily indisposed.

"I would be too if I was with whoever owns that delicious voice," Kelly remarked before I also muted the video call. I could see her motioning beside herself like she was caressing an invisible man beside her and making out with him. I smiled because she was facing the wrong direction for it to be towards the man in question. Right now, her image was dry humping the elevator wall. I made a mental note to remind her that's exactly how I saw it on my end later.

"Obviously, I was about to go up to your office," I lied. This whole check in, check out crap was bullshit.

Like he could tell I was full of as much shit as the demands were, I noticed him narrow his deep brown eyes at me before letting it slide. "Before you leave, please report on how the recent download went in your sector."

Clearing my throat, my mouth felt dry as I swallowed. Out of all the questions he could have asked, he had to ask the one that could get me fired. This was my chance to set up the code to counteract Jessi's sabotage. Her authorization codes would be all over the reports for the software testing this morning. In casual conversation I could hammer the nail in her coffin by simply saying, Jessi was nice enough to do the testing this morning for me. I was late to work, I could say, which wasn't a lie, and sector B33 is big on teamwork makes the dream work, so everything was smooth as cream. I spent an awkward silence mulling this whole conversation out while watching my best friend mime in front of me. I closed my eyes and huffed.

I couldn't do it.

"Nothing too exciting to report, but one of the drones has been flagged for engineering to take a look at. Its indicators lead me to believe some hardware is loose, interfering with the download." It wasn't the indicators that made me believe it was loose hardware. It was because I manually operated it and its functions were still operational. It had to be an interference stopping the download. Engineering would do a full scan and go over every inch for safety before it gets redeployed. "Just being extra cautious is all, want to make sure everything checks out."

"I see." His voice dropped, and I didn't know if it was just me that he didn't trust, or if he just naturally sounded like a skeptic. Not calling me out on it he let me exit at the drone pickup zone on the fourteenth floor. I was bored enough during my work hours to actually schedule this pickup, and the passenger drone waited patiently for me, it didn't hurt that I worked for the hub where all the drones chilled out before being deployed.

"This is me," I said lamely, because I couldn't think of another way of ending our awkward conversation.

"No need to come back for your manual training hours today, your authorizations will not be activated until the morning."

My shoulders slumped, of course the one thing I kept repeating to myself through the day to get through it was canceled. I waved at him without turning back, part of me wishing the only thing I was waving was a particular finger, and popped a wheelie into the drone and pulled myself in.

Unmuting my video call I immediately hear Kelly mid-sentence, "…Go. I've already signed up to give us another shot at it. What do you say?"

"Sorry, I only now unmuted you. It was work, and I don't even want to get into it right now."

"I was saying, it's time for you to empty your pitiful excuse of a savings account and use your superhuman piloting skills to win the only thing you've been obsessing about since obsessing became a game on Tuesdays. On the note of obsession, usually you're super bored at work, where were you today? Please tell me you were with whoever I heard earlier. I would give both nuts to have him talk to me all day."

"It wouldn't be worth it. Whatever nonexistent nuts you have would be wasted on listening to him talk about how you almost measure up, and broody silent treatments with skeptical stares that would make your mother roll in her grave. I don't recommend it."

"Speak for yourself. I'd take my chances. Tell me he's as dreamy to look at as he sounds."

Ignoring her I redirected her attention back to the main course, "Is there a race this week?"

"You need to start checking your emails!"

"I've told you, notifications like that will ruin your life. I won't be a slave to technology like you. Every ding of attention from advertisers, and random people I don't even know giving my body an unnatural shot of endorphins that should be reserved for actual human contact."

"Whatever, save your freedom speeches for after

you practically steal the chance of a lifetime away from snobby rich kids that don't even need it."

"Are you saying what I think you're saying?"

Kelly was the reason I even got into illegal drone races. She started off blackmailing me when I stole her family's drone. If I won a race for her, she'd keep the winnings and forget about calling the police on me. I didn't win that race, but I did make her money by beating the person she actually made the side bet with. She was the one that won the race herself, and I had enough info on her to ensure mutual destruction should she have decided to turn me in.

She quickly turned into the best friend I never knew I needed, and all of this without ever actually meeting her in person. All of our communications have been through links.

"Read my lips you handsome devil. AM.BU.LAR.GOing straight to the finish before all those other trust fund suckers."

"I love it when you call me handsome."

"You love it more when I tell you I already dumped my whole lifesavings into getting us invites!"

"Wait… what?" I mean, her whole lifesavings really wasn't much, considering I didn't even realize she knew what the word save meant.

"AM.BU.LAR.GO. AM.BU.LAR.GO," she chanted.

"No, really. Backup and explain yourself, do you even have an account that shows positive credits?"

"Of course not… At least, not anymore. This is a once in a lifetime race, these things don't just appear all the time, and when you win, and I get second place we'll have won all the money back and then some. Can you imagine being able to walk up to your boss and say all the things you've always wanted to say, but don't because, well, you're sane?"

If only she knew the things I already said to my boss already, she wouldn't be calling me sane then.

"No race would be able to give us that kind of freedom, plus… it'll be a bit more difficult for me to hijack one of the drones from work to even enter a race now."

"What happened?"

"It's the work thing I don't want to get into right now."

"You have to get into this race, I got us the invites. I can't back out now."

"How much are you in for?"

"That's not what matters, especially if we win."

"When is the race?"

"Friday, no details until it starts, five-minute prep time, the usual."

"What happens if I can't figure out how to fix a drone before then?"

"Do you have room at your place for an extra body?" She smiled big.

"For you…" I pretended like she would be the worst roommate ever before winking at her, "always, but I'll see what I can do so that you don't lose the roof over your head because of your overly optimistic attitude towards gambling your money on races."

"It's not a gamble when it's on you," she said sweetly.

"There's always a first time for everything. I'll figure something out." It was then that I realized that if I lost this race and she really did need a place to stay, it would be the first time we met in person. I talked with her every day, and we video linked up all the time, but there was no need. How odd. I made a mental note to figure out a time that we could make a date to go eat together or something. What kind of friend was I that the closest I've ever got to my best friend was in a drone flying in illegal races.

Figures.

I laughed, and said, "I've got to go so I can focus on a plan."

"Scheme away!" She said before ending the link.

And I'd have to pull out all the stops and risk a lot more than my job to get us out of this one.

## Chapter Five

*Flight Schooled*

My NeuralGo sending pulses through my brain to wake me up gently should have been annoying, but strangely enough, I understood why more people actually used the feature. It felt like it was triggering my pleasure sensors, and not in a touch myself kind of way, just like waking up to satisfaction. I'm pretty sure this was the same technology they used on addicts to keep them clean, rewarding good behavior like waking up on time. Either way, I usually kept that function disabled because well, my pleasure centers were mine to ignore, and mine to decide when to wipe away the cobwebs.

Suddenly, I found myself imagining a certain someone using those strong hands to defeat spiders and those lips in that silky voice telling me, you're all set to go. I thought I would hate him starting up my interface in the morning, but the way Jessi fumed seeing him get my cube set up was priceless.

I stared at my brown drab hair in the mirror and took out my old flat iron from the drawer. Peeling a strand of crunchy hair that got stuck between the plates, I cringed. Maybe my hair might be better off being frizzy and untamed. I decided to just wet my palms and try to tug at my unruly trundles, if it was good enough for men then it was good enough for me. It did all right, I mean, it wasn't ready for a photo shoot by any means, but I didn't want to come across as wanting his attention either.

His attention, now that I thought about it, I groaned. Was I really giving two shits about what he thought about me? He'd already seen me like a slob, what did it matter if the trend continued. I took my fresh clothes out of the dryer and convinced myself that I only did that because it felt awesome to put on warm clothes in the morning. It had nothing to do with being more presentable, it was for my comfort only.

My button up was sheer, with a camisole underneath, that was also because I thought it was pretty... not because it showed off my cleavage in a very demure way. I grabbed a black tie from a drawer and quickly put it on to cover it up. There was no need for anyone to see that. It was for me anyways.

I rolled out, with my drone transport already waiting for me. It was off hours for most people, so a majority of the drones were available. I was going to be more than on time... I would be early, and I didn't even need to take out my joysticks or bypass the speed restrictions. Like a regular law-abiding citizen, I rode a normal passenger drone to work. Not that I had much of a choice, I still had to get in contact with Kelly's guy to find an upgraded chip that had better link fixing hacks than the one I had. I bought the cheapest one on the market that still required borrowing an active authorization code. So, unless I wanted to add stealing someone's authorization codes to my list of offenses, I had to shell out some more credits.

I arrived five minutes before the designated time

and made it to the training floor with ease. Inside were a dozen stationary drones surrounded by glass cubes and suspended over magnetic fields. All capable of creating visual fields to simulate real airspace, and completely mobile within its cube to do any and all maneuvers realistically without ever having to actually crash into anything or leave the designated area. It was the best money could buy, and the opportunity to play with them was a luxury.

A scan went over me, and the cube opened up. A friendly female voice said, "Welcome to the ELO, Ms. Beryl, the state-of-the-art training and leisure activity flight simulation. Exercise Lift Ordinances, your authorization is good for two hours with on-site supervision, please wait for your on-deck trainer."

I tried to open the hatch for the drone, only for it to repeat, "Please wait for your on-deck trainer." I groaned, what did that even mean? The whole system was state-of-the-art and top notch A.I., it already had a trainer programed in.

What was I waiting for?

From behind me I heard the same female voice, "Welcome Regent Azel."

I turned around to see Mr. Azel with a small towel around his neck and watched him pull it up through his brown hair which did nothing to dampen the still glistening water on his exposed chest. He was wearing exercise loose pants, hanging off of his hips and giving me a clear view of a cut into his abs that only made me believe he starved himself of anything delicious to eat. I mean eat some donuts occasionally to make the rest of us feel better about ourselves like a proper human.

Plus, what was he doing coming here like a

shampoo commercial?

"Am I early?" I wanted to scowl at him, but all I could muster was making sure my mouth wasn't catching any flies.

"Considering your history of tardiness, everything is early for you." Was that a joke I heard in his tone? Was he joking? Did I get transported to another universe where my boss was half naked, and being friendly? This was a dream, or a prequel to a nightmare. I smiled to myself before I could catch it. Digging my fingernail into my hand just to make sure, I raised an eyebrow at him curiously. Nope, this was real.

"These things cost a fortune to rent, and you're wasting my training time. I'm not even sure how you convinced the board to even allow me to touch one," I admitted, and was confused at my candor with him. I pulled my gaze from his eyes and settled on his chest, only to blink several times to force myself to look anywhere else. Could he at least put a shirt on?

"I'm a very persuasive guy, and I have use for someone with your piloting ability. Shall we begin?" He pulled a black shirt on, and a part of me was disappointed before he added, "We wouldn't want you accusing me of caring about your wellbeing here at Zeiten, so we'll keep these sessions between us, and you'll continue to have access to them during off hours."

"Because I was *so* looking forward to Jessi's enthusiasm," I mocked, "for a slacker, such as myself, being given access to an ELO training module worth more than what I could make in my lifetime."

"Don't break them," he teased. Was he actually being funny? I smiled at him, and quickly turned away to keep a straight face. This was for work, he obviously needs my piloting skills for some project, but I needed to be prepared for it. What exactly would I be doing for him? What secret project was it? I didn't see any newsletters with any upcoming events. Maybe it was a government job outsourced to the commercial sector because it's cheaper than doing it themselves?

I could be the next government drone spy pilot… I was getting a head of myself.

Mr. Azel seemed to appear in front of me like magic, but I was preoccupied with my future spy missions that he could have easily simply walked up while I wasn't paying attention. He flourished his hand to the open drone latch. "After you."

He didn't offer to help me into the drone, which was refreshing. I popped up the wheels and used the handles on the inside to lift myself the rest of the way in. I was a pro at maneuvering myself in my wheelchair, after years of building neuron connections to this software, it was like it was an extension of me.

Once inside, I was about to close the door but stopped short when I saw my boss climb in after me. He proceeded to shut the latch and strap himself in. I've never had to strap myself in since my wheelchair used magnetic locks into the ground of the drone, and I was pretty much already on lock down.

Mr. Azel adjusted something around his wrist, a computer chip slipping out from his battery compartment. It wasn't anything fancy, like I would expect on an executive, but it was an interesting enough watch. Not that he had to wear a watch at all with contacts linked up to a NeuralGo. Watches were for the joy of accessorizing, like earrings, and rings. He saw where my eyes landed, and his expression turned serious.

"Proceed," he mono-voiced, obviously not willing to discuss why he had a secret compartment in his watch.

"Right…" I snapped my head back to the screen, and finally appreciated the sight of a drone purposefully built for manual flights. It had an interface screen, its own joysticks, and buttons… so many buttons. I wanted to press them all, but these buttons weren't even necessary unless the interface failed. This was a drone made for anything, any software malfunction, or virus would weep in defeat with this setup. For every function there was a manual trigger to override the software that directly linked up with its corresponding part. It was beautiful.

My contact linked up with the interface, and the glass walls around us transitioned into the fourteenth floor drone pickup zone. It was like I was there, and not in a cube.

Gripping the joysticks, I guided the drone through the runways, avoiding purposefully placed pedestrians, and incoming and outgoing drone traffic from automated transports. My heart rate was increasing like I was about to start an illegal drone race. A huge smile was plastered on my face, and I didn't care that my boss was behind me. I almost forgot he was even there, he was so quiet.

As I was exiting the building, a drone was coming in the hangar, and it was easy to maneuver considering all the drones followed protocol and were essentially predictable. Until my whole body tensed up and on instinct, I pulled hard on the joystick to ascend sharply.

But I hadn't removed the speed restrictions on the drone, like I normally would during a race. The drone didn't react fast enough to match my commands, and the whole thing shuddered making me wish I had added my extra wheelchair strap for my chest to keep me steady.

My hands slipped from the joystick on the impact, and the back half of the drone's viewing field lit up red. My body flung forward, and my leg straps weren't enough to keep me in. Strong arms wrapped around my shoulders pulling me back into my chair. My contacts were giving me a headache with the flashing notifications telling me simulation failure. I muted the notification, and realized that Mr. Azel was hugging me, and he was no longer strapped into his seat.

How did he unbuckle himself to secure me faster than I could anticipate a rogue drone in the simulation? That drone was purposefully trying to hit us. I barely got us out of the way for a complete crash. My heart was racing, and my palms were sweaty... we could have died. I was a horrible pilot. My first simulation and I failed. This wasn't anything like what I thought it would be. Would he even let me keep training with a crash on my record?

I closed my eyes and let my head lull onto his forearm. I felt fresh moisture creep up on me, but I refused to let him know how real this all felt. Refusing to let my weakness show, I willed my eyes to dry before he could see. His body wash smelled like pine trees. We both stayed there unmoving until my breathing wasn't so haggard. My shoulder flinched and he felt the adjustment and slowly pulled away from me leaving a coolness in his absence.

Without skipping a beat, he broke the silence, "You are the second pilot to ever successfully avoid a fatal collision on the first simulation."

"But I failed…"

"No, you dodged the drone just enough to save the occupants, and your upward momentum if you had continued the simulation would have flipped the drone back into the hangar. Upside down maybe, but alive, avoiding a full fourteen story fall into air traffic," he explained.

"Who was the first?"

"Me," he said.

Chapter Six

*Night Crew*

Mr. Azel unfastened my magnetic field, rolled me back, and re-secured the wheelchair. I was a side companion now with my boss in charge of the manual drone. His hands gripped the joysticks with a tenderness that made me want to be an inanimate object, unlike the way I preferred to strangle the things with all of my enthusiasm. His black jersey tee clung to his back muscles in a way that his button-ups didn't do justice. Connected to the interface, the simulation restarted. It started off the same, the fourteenth floor with pedestrians and regular drone traffic. Even knowing what was coming I still clenched my fingers into my pant legs, but this time I decided I'd prepare and strap my shoulders into my chair so I wouldn't budge.

The exit out of the hangar was coming up, and my hand reached out, grabbing his forearm accidentally instead of my chain handle. Those hard eyes seemed to soften when they met mine, but it was too fast for me to be sure before his features were stone. I eased my hand back to my handle, instead of his firm muscles, knowing it wasn't the time to be distracting him from the flight when a drone was going to be crashing at us any second.

We ascended into airspace, and no drone attack… I wondered if we were in the same simulation program, until he quickly turned right, without me even noticing he moved until the joystick was already full-throttle. I didn't even see any drone on the overlay screen, until out the side window I saw another drone literally inches away from us, like we were doing an air show with synchronized flight, that's how close it was.

He didn't miss a step. Inside the drone I saw another passenger screaming. It was so realistic, down to the terror in their eyes as they waved at us as if to say, move, quickly, move.

Before I could even react, the drone sped up to get in front of us and then immediately threw back in reverse. The drone was purposefully trying to hit us, like someone else was driving it, and completely on a suicide mission, with a passenger on board.

Our drone casually lifted into the air, like he had anticipated the attacker's actions and we were merely dancing with it. Mr. Azel finally slipped out the chip from his watch and plugged it into the terminal. Next thing I saw was our drone hovering stationary, but my boss' hands still guiding the joysticks. The other drone landed safely on top of a building's drone pad, and the passenger quickly flung himself out of the vehicle only to kiss the roof beneath him.

The simulation ended, and he redeposited the chip back into his watch.

"What was that?" I said, breathless.

"The future," he warned, looking grim. "I think that's enough for today, we'll pick this up tomorrow." He opened the hatch and offered me his hand like I was a normal lady. On autopilot I took his hand and wheeled myself off the ramp that even had time to come out in my daze. I nodded at him still reeling from what I'd just witnessed, this was more intense than any of the illegal drone races I'd been in.

Sure, they were ruthless and tried to send us through traffic, and tricky landscapes. They'd give us strict time limits, and sometimes you'd have a fellow pilot try to herd you… but never so far as to risk their own lives. They were inside the drone they were flying after all. It was risky enough as it was, given the added stress of avoiding police drones.

"I've already unlocked your interface for you," he finally said, "Let me know if anything out of the ordinary should interrupt your work schedule." He released my hand, and before I could even think to ask what he meant by that, he was gone. Even the automated A.I. lady had a delayed response after him, "Have a good day, Regent Azel."

As I left it didn't even give me a goodbye greeting. It merely said, "Authorizations suspended until accompanied by a registered trainer. Please vacate the premises." At least it said please, and he thought my customer service was below pleasant. I scoffed, and returned to my desk, wondering if my training time counted towards my worked hours, since he was the one who had arranged it.

The floor was silent, and only a few workers were manning their interfaces. They were the night crew, and business attire wasn't required. One of them shooting those foam darts with suction cups at the ceiling. The magnetic strips on the bottoms would activate and realign back into the fake bazooka, and she'd fire them at the ceiling all over again. Automatic retrieval systems even in the toys, I laughed.

The girl stumbled, falling back over the top of her chair that she was leaning in, and onto the floor.

"Hey!" she said, thrilled to see another human. "Cameron! What time is it? Is our shift over?" Then it made sense why she was so happy to see me. I was a sign that she could go home and sleep or do whatever night crew did when they got off work.

"No, one more hour," Cameron replied, stoic.

"Really? Are you sure?"

"Positive. You know your hours are on your screen if you just looked at it for once."

"You know it only matters if a notification pops up. I have it on my contact screen. Plus, not even the shit faced are out during this time."

Then Cameron turned around to see me, "What kind of nut job are you to come in an hour early to work?"

I would definitely ask myself the same question in their shoes. I liked them. The girl got back into her chair and rolled it up to me. It was one of those rare occurrences where someone didn't seem so tall as they approached me. It was like she was like me, at least for a moment.

"Bailey," she said but didn't offer her hand. She tilted her head waiting for my response.

"Tyler."

"Who did you piss off?" She wiggled her eyebrows at me.

"You're good." I smiled at her. Was it that obvious that I was hanging on by a thread in this company?

Shrugging, she wheeled back to her desk. "I'm a natural, plus why do you think we're here at this godforsaken hour?"

"You're here because you didn't want to wear a suit," Cameron corrected.

She waved her off. "This," she flourished over her body, "cannot be contained." Her dreadlocks were braided to the side, and her outfit was a gothic hipster kind of vibe with a loose, comfortable t-shirt, ripped jeans, and combat boots.

"I didn't get in trouble. I volunteered because you begged me to switch shifts to be with you."

"Semantics," Bailey objected.

As I linked up to my interface, I noticed my hours were not reduced by going to ELO training. I groaned. At least I'd be off at four instead of five, because I was starting an hour earlier.

"We got a live one!" Cameron announced like we were at an event and she was the host.

"Ooo, put it on, put it on!" Bailey squealed, "New girl, you won't rat on us, right?"

"No," I said hesitantly, not knowing what I was agreeing to, but having been wrapped up in illegal racing made it easy to quickly answer. Though, my moral compass was off, I did have my lines when it came to customer privacy, and safety. I really hoped what they were doing wasn't violating those core principals, like some creeps that like to listen in on their drones in hopes of catching some drunks in lewd acts. There was a reason there were different clearance levels for pilots, some political figures chose our company over others for this very reason. Only the highest authorizations had access to listen without being prompted by the call button.

"Link her up!" Bailey twirled in her chair.

A notification offered to link to me through my contact. I accepted, and I could hear audio of a guy.

"Doctor B? Are you there?"

"We're here for you, babe," Bailey offered, "Tell it to me straight."

"I need you to send me to the last transport."

My eyes widened. I was known for not following protocols and being on the wrong side of the law from time to time, but I'd never done anything that I thought would put anyone else in danger. If this was what I thought it was, this could get the company in a lot of trouble.

"On it! Have fun you rascal you," she cooed and swiveled her chair to wink at me like what she was doing wasn't completely wrong. If she was sending this person to the last customer's location this was a violation of privacy beyond anything I'd ever heard of. He could be a stalker for all we knew.

I stared at the call button located on my interface that would let Mr. Azel know I needed extra authorizations to handle a work problem. If I had my own access, I could have intercepted this whole thing without having to bring him into it. I thought about it and the button lit up but didn't engage. Lingering there uncertain about my choice.

"Have you been there before?" Cameron asked me, interrupting my train of thought.

"Been there?" I said dazed.

"To Last Transport?" Bailey chimed in, and I quickly pushed myself away from my desk to prevent activating the call button, but saw it blinking like a beacon already. Shit. Interrupting my concentration made my link follow my thought's command to press the button.

"It's like the modern day speak easy, invite only kind of place. We're kind of double dipping by being the go-between for transporting those high-end mo-fos to their secret hidey hole. Shh," she lifted her finger to her lips.

"It's not really against policy B. It's just frowned upon," Cameron clarified.

"So, you get paid to direct the transport drones to a location the occupants don't even know where it is?"

"Exactly," Cameron answered.

"Well, it's more like we're paid for what this company is known for. I think the big heads above us would agree that security and privacy are on brand, but we've never really been given an invite yet, have we Cam? Those greedy knockers."

"Privacy and safety are the spirit of Zeiten, I couldn't agree more," a recently all too familiar silky voice agreed. How did he get here so fast? And why didn't I hear the elevator chime to announce his presence.

Bailey pursed her lips together and then smiled awkwardly. "We've quite the initiative at the night shift to ensure high customer satisfaction, isn't that right Cam?"

Cameron cleared her throat and then nodded instead of adding anything further.

"And what do you think on this matter?" My boss was looking straight at me. I was the one to press the damned panic button.

"I think it's something to look into, could be an under-utilized market. It's lucky that you have such aspiring employees to help expand the business." I tried to mitigate any of us getting in trouble but wasn't sure if I was swinging in the right direction.

"And how do you secure our clients information?" Mr. Azel asked Bailey.

Crumbling slightly under the pressure, Bailey began mumbling under her breath before Cameron stepped in to answer, "We don't actually know where it is either…"

"Yeah, it's all encrypted." Bailey finally added.

"So, tell me what it is that you're doing for the client then." He stood there with his arms crossed. I could hear the skepticism in his voice, but something in the way he said that made me think he was being a bit cheeky. Though, you wouldn't tell by the statuesque features on his face.

"We override the screen features in the drone to black out the route," Cameron offered.

"I'm pretty sure the value is in adding that encrypted code into the drone," I added, "that's not a standard feature in our current location programming."

Bailey glared at me, because I'm pretty sure that was the part of the deal she didn't want to fess up to. Without cringing I continued to add, "It should be something that's an upgrade for our elite clientèle base. This could mean a lot more credits for the company if marketed correctly. If anything, maybe you could discuss a bonus for Bailey and Cameron's innovative product discovery."

At the word bonus, Bailey's eyes lit up and she leaned forward in her chair. Cameron fidgeted with her shirt hem, and I couldn't even bring myself to see anything higher than Mr. Azel's shoes, which were markedly different than this morning's sneakers and bare chest. They were pointed toe suede in a deep green, both bold yet muted business shoes. He was in a pair of black slacks, and a white button up with a black color-block and splatter paint design. I couldn't even dream of being so professionally fancy with an artist flare.

"Was your intention to add a new revenue stream for the company?" He asked, looking from one to the other. Bailey nodded fast to go along with it, while Cameron winced like they'd been pinched. "Which one of you should be rewarded for your," he paused to emphasize, "*innovative product discovery*, as Ms. Beryl so aptly put?" His voice was too smooth, it was difficult to catch the subtle sourness in how he quoted my words.

I wanted to warn Bailey and Cameron, if they hadn't dealt with our boss before, that this reminded me all too much of when I thought I was being fired... but instead got all of my privileges taken away. They were not going to be rewarded, and it would be all my fault.

Bailey didn't budge to see the worry plastered on my face, and her mouth began to open to say something she might never be able to take back.

I had to think fast.

"Adding code to the drones is a standard feature for all drone pilots, or they wouldn't be able to initiate the new download protocols, wouldn't you say so?" I said sweetly to our boss, who turned his attention on me. Those eyes seemed to crinkle in amusement.

"So it is," he conceded before adding, "Will you ladies see me in my office when you're finished?" Without waiting for their answer, he gave a subtle head nod to the night crew, and then to me before ending the conversation by walking away.

"Yes, sir." Cameron saluted him.

Bailey raised an eyebrow at me and shrugged. "Sure thing, boss."

"Where did he come from anyways?" Bailey motioned to the elevator he just disappeared through.

"He's like a ghost." Cameron shivered.

"The kind you want to haunt you forever." Bailey wiggled her eyebrows.

"Uh, I'm so sorry," I blurted.

"It's not like you made him sneak up on us," Cameron tried to soothe, but I wanted to cringe. I felt like I was slathered in dirt and couldn't clean it off even if I tried. I was the one who called him, accidentally, but still the culprit.

"Plus, maybe he wants in on the action. Monetize that shit, just like you said." Bailey twirled in her chair.

"It just doesn't sit well with me." It was the best I could muster at admitting I did it, but anything else more blunt wedged itself in my throat and made my chest tighten up. I was no shining star of following the rules, but something about breaking privacy triggered me to act. Slack off all you want to, it was a boring job I could understand even adding code to entertain yourself, or even in my case borrowing some drones for a little fun. But people's business was their own, and that rando could have been a stalker. He wasn't... but he could have been. I tried to remove the alert as soon as I realized it was just a party, but the damage was done.

Glass houses and rocks, I knew.

"How did you hide the code in the download?" I asked out of curiosity.

"Since this is probably our last night, I'll do you one better." Bailey sent me a link request with her NeuralGo comm ID. Her contact was added, and we could now communicate outside of immediate range. I would never link her, because my guilt would be much too heavy to face her again if she were fired.

A notification message appeared in my contact: Meet you at The Last Transport, and I'll tell you everything you want to know.

The elevator chimed, and this time I noticed it. Even if I didn't, it'd be hard not to notice the loud clap of those heels, or the annoying voice that came after.

"Early doesn't suit you, you might actually have to work when there's less people around to manage the interfaces," Jessi said in a sickeningly sweet voice, as if the words coming out of her mouth were candy instead of the vomit that was obvious to me.

"Don't worry, I knew you were coming, and I didn't want to risk any report discrepancies," I smiled back at her trying not to twitch at the unnatural nice mask I was wearing. It was a beautiful zinger, and I couldn't have been more happy with it.

She sucked in a breath, and I knew deep down she was fuming, and it brought an unhealthy amount of joy as I watched her stiff leg it back to her cube.

"Don't you have somewhere to be?" Jessi snarled at Bailey, who simply pushed away from her computer on her chair. Swiveling she bounced to her feet, and as she passed my cube winked at me. Jessi walked back to grab the chair as Cameron brushed passed and nudged it a little farther away from her with a fake stumble.

"Bailey, you know I need the entire walkway to keep my ego from deflating." Cameron caught up with her, and at the elevator they pressed the up button instead of down to the fourteenth floor below us. I hoped I'd get to see them again, but my stomach clenched at even thinking about coming clean to them. They had both just stood up to Jessi for me, and that made it even more difficult. These girls were my people, they understood me, and I had misjudged them. To be fair, I didn't know them, but that didn't matter anymore. I felt like I stabbed my own self in the back.

I had to find a way to make it up to them.

Not sure what I was going to do, but maybe I could at the very least convince Mr. Azel to give the same treatment given to me. Suspend their authorizations.

It was better than getting fired. Well, the jury was still out on that one, but probably better than getting fired.

Chapter Seven

*The Boss*

Four o' clock didn't come as soon as I'd hoped. If time were a hotdog on a spigot, the flame was out, and I wasn't eating anytime soon, unless I liked em cold. Lucky for me, I've eaten plenty of cold dogs, and I was just happy that my hours were up.

Entering the elevator, I realized I couldn't get fourteen to light up. I'd never had a problem with my NeuralGo, but I supposed this week would be the week for that to be dumped on me. Until I realized the elevator was moving up.

The only lit floor was the last one, unlabeled. It was just a button in your lens that was only viewable when in route, like an Easter egg, or when your boss had specifically requested your presence.

When the doors opened, my boss was sitting in his chair already. Facing away from me, actually working this time, but the interface was blurred so only the linked-up contacts could see. Typical privacy screening. I passed over the authorization scanner, and the friendly voice said, "Would you like a beverage while you wait?"

"Wait?" He was right there, wasn't he only supposed to confirm my cube was unlinked and let me be on my way? He ran his fingers through his hair and

65

his perfectly sculpted follicles weren't worse for the action. Instead of being messed up, he was stylishly fluffed, like they do in the hair salons. Not a hair that didn't belong where it landed.

I linked up to the beverages and could see that all of the alcoholic beverages listed there before were no longer options. My face flushed, and I looked back to see if he was watching. He wasn't. I choose that delicious coffee with the heated twist again.

Rolling up to the couch, I tried to blend into the furniture. It wasn't like it should take that long, right?

My coffee was gone, and staring at the back of his head was losing its original appeal. I groaned, which came out more like a growl that I secretly hoped he could hear. Rolling my eyes, I went to leave only to have the scanner turn red and the A.I. receptionist say, "Authorization denied. Please wait for assistance."

I spun around on my wheels, and glared at the back of his head behind the glass room he was in. Before I could even think about asking him what the deal was, the walls went frosty, and turned into a serene landscape of a forest. He knew I was going to come into his office, and he preemptively said screw you with a pretty visual. I'd never look at trees the same way again.

Waiting in that damned lounge area for so long I even drank another cup of coffee, and really needed to pee. It was a matter of life or death by embarrassment that I found a bathroom. I passed the now enclosed office and found a room that could be promising. Though immediately I regretted it upon seeing the all-white, luxurious beach resort bed.

Did he live here?

Before I turned around, I caught the sight of what I was searching for. I didn't have much time for indecision. Thankfully, the whole place was large, and allowed ample space for me to maneuver around. I found the toilet, or more aptly called some sort of super deluxe computer for the sole purpose of human waste. It tried to link up to me as soon as I entered the space. I didn't really want there to be any evidence that I had even been in this room, so it was best if I used the manual features on this thing like a normal human.

As soon as I came up to it, I realized there wasn't any handlebar nearby for me to grab on to. Quickly, I abandoned the idea of using his restroom and instead became distracted by snooping at the things left on the counter. There was a display of watches on a rotation device, and a pill bottle. I knew I shouldn't snoop, but it was right there. Melanin enhancers. Was he trying to have the perfect tan from the inside out? I'd only known these pills being used by people who have light sensitivity, or recently for models who want to appear sun-kissed without the actual UV rays.

A click sounded from the wall, and a bar came out of a hidden compartment. I panicked, sending the whole bottle clattering in the sink.

His voice from behind the door said, "If you'd link up to the device, it would customize to your preferences."

"Uh, right…" Then I thought about it more and yelled back, "Don't tell me you have a fetish for listening to women pee."

"I'm not accustomed to having to babysit while I try to get my work done, so when I saw the time, I realized you may have needed a tour. When you weren't at the entrance, I wanted to make sure you were taken care of."

"You aren't babysitting me. You're keeping me hostage. Those are two very different things." I folded my arms and glared through the door, hoping he could feel it.

"Consider it being paid to be available until I'm ready to leave," he said sweetly.

"I'm not your personal assistant, can't you just clock me out, and let me 'wait' at home." Then I replayed his words back in my head, particularly where he said paid. Was I still getting paid?

"Actually, that is exactly why I needed you to wait for me to be finished. So that we can talk. Please come to my office when you're finished."

"Like I have a choice," I huffed under my breath and then gently placed the pill bottle where I thought it was before. Then adjusted the label to be slightly turned; I was pretty sure it was facing that direction.

His office was still hidden behind a forest screen, but with the sliding door open. Inside were so many blurred screens plastered all over the place, I wondered how he kept track of them all, and what he was working on. He gestured his hand in a wave, and the screens disappeared. Turning towards me, I hesitated before rolling up to the same uncomfortable spot I was in the day before.

"Thank you for waiting," he started, and I scoffed. Ignoring my attitude, he continued, "As of today, you are under my sole jurisdiction."

"I'm not sure I follow."

"You, Ms. Beryl, are no longer employed by Zeiten Drone Transportation," he let that sink in, and my chest tightened, "You are my personal employee, and I have taken full responsibility for your future actions here on the premises."

"Why?" I choked out.

"As I said before, I have use for your skill set, but I cannot condone your current ethics without making sure you have no room for your *side projects* on company time." Mr. Azel loosened his tie and unbuttoned his shirt cuffs. The time was almost eight p.m. and he pulled a new, more comfortable shirt from under his chair. He had a secret compartment just like mine. My jaw slacked, and I possessively clamped my hand over the triggering mechanism hoping he wouldn't try to confiscate my joysticks.

"That being said," he continued, "I expect you to be on your best behavior and be my extra assist when I need it."

"What exactly do you need assistance with?"

Mr. Azel popped one button at a time, too slowly for my comfort, and I regretted asking that particular question right then. He was walking to the door and changing his shirt at the same time. Like nothing was odd about this behavior, the elevator chimed, as I was watching him from the door of his office.

"I realize this is a bit jarring for you, but once I leave this elevator, it's either with you or without you. I won't force you to continue, but there will be some differences between working for the corporation and working for me."

The elevator door was about to close, and I quickly turned off my speed regulators and stopped it with my wheel. As the door rotated back open, he stepped to the side for me to join him.

"I won't scrub toilets," I broke the silence.

A small smile crept up the side of his mouth.

"They clean themselves, Ms. Beryl."

"No funny business," I added.

"I wouldn't dream of it," he said deadpan, and I felt like those words stung me. I mean, was I that much of a mess? It wouldn't hurt to dream a little, would it? I shook my head and folded my arms. Wouldn't dream of that soft hair, or firm hands of his either. "Please try to be a bit more discreet with your illegal activities outside of work, would you?"

"No promises," I grumbled. Pressing my lips in a flat line I forced myself not to be shocked at him knowing that much about me.

The floor opened up to the ELO training cubes, and the familiar voice greeted us, "Hello Mr. Azel, and Ms. Beryl," but the programing said it in a way where hearing our names together almost sounded indistinguishable. I looked up at him, to see if he noticed it to, and as usual not a twitch for me to distinguish.

Chapter Eight

*Simulation*

The simulation began, and as the exit to the drone hangar came up, I could feel my blood throb even to the tips of my ears. It may not have been real, but knowing what was coming didn't change the adrenaline pumping. With one of these babies, I'd never feel the need to enter a manual drone race again, it was so realistic. That similar feeling came over me, and I knew the rogue drone was coming in. It was like my body hummed, and the energy around me prickled. I quickly yanked up, like last time, but also at an angle to account for the extra pull.

Not as smooth as when Mr. Azel was when driving, but we survived the collision. I knew it was coming. The drone attacker veered off like it was giving up, but it was all too easy. I also didn't expect for the first attack to be so simple of an escape. My maneuvering more than overcompensated for where the drone ended up appearing, it wasn't exactly the same as the first simulation.

Behind me I could hear Mr. Azel moving around, and the clank of metal paneling being shifted. I would have checked behind me, but I didn't want to miss something on the screens. Before I knew it, the drone was accompanied by another one flanking me on either side. I could go up or down, and I only had seconds to decide. Up was into traffic, and down was just as dangerous with the tops of buildings to contend with. I decided to override the speed restrictions on my interface and sped up, but only slightly at first.

They matched my pacing, and as they closed in just like last time there were scared passengers and they obviously weren't the ones controlling the moves. Whoever was responsible for the drones in this simulation was a Link Fixer, and they didn't care if there were casualties to take us down. Why would a simulation like this even be necessary with all the quantum encryptions these days? Even with another quantum computer, the more you try to fix into a link the more the encryption changed until it was nearly unidentifiable. What this simulation was expecting was for a Link Fixer to be able to hack an encryption fast enough to prevent the code from morphing into something unbeatable even with millions of years to dedicate to breaking it.

It didn't make sense.

Link fixers primarily got access to drone software with direct connections, and or gaining access to someone's authorizations.

I slammed on the throttle to go forward for only long enough to trick the operators of the other drones to full throttle forward before I stopped the trajectory and launched down towards the streets. Dodging through the buildings and avoiding the incoming and outgoing regular drone traffic was a lot easier, since they all had speed restrictions this low. And I now, did not, allowing me to dodge away from my pursuers long enough to hide my drone by sending a magnetic pulse disabling my drone and landing on the roof of a small, out-of-the-way building that I aimed for with a few magnetic pulses to soften the landing but allowing my drone to disappear from any interface radars and disrupting any communication between my drone and theirs.

"This simulation is very improbable… Fun, but ridiculous," I admitted to Mr. Azel.

"That would be true."

"I sense a 'but' coming."

"That is if you were considering only outside Link Fixers. What if they had a direct link? Quantum keys can be stolen, and if stolen in a way where no one knows anything is missing, then the key is still usable."

"So, you're saying you need me to train as if someone out there has a key to taking over any drone without an authorization code that can be disrupted by any of the drone pilots on staff."

"Human error Ms. Beryl. How dedicated were you in watching your interface for outside authorizations?"

I shrugged. He had a point. It was the most boring job to be caring about if an authorized code is used outside the office. I mean, I did that all the time to reroute drones to come pick me up. But I wasn't putting anyone in danger.

"Keep in mind that you won't always have things to obstruct the view between you and the other pilots to pull this maneuver," he lectured.

As we sat there, waiting to see if the pursuers would find me in the simulation, I finally had the guts to ask him, "What happened to Cameron and B—?"

"They're fired," he said, icy like a stone-cold mammoth.

"Crushing." I cringed.

"You don't think I should have." It wasn't a question, it was just stating the facts, but I felt compelled to confirm it anyways.

"What they did wasn't as bad as my track record, so no."

"You were also fired." He salted my wounds.

"Did you hire them onto your entourage too?"

"No." He was serious sounding, like I had crossed a weird line with him that I hadn't crossed with all my earlier commentary.

I said nothing.

"Do not presume to know their merits, Ms. Beryl. I suggest you stay away from them," he added, and I detected a bit of a growl to his tone.

If he had known me better, he would have known that if he wanted my compliance, the worst thing he could have done was think he knew best for me. Telling me what I shouldn't do was not an endearing quality, especially since whether I did or did not hangout with Bailey and Cameron was outside of work, and therefore outside of his purview. If anything, he merely helped solidify my nerves to actually call up Bailey despite my guilt about getting her fired.

"Fortunately for both of us, what I do outside of work isn't really your business. Speaking of which, as I noticed earlier my training hours are not covered under required working hours, so I think we're done here." It took all of my willpower to press the end simulation button, terminating the training early. I loved the feel of the manual control in my hands, and the feeling of real piloting within my grasp, but the company was less than to be desired. Linked to the hatch control, the door lifted, and I descended down the ramp without waiting to be dismissed.

I'd already been in this building way longer than a normal human would ever tolerate. I woke up at the ass crack of dawn and it was now nearly time to sleep. This schedule would not be sustainable, and glaring back at him only served to amuse him. If I didn't know better, I'd say he was trying to make me quit my new employment, or it was his twisted way of keeping me out of trouble. Didn't he have anything better to do than to mess with my life?

I shivered. Letting the training deck A.I. give me a goodbye Ms. Beryl, which still suspiciously sounded like it was saying his last name and not my own. I gave one last glance back, and he wasn't anywhere to be seen. Cameron was right, he was a ghost. I tried to shake off the chilled feeling I got, but all it did was make my mind wander. Was I like one of those real-life simulations for him?

It was always pretty creepy to be one of the simulation consorts that basically live streamed their whole life and let people pay them to make their daily decisions for them. Were they really living at that point? When did they actually get to enjoy the credits they accumulated from it?

I quickly linked up Kelly to help distract myself. The whole place felt eerily quiet and vacant. To break up the silence I needed to have someone with me, at least until I got home.

Kelly's NeuralGo continued to try to connect, the little refresh circle kept rotating. It was very unlike her, but it was also a lot later than when I normally called. Then I quickly summoned a drone to be ready when I got out of the elevator, I didn't want to wait by myself.

My best friend not answering only added to my uneasiness, and then I couldn't help but wonder why I didn't have a missed call from her.

This would be the first day I didn't get to hear her voice.

My uneasiness amplified.

Chapter Nine

*Stolen*

Kelly remained AWOL, avoiding my link requests for the last few days. My boss has been monopolizing my time from the beginning of the day to the end of the day, making it difficult for me to figure out how to get a hold of a drone for the race Kelly signed us up for. A new pair of employees were transferred to the night crew where Bailey and Cameron used to be, they weren't as entertaining. Minding their own business, they quietly monitored their interfaces, and if they got any random calls for The Last Transport, they didn't show any interest. Probably only using the automated customer response protocols.

My boss was mute for the last several training sessions, observing my efforts on the simulation with only the smallest of grunts before stalking off all broody when the time eclipsed. It was for the best, luckily, he hadn't requested anything from me that wasn't part of normal drone pilot protocols outside of training. I'd gotten to know the space of his penthouse office suite quite well the last few days. Found an actual library with real books and found a fun fantasy history section made with leather binding and sewn through pages. Some author called Acatalec described the weirdest of places, where the citizens of various districts had some fun magical talents… but some of the pages were torn out, including a whole section called Tarquin.

I think it was the handwriting in a fun cursive that really made reading it a lot more fun. Maybe Mr. Azel was into collecting memorabilia from obscure fiction authors. Hearing my boss leave his office, the elevator chimed, and I knew he had left without giving me the option to leave. He was so inconsiderate sometimes.

Gently placing the book back on the shelf, I went to go after him, and noticed the elevator was still open and my boss nowhere to be seen. Looking around just to make sure he wasn't watching me from somewhere, I entered the elevator. To my surprise, it didn't scan me, allowing me to leave.

Having plenty of spare time to think about things during my workday, I decided to go to engineering on the first floor. Extra tall ceilings made the whole place like a showroom, and even the drones in pieces were like artwork in their own organized compartments. Robotic arms took the different parts and placed them in designated containers, where they were scanned, repaired or cleaned, then reassembled.

In the back of the assembly line, there was a rotating lift contraption that held the drones in storage. The one up next for repair, was the same one I'd sent there early this week. I knew that because all of the drones for my sector had a black stripe, and my units were always numbered with the letter B, for district B33, on the propeller's ring under the drone. It was exactly what I was searching for, a drone that hadn't downloaded any new information about my authorization codes.

It still thought I was an authorized pilot operator, and I knew there was nothing wrong with its other functions. Going up to the control interface for engineering, I went into the schedule and marked a bunch more drones to be expedited for repair. Those would jump the line and prevent my drone from being worked on until after Friday. Mr. Azel wasn't going to put a damper on my extracurricular activities this week. I smiled to myself, not if I had anything to do with it.

I'd have to make a note to tell Jessi thank you, if it weren't for her, then I wouldn't have known about a drone that needed servicing, because she could have easily checked the report and sent that sucker into engineering herself.

A notification popped up on my screen requesting anonymous link verification. It was 7:45 p.m. and on the off chance that maybe Bailey gave Cameron my information, I accepted but only with temporary access.

"Take your positions. You've been summoned to the race for the future!" An enthusiastic male voice vibrated in my comms, along with background hype music. "For returning racers, you know the drill. For you newbies, you have exactly ten minutes to get dressed in your finest before we send you coordinates. This isn't shabby chic, this is paint the town in precious metals."

"Pilots, this year is bigger than ever before. More bounties, more credits, and more pride. With the Courts watching, this is the time to show them what you're made of and bring honor to your families. Only the best will join us for the Seven Sun Celebration. Don't disappoint!"

End of transmission. At the top of my contacts was

a timer counting down from ten minutes. The engineering deck screen showed my drone was next in the queue to be rotated out from where it was currently sitting. I had a minute at most to get to the wait deck before it disappeared into the basement storage below.

I tried to ring up Kelly while I rushed to the end of the engineering floor at the fastest possible speed my chair could go. It was one of those moments that I was super thankful for my trusty wheels, I don't think legs would have done me any good.

Kelly's transmission went straight to voice mail again, but this time I actually decided to leave a message.

"You're probably rushing just like I am right now, but seriously call me back!"

There was no need to lock the drones down as they had magnetic field attachment that would stay engaged until commanded otherwise, so all I had to worry about was if I was wrong about still having authorization active on it.

Before I even approached it, I linked up, and made sure the door hatch was opening. The platform it was on shifted. The drone rotated forward, and I knew it was going to be close, before it sank into the ground. The door was fully opened, and the drone inched in its decent into the basement. I'd have to make a choice to fall into the drone off the floor ledge or stop now. I prayed that I wasn't about to commit suicide by mangling myself and my chair into the side of a moving drone.

I fell off the ledge of the floor, and for a moment it felt like I was flying before I was actually falling into the hole. It was almost as if I was suspended in the air, just for a moment as my mind caught up with my body. I activated my own magnetic locking mechanisms in my wheelchair midair to suck myself into the drone slamming inside at an angle.

My shoulder took the brunt of the force before I smacked my head on the thick glass encasement and the magnetics could realign me from the force of the fall.

Moaning, I held my head with my hand and quickly retracted it at the sting of the pressure. A small trickle of blood dripped from a gash at my temple. I didn't have long to let the air in my lungs refill before the open hole above me closed up, leaving me stuck inside a drone... inside the basement storage.

Pulling out my joysticks I forcefully plugged them in, to interface, and winced at the quick movement of my shoulder. The drone latch closed, and I held my breath as the circle rotated on my screen at my authorization codes.

Drone Pilot Class A... Authorized.

"Holy shit," I huffed under my breath. Relief at the hardware not having updated to know my authorizations weren't active anymore was short lived.

I disengaged the magnetic locks on the drone and pulled out of the sunk-in hangar just as the floor was sliding over. Hovering in the engineering floor, I only had eight minutes to get back to my house and get my fanciest clothes that were probably not fancy enough. I could make it, but I didn't know where the next destination would be, and as soon as eight o' clock rolled around Mr. Azel would know I was gone.

If this race was as big as Kelly made it out to be, I wouldn't need the job anyways. Plus, I couldn't let Kelly down. She'd spent her life savings to get us entry into this race. My heart was beating out of my chest, and I peered around trying to figure out how to get out of here. One of the robots finally finished polishing a drone and it was on a conveyor belt leading up to a big garage contraption. I took a chance that it was my way out and followed it. Wasting precious time. I only had five minutes to figure out what to wear, before I resigned myself to just being a bum. I'd have to make do with my work attire, it wasn't like I could just order a dress and have it work with my chair. That shit had to be special ordered, or manually altered. With the invention of AmbularGo, there really wasn't any incentive for fashion designers to pay much attention to the particulars of sitting down regularly.

The large hangar door rolled up, and to my surprise it was outside of the building. The drone in front of me automatically piloted from engineering bay to what I assumed was back into the fourteenth-floor transport rotation.

It was my lucky day.

As I was waiting for the next instruction to the race, I noticed something in the seat behind me.

A box. Wrapped in fancy black paper with a bit of shimmer, like a sophisticated secret, and tied with a delicate white ribbon. Even the box was ready for a black-tie event.

Chapter Ten

*Pilot Sixteen*

Curiosity got the best of me, and while I waited for the last two minutes to count down on my lens, I picked up the sleek box and placed it on my lap. I slid the ribbon off, so that I could put it back on after snooping, even though a part of me wanted to pull the bow and open it lavishly. The box wasn't a traditional lift top, I had to push the box out from the slipcover like a drawer. Inside was a bunch of fancy tissue paper with more ribbon, and within was an intricate lace bodice with corset snaps on the side, as opposed to the traditional back closures. A very thoughtful design if I had to wear it myself. Underneath it was a beaded sheer shawl that paired with it beautifully. The last known person to have used this drone was Mr. Azel before I sent it to engineering. He had to have left it in here. Whoever he was giving this to was a very lucky lady, but now that I thought about it, maybe a very pissed off one since it'd been sitting in this drone for almost a week.

I hadn't really thought about Mr. Azel dating anyone, but he was too pretty not to have been taken, so it made sense. Checking the size of the garment, I lifted it up to myself and couldn't help but hug it into my chest at how fancy it was. Whoever she was obviously went to special dinners with the boss man at expensive restaurants with dress codes. And lucky for me she wasn't some skinny ass model stick figure, I might actually be able to borrow it for tonight.

Giddy, I dimmed the glass to blackout any lookieloos. The stiff nature of the corset was perfect for me to position it behind my back with little trouble at all, and the side enclosures were a gift from the fashion gods. As I picked up the shawl, a pair of lacy flats were hidden underneath that matched the top.

The notification link request sounded before I could indulge in playing dress up any longer.

Turning the dimmer off, I prepared to haul ass to the given location.

It was now 7:55 p.m.

"You have five minutes to join us before the party leaves without you! Good luck!"

The coordinates flashed on my contacts, and I bypassed the speed restrictions to make it there on time. Traditional drone travel would have taken an estimated ten minutes to get there, eight minutes if you respected air traffic, and five if you ignored everything, which I supposed was the point.

Just like in training this morning, I stuck to the traffic below skyline roof levels that way I could easily move around buildings, and regulated speed reductions of incoming and outgoing drones. It was a lot easier for me to manually avoid drones when they were slowing down, and buildings were stagnant so I could go a lot faster than in air traffic above. I would barely make the time limit, despite having to do a lot more maneuvering between buildings and avoiding drone landing zones. All drones were highlighted on my flight overlay so I could anticipate where to go, and how to avoid collisions.

Three minutes later, I got that prickly feeling to keep my eyes peeled for more than just the plotted course on my interface. Instead of going straight, which would have been faster, I turned off down a different roadway that vehicles used to occupy before drone travel took over. You can still see a few vintage clunkers rolling down the streets sometimes, for those that had collector passes for road use.

As I turned off, I saw another drone, not reflected on the interface, plummeting down to street level at top speeds. They spotted me and decided to rush down the side street to catch up. Coming up fast behind me, I moved up to allow them to pass if they thought they could handle going faster than what I was already going.

Like a parasite they followed suit, lifting up to my altitude and closing in.

What were they doing?

The drone matched my speed and came up on my side right before a turn off, and we had to adjust together to avoid crashing into each other, or the buildings while maintaining our speed. I risked a glance over at the other drone to see a girl with her hair all in ringlets, and blinding jewelry in her ears and even a tiara of diamonds. She grinned at me beneath a bejeweled mask before her drone eased over trying to guide me straight into an upcoming garage opening, while she would continue on the straight away past the building. At least she was being kind about it, making sure if I crashed it was where I could park my drone.

I gritted my teeth and clamped down on my

joysticks. Game on, princess.

Checking the garage layout, I could see this one had a through and through garage layout. It would be risky, but if I went through on purpose, I might make it out without having to fight this crazy lady. Aiming for the entrance, I stole a moment to see the shock on her face, which was what I was going for.

I could see her thinking, was she nuts? And I would respond simply, if I could, it's only nuts for someone with half of my experience. The hair on my arms stood as I followed the pattern of drones making their way through the drop zone and watched as shocked civilians ran out of the way, even though they weren't in the way to begin with. This was the riskiest move of all, being noticed. I could only hope that they didn't alert the police, security cameras would do that job if I didn't follow designated drone pathways. But another drone was coming in making me have to swerve off the path. If the police weren't notified already, they would be as soon as the footage was analyzed.

Before zooming out of the garage, I turned my flight deck off, losing all drone overlay on my screen. It was risky, but with the police potentially on the way, and that rogue drone not far off it was actually more safe than keeping it active. I'd have to rely on my eyes, and intuition.

There was another building directly in front of the exit, and I quickly pulled up, ascending above the rooftop, and closing in on drone airspace, without an overlay to be alerted to the incoming drones going at speeds quadruple what was allowed in the building zones. I had lost precious time in the garage, and I could see the rogue drone in the distance ahead of me, also taking the airways above, probably searching for her next victim, or trying to make up time for her detour of running me off my course.

The clock in my contact was counting down the seconds. This was the most nervous I'd ever been in a drone, flying blind. My palms were sweating as I cruised through the traffic, avoiding the drones on their automated pathways. Based on my calculations, I wasn't going fast enough to make it on time. Not unless I sped up, and if I went any faster, my reaction time to seeing any drone traffic in time to correct course, was not ideal. It would be the fastest I'd ever flown without interface assist.

Swallowing down my nerves, I took a deep breath because I would literally be holding my breath the rest of the way. This was it. I turned on my pilot playlist and upped the throttle. I could hear the pounding of my own blood heating up my ears. I whizzed by drones, skirting on the very edge between traditional pathways. It required moving back and forth more often, but with less space needed to clear incoming traffic. I got into a rhythm knowing that drones entering the air traffic had a set pattern they stuck to.

Sway left, sway right. Until someone with familiar erratic movements weaving through the traffic was coming up fast. Princess was on full throttle, and I was torn between revenge or hiding.

I didn't get to choose, because she obviously spotted me coming up on her tail. As soon as I caught up, she moved on top of me and began lowering her propellers on top of my glass dome. An incoming drone was coming at us, and we both moved to the side to avoid it. Her drone tapped the top of mine and sent me inches into oncoming. The automated drone nicked my glider and went spinning out, along with me.

I torqued my joystick up at an angle just in time to jam my other glider into her propeller system as I rotated down. Transport drones weren't really meant for any showmanship flips, and I clung onto the joysticks, and tried to correct all of the flashing notifications in my interface as fast as I could think. The top speeds didn't help any, and I immediately turned off my propellers to free fall in a counter intuitive attempt to fix my alignment.

My drone passed through drone airspace with only one more small ding from outgoing traffic, before I saw the top of my first building. I quickly turned on the propellers and rotated them to stop just above a drone pad on luckily a lower roof than its neighbors.

The clock in my contact was counting down from thirty. I didn't even know what happened to the other drone pilot, but I knew I barely even dinged the other automatic transports, so they should have been fine. No time to let my nerves settle, I quickly sped through the buildings, wobbling from it being harder to control with the tips of my gliders broken. Up ahead I saw the marker of the coordinates in a parking garage. Behind me I could hear sirens in the distance.

The clock disappeared as soon as it reached ten seconds.

Screeching into the garage, the door closed behind me, muffling the sounds of police drones closing in. My gliders ground into the concrete breaking off more chunks, and I knew this thing wasn't going to be flying me home, and definitely wouldn't be flying in any race after this. I waited for the garage doors to reopen for the police and take me away.

The trip was over.

I'd let Kelly down.

Whatever debt she got herself into, she'd have to figure it out.

I'd have to thank her later for finding a race that finally beat me. I wasn't looking forward to explaining myself to the police.

Slumping into my chair, I let my head lull back in exhaustion, and all I wanted to do was curl up and sleep until I convinced myself this was all a dream. A really bad dream.

A tap sounded on my stolen drone, and I rolled my head over to see a man in a tux, and face hidden behind a mask. He didn't need my permission to get into the drone, whatever device he had in his hands hacked into the programming, and the hatch lifted.

"Pilot Sixteen, you must exit your drone and come with me."

I groaned. Was he some sort of creepy police officer?

"Are you injured?" he asked seeing I wasn't making any moves to exit.

"Mentally."

"You have exactly forty seconds before the police gain entry." He took in my wheelchair and hesitated before asking, "Do you need me to carry you?" Moving towards me with his hands at ready I swatted at him.

"I'm not an invalid," I protested, "I'm very capable of getting out myself." I wondered why so many men were interested in invading my personal space this week. This was becoming a social habit I wasn't fond of, screw the chivalry.

I disengaged the magnetic locks on my chair and popped my wheel up. He moved out of the way as I launched myself out of the drone without enabling the ramp. I saw the box with the shoes crumpled, and one shoe on the passenger seat, and one wedged near the hatch.

Sweetly, I asked, "Could you get those?" I felt bad for yelling at him when he tried to help, but it was a touchy subject for me, and I was more than a bit on edge. He nodded and plucked the shoes. He then scanned the drone with his device and walked away expecting me to follow. Which, of course, I did and quickly.

When we were at the elevator of the building, the garage lift gate opened, and sirens flooded the floor as the mystery man casual offered, "I've wiped your digital data from the drone. I'll have to ask you to wait in the lobby until you can be escorted to The Last Transport."

"Last transport? I don't have a drone anymore," I said it like it was obvious that I wouldn't be continuing the race, if that's where he was from.

"You didn't have that drone to begin with," he corrected me.

He had a point, but I didn't like how matter of fact he was being, like that didn't matter that the drone was totalled.

"Well, now that the excitement is over. Thank you for helping me out, but it's now eight, and—"

"Eight O' two," he corrected again.

"Yah, okay. I have to get back to my boss before he figures out that I'm missing, since I didn't make it in time, and I no longer have his drone."

"The other pilot matched against you did not make it to the pickup point, your time would normally disqualify you, but your tenacity in taking out your opponent has actually added bonus time to your allotment, making you in the top twenty. You will be going to The Last Transport."

Then it clicked… he wasn't just talking about the last transport in the drone race… this was what Cameron and Bailey were talking about. This was The Last Transport, some sort of exclusive club. Was that other guy earlier this week a part of the set up crew for this race? I had so many questions, I only hoped I had enough time, and or would be allowed to ask them.

In the lobby of what must have been a business district filled with many small retailers, the guy turned to leave me.

"I have no drone to get there…" I repeated.

"No one uses their own drones for this race, creates too many chances for cheating outside of the rules. You'll be escorted shortly. Please wait for your escort to provide you with a mask."

I opened my mouth to ask another question, only to notice him seamlessly walk beside the next person to pass us like they were always walking together, and as that person turned off, he was no longer there.

My heart hammered in my chest, still hyped up from what had just happened, when a notification link came up as priority, but with no identifier.

I hesitated, but the longer I waited the more urgent the notification became in my contact. I accepted it despite not wanting to.

"Ms. Beryl," he remarked in an oddly calm manner.

"Mr. Azel," I said back to him, trying my best to match his calm. I had forgotten that, as my employer, he had access to my link I.D.

Chapter Eleven

*My Escort*

This was it. He was going to fire me. How did he already know the drone was stolen? The police couldn't have already called him this quick, could they?

"How was your training today?" Mr. Azel asked, and I was taken aback. The clock in my contact showed 8:05 P.M.

I cleared my throat. "I think I've really started to appreciate the highly unlikely simulations you've been supervising."

"I thought you might," he seemed glib and I wanted to die right there. How did he know?

"Is this what being fired feels like? I thought for sure you'd wait to do it in person," I admitted, and prepared myself for the punches. My nerves were too shot to be dealing with the stress of letting it linger. Just burn me now, instead of staring at the sun waiting for it to consume me.

"I always have my important conversations in person," his voice so close I even thought I felt his breath behind my ear. My skin prickled, and I begrudgingly turned around to my boss standing there like the poster boy for those mystery date niche dating programs. His dark hair was styled, a white mask hid three quarters of his face only showing part of his mouth, and those dark chocolate eyes. Even if he wasn't talking to me in that criminally smooth voice of his, I'd recognize him, especially those fancy shoes. He spotted the pair of beaded flats in my lap and smiled.

Instantly, I lifted them up to him. "I'm sorry for stealing your girlfriend's shoes." He delicately took them from me, and I turned away from him ashamed. I wasn't going to strip, and give him the bodice, but I did pull off the shawl that I wrapped around my legs to hide my black slacks. I grimaced seeing that the item was snagged at the end, with a huge tear in it, probably during the whole falling through the air bit and caught on a bolt or something.

Without saying a word, he knelt down to meet me at face level, and all the heat flushed my chest and up my neck. Placing the shoes on the ground beside him, he lifted my foot from its holster strap. My jaw dropped, and I stared at him confused. Too stunned to punch him in the face for touching a part of me I've never let anyone but my mother, and my doctor touch. If I could kick him, I probably would have on instinct alone. His fingers were soft as he eased my black ankle boot off to reveal my embarrassing fun sock of little penguins flying drones. He smiled, and I blushed.

I wasn't blind to the delicate way he held my limp appendage in his hands.

Stammering I suddenly found my voice. "What are you doing?"

His finger slipped along my ankle, and even though I couldn't feel it my pulse quickened as if I had. Being so gentle, he slid the sock off in one smooth motion and tucked it into his coat pocket before taking the shoe and slipping it onto my painted toenails, that my mom insisted on doing for me the last time she came to visit. Thank you, Mom, for at least making my feet presentable for the current indescribable feeling I had watching him take such care in placing a shoe on my foot.

"Ms. Beryl," he said so formally, "It's time I escort you to The Last Transport," he surprised me, and all of the nanochips fluttering in my stomach must have just been gas because he wasn't flirting with me at all, he was my escort to the most dangerous race of my life, if earlier was any indicator.

"Oh," I responded dumbly, "So, not fired?"

"As my pick for this race, I expect you to win." He continued to put the second shoe on, but this time I was trying not to pay attention to how thoughtful he was and reminded myself that he wasn't doing it because he liked me, he just wanted me to win.

This was one of those stupid filthy rich games of his, and I was merely a thing he found entertaining. When you had everything else, meddling with people was all there was left to do. I understood it, but it didn't mean I had to like it.

The training all made sense now.

"How did you know I would come?"

"Honestly, I was hoping you wouldn't." He stood up, and from inside his coat pocket he pulled out a lace mask that matched the bodice I was wearing. Full of contradictions, I didn't know what to make of his confession.

"Why?"

He pondered my question for a moment before walking away and having me catch up and repeat the question.

S.M. McCoy

"Staying off the radar has its advantages, and there are some at this kind of event that are better off not knowing," is all he would say on the matter before we walked into a lawyer's office. Nodding to the clerk, they opened a door for us like we were royalty, even though the door would have automatically opened without their assistance. Hovering outside the window was Mr. Azel's personal drone. The best credits could buy.

The clerk quickly pushed the window that was as tall as the room over. This one was not automated and seemed to be custom built. I didn't think this feature was added to the building's schematics, my boss had more mystery than just the mask he wore. Why would he have need of a secret escape route from a business building, except now with the police in the drone garage?

He entered the drone and offered his hand to help pull me in across the small gap between the drone and the building window. I looked down and saw how high up we were down that small sliver, and with the wrong push of my weight it could open up to swallow me in an instant.

Grabbing his hand, I appreciated that he didn't just pick me up like last time in his office, but these were different circumstances. I closed my eyes, and instead of rolling forward like I expected, his arms wrapped around me pulling me the rest of the way. I felt safe in his arms, and stared up into his masked face, as the hatch closed behind us.

I worried he could feel my heart beating out of my chest and was thankful my lace mask covered most of my cheeks.

"What kind of race is this?" I asked seriously.

"For both our sakes, the kind you'll win." Breaking the spell over my eyes, I activated my magnetic locks and felt myself being pulled into position away from him. That's all that mattered to him, was that I'd win. Lucky for him, it was in Kelly's best interest that I did, because I wasn't doing it for him.

Chapter Twelve

*Gangsters*

Mr. Azel's personal drone was larger than a normal passenger drone that could fit four people. This thing was like a stretch drone that could fit ten people with how long it was. It could have been considered a small plane.

The glass enclosure was rolling augmented reality across the surface, to make it seem like we were hanging out in the rain forest. Even the speakers had the sounds of extinct birds, the occasional predator growls, and light water drizzling through the canopies. An aroma spritzer included the fresh scent like we were there, and even though I've never been, and had no idea if that's what a rain forest actually smelled like, it made me think it was real except for the seats that seemed to float through the scene.

It took all of my self-control not to keep asking Mr. Azel questions, but I didn't because I was determined not to talk to him. I pressed my lips together tight and avoided direct contact, busying myself with staring at the forest scenery that I knew was only there to prevent me from seeing where we were going.

Wherever The Last Transport was, it was secret, and they didn't want anyone knowing where it was. I tried to link up to the drone to search its data for the coordinates only to be met with limited access and a password prompt. Trying to crack a quantum password was beyond my link fixing abilities, I'd need a special fix chip installed in his drone's panel to even have a chance at getting past the firewalls.

The more I tried not to look at him, when I was literally facing him, the more I found myself seeing him in my mind. Don't meet his eyes, I'd tell myself, and then I'd think about how dark and chocolatey they were.

Don't even peek at his mask I'd say, and then I'd think about how his lips were the only thing besides his eyes that I could see if I did.

Don't glance at his hands as one was lying gently on an armrest and the other was on his thigh. A thigh that was muscular and led me to thinking about how his leg crossed over his knee as he leaned back casually, and last I checked he stared off to the side avoiding eye contact with me.

In a split-second decision, I turned my head to face the other direction and took a glance at him as I did. Before I could finish turning my head, I stopped. Our eyes locked, and I couldn't turn away. His face was hidden, and then I heard his fingers tap. I followed the noise, and my eye caught on his opened jacket where my character socks peeked out from his inside pocket. Matching my smile, he took one sock out, folded it, then placed it in his front pocket like a decorative square, but with penguins driving drones.

I giggled and broke my own rule to not talk to him. "I'm not sure that matches your wardrobe."

"It's quite the conversation starter though, don't you think?" He patted the folded over sock in his pocket like he was going to keep it there.

"I'm sure your girlfriend will love it. I can only hope she doesn't know I stole her gifts for this." I laughed and tried to make light of stealing his present for her.

He raised an eyebrow and uncrossed his legs to lean forward which made me almost choke on my nervous laughter. "Those," his focus never leaving my eyes he told me seriously, "I bought for you."

I gulped despite my mouth being dry and stared at him, digesting that information.

The top was exactly my size, had enclosures where I could reach them, the shawl fit perfect around my legs like a skirt overlay, and the shoes were practical flats that didn't get in the way of my footholds. It was the most thoughtful gift anyone had ever given me, and we barely knew each other. Wait, a gift… from my boss.

"Why?"

"I couldn't have you defying my orders to go to an illegal drone race, and not go in style." He leaned back in his seat again, and I realized then that it had nothing to do with me that he got me these things. If I was a representative of him in the race, then he couldn't have me embarrassing him in front of his elite drone racing buddies.

It made sense, and I gave him a small nod before avoiding those eyes that made me feel like he cared. I swallowed down the lump in my throat and tried to focus on the reason why I was even here with him. He was my boss, and this was probably why I was hired direct by him after being fired by the company.

"Why are we so dressed up for a race anyways?" I asked sobering the mood.

"Every year the Lord Prince likes to hold a race to bring all of the regents together before a big summit. There are seven regions, four racers from each region are selected, and four wild cards. Only the top sixteen from these are allowed to actually race, and only the most influential of the regions watch the races from The Last Transport, while most everyone else who knows about it will watch from their home interfaces… for a price," he explained, and I was left feeling more confused than when he started. Who the hell was the Lord Prince? Some sort of mobster with a pompous alias that lords over regions of gangsters? I was lost, and my boss could tell.

He sighed. "The less you know about these people the better."

So they were mobsters, I confirmed to myself. I mean, anyone hosting an illegal drone race couldn't be considered a quote unquote good guy, but I hadn't really thought about it before. I merely liked the extra cash that most of these races provided, but this race was much riskier than anything I'd ever been involved with.

"Got it."

"If we win the race, you can get through this whole thing without anyone knowing who you are. You keep your mask on, and you stay in the drone assigned to you. It isn't uncommon for winners to take on a persona, but if you lose you will be forced to pay off your debt, and we don't want to owe these people, they don't take credits. You will be forced to join the Drone Guard, as you are now considered one of the top pilots, and that is more valuable than credit."

"Like indentured service? They can't do that… can they?"

"They can, and they do, though most are more than happy to devote themselves to the cause." He smirked at me. "I don't see you as being a follow orders kind of pilot," he joked, "If you were, we wouldn't be here."

I glared at him. "This isn't funny. You could have been more upfront and said, 'Tyler, I know you're a sucker for illegal drone races, but you've been getting yourself involved with gangsters. Please sit this one out.' Would have been a nice heads-up." I lowered my voice and did a horrible impression of his silky deep tone that sounded more like a gruff cartoon character.

He leaned forward and grabbed my hand in his, then smoothly said, "Tyler, don't get involved with illegal drone races. Being as they are illegal, they are usually run by powerful overlords that don't care about your wellbeing. Please listen to me next time."

I pulled my hand from his and swatted at him. He laughed, and leaned back into his seat, and this was the most relaxed I'd ever seen him. Which was surprising considering we were going to an evil overlord's lair and trying to win a drone race to save my friend Kelly from financial ruin, and now make sure I didn't become an indentured pilot to amoral goons.

"Would that have made a difference," he asked seriously to me.

I frowned and shook my head. "Probably not. I wouldn't have believed you."

"And you believe me now?" He quirked a brow. He was quite handsome when he wasn't reprimanding me.

"After the cutthroat race to even be here right now, unfortunately yes. Plus," I stopped and shook my head, changing my mind about telling him how much I was worried that I still hadn't heard from Kelly. She was the one who even signed us up for this race, and it made me nervous knowing who we were racing for was dangerous. What if she didn't make it through the first race, and was lying in a ditch somewhere, or worse at the hospital because another racer crashed her into oncoming traffic? Picking at my nail cuticle I flexed my fingers and then dug them into my pant legs to stop myself from picking until I had no more skin to pick.

He watched me expectantly, waiting for me to finish. The way his eyes tore into my soul made me want to tell him all of my secrets, my lip quivered because my insides hurt thinking about anything happening to Kelly. She was all I had when this was all over, at least I hoped I still had her after this was over. Misinterpreting why I was so emotional he nodded and tried to reassure me, "You've far surpassed most pilots I've seen in this race during training, but fear will help you stay sharp. Let your instincts help protect you when the time comes."

"My instincts are what I fear most right now." Instinct told me something was wrong with Kelly. Then it occurred to me this whole thing was run by mobsters, and I was his pick… I turned my attention over at Mr. Azel with a new understanding. He was part of this.

"You could have told me this was what you hired me for."

"Could I?" His brown eyes blazed.

Through the window the tranquil forest faded from view revealing a frosted glass building towering below us like an ice sculpture. A soft hum vibrated through the drone as the propellers turned off, and the hatch opened us up onto the platform. Where was something like this in Washington? We couldn't have traveled outside of the state with such a smooth ride, could we?

This was The Last Transport.

## Chapter Thirteen

*The Last Transport*

Floating tabloid drones buzzed around us, little twinkling stars in the dusk, flashing with each photo snapped. With my mask in place, and an outfit I'd never usually wear I guessed that the face recognition software would probably have a tough time identifying me, but fewer and fewer people were in wheelchairs like me. I looked over to my boss nervously and wondered why he didn't tell me about the paparazzi. He did say something about people of influence, and watching, but I didn't think on it too much. Squaring my shoulders, not waiting for the dumb off ramp I popped out of the drone in my traditional flair, ignoring the hand offered to me by my masked employer.

Instead of feeling snubbed, he flourished his hand in my direction, like that was what he intended on doing anyway, merely displaying me like the commodity I was to him.

He walked beside me as we followed the pathway inside lit up by the drones snapping pictures of us as the sun dropped behind the building creating soft star bursts, and pretty violet hues mixed with oranges. I smiled awkward as Mr. Azel rested his hand on my shoulder and resisted the urge to scrunch up my neck to shrug him off. He was so close that despite being outside I could still smell the rain forest on him from the drone's humidifier spray.

A green scanner rolled over us before the door would open, and even with his mask the door opened greeting him, "Welcome Regent Azel, and Pilot Sixteen."

Under my breath I huffed at him without moving my mouth, ventriloquist style so the photo drones didn't catch me, "How?"

He squeezed my shoulder reassuringly, and even though it seemed a bit possessive, part of me, a deep, deep, down part of me, felt comforted, and didn't want the feeling to stop.

Once inside the building he whispered, "They weren't scanning you, they were scanning your NeuralGo." Seeing my unease, he added, "Only a surface scan, they have your temporary ID that was used to join the race. I'll scrub your files after we leave so they can't track you." His voice became gruff, and masculine as he explained how he would protect my data.

I didn't think talking about Link Fixing traits would get me so excited, but when he said it, I was at a loss to think of anything else. At the very least, he made me feel safe even when rolling into a mobster's hideout.

Like a grand ballroom, the halls were huge and wide, every wall was interfaced augmented glass, and seamlessly transitioned from glass to what I would imagine the inside of a mansion taken over by forest fairies would resemble. It was magical.

A sliding door opened up, and the sound of a party in mid-swing filled the air. A few masked guards in full-on black leather armor were at the doors we passed bowing to us, before standing tall yet again to repeat our names to the crowd, though my title really wasn't a name, but a number. I wasn't part of the influential filthy rich people in the room, I was an object of entertainment.

The music hushed, and a tall man parted the people between us. He was young, didn't seem much older than me, and wore a gold accented suit that was more like an elaborate uniform that was part armor, and part costume like… a Lord? I could only assume he was the Lord Prince that Mr. Azel was talking about earlier, and he was headed right for us. He wasn't hard on the eyes, and all of them were on him.

"Regent Azel, what a rare occasion to have you join us on this momentous of events. The Summit isn't until after the Seven Suns Races, but maybe the changes this year have piqued your interest." He smiled big, and the charisma flowed off of him in waves. The whole crowd hung on every word, and then he moved again without the distraction of the parting people. I had trouble keeping my mouth shut, my lips parted unable to keep the shock off my face, because I was obviously hallucinating. He didn't walk at all, he hovered without any magnetic tracks, or anything remotely obvious technological assist. It was the most brilliant display of technology, that if I wasn't a true believer in science, I would swear he was a magician.

"Any changes should have been addressed with all the regents before the race," he growled at the most powerful man in the room, and I was both in awe, and terrified. Then I wondered why everyone kept calling Mr. Azel a regent…was he a high-ranking member of this illegal mob squad? What had I got myself into?

S.M. McCoy

Even if I got out of this race intact, my boss was one of them. I recalled that even the ELO trainer A.I. had greeted him with that same preface, regent.

The prince's smile turned dark, and my wheels rolled back a bit with my unconscious thought to escape, but with Mr. Azel's hand on my shoulder I wasn't going anywhere. "That's the thing, it was a request by a majority of the other regions that this issue be addressed. It was merely convenient to combine the two events. Many of the regents are getting impatient with waiting for another hand offering, and only the best make it in this race. It's only natural that we should choose the winner to compete for the honor. And how wonderful is it that it'll be the first time you've decided to sponsor one of the pilots."

"No one has survived such an honor," he said scathing under his breath so the crowd wouldn't overhear.

"Another first is always welcomed," the prince said cheerfully before bowing to Mr. Azel, and nodding to the crowd for the music to resume.

Mr. Azel's grip on my shoulder was hurting me, and I placed my hand on his and pinched him with my nails so he'd remove his hand, but instead of flinching away, he softened his hold and kept it there before whispering to me, "You will lose this race, Ms. Beryl."

"You just said—"

"I know what I said," he hissed, "and it is now more pressing that you survive throwing the race."

"Aren't surviving and winning mutually exclusive?"

"No, let me take care of it." His teeth gritted, and those brown eyes, embers, ready to burn down the building. He clearly wasn't used to not getting his way about things, and this Lord Prince seemed to press Mr. Azel's buttons like Jessi prodded mine. He always seemed to keep his cool, but he had a fire about him today I'd never have expected from someone who seemed so calculated.

Releasing my shoulder, he disappeared into the crowd of finely dressed thrill seekers. I'm sure among them were the other fifteen pilots, their escorts, and of course the people who had too much money that they preferred to watch other people risk their lives in a full-throttle drone death match. I cringed, wondering if that other chick that I'd raced against earlier was all right after her propeller was damaged by my glider.

I would have thought on it longer, but movement caught my eye from the edge of the room that I hadn't noticed before. Strange small glass cages were displayed near the food and beverage station, but it was more of an ornately decorated display which happen to be made of food and beverages. The wine flowed over a fountain made entirely out of ice. The food was just as beautiful, I wasn't sure how anyone would dare eat the artwork. Inside the cages were people seductively dancing to the music like a weird voyeuristic dance club.

Except one cage in particular was the worst dancer of the bunch, and they seemed to be breathing on the glass and writing in the wake of their own moisture and waving. All the other dancers seemed like they wanted to be there, but there was something different about this one. I headed in that direction to see what was going on. As I passed down the row of human captivity, both filled with some men, and some women they all seemed preoccupied with having a good time, so my level of concern for the odd one of the bunch was reserved until I found out more.

The closer I got the more erratic the dancer became, and suddenly my heart rose up into my throat. Black hair with auburn highlights were expertly tamed back and straightened in a beautiful design, and that deep perfect ebony skin behind a sleek diamond encrusted mask were unmistakable. Legs for days were on full display in a sexy matching white cocktail dress. As I approached the cube, it rose up in the air so I couldn't touch it. The glass cube lit up flashing like a disco ball, and as I backed away it came back down. Obviously, I wasn't meant to get too close. No one paid me any attention, the light show only added to the dance ambiance.

I turned up my audio synthesizer so only voices would be heard, muting out the extra music in the background. Wide eyed, I felt my heart pounding in my ribcage, and no idea what to do other than say, "What the hell?"

Kelly crouched down in her glass cage and waved at me sheepishly.

Chapter Fourteen

*The Bounty*

Kelly fanned herself in relief and slumped against the wall of her glass enclosure. "I'm so glad you made it. You didn't tell anyone here who you are, right?"

"Of course not." At least, not anyone else outside of my boss, but I didn't think she needed to know that. I wasn't in the mood for her to razz me about how his voice was devilish, part of me always knew she only did that because it rattled me. For a long time, I've suspected she'd never been into men, and her commentary on them was so over the top, and comical that it only added to that suspicion.

"You'll be a slam to win this thing. Just don't talk to anyone else, okay?"

"What did you get us into?" I yelled at her.

She grimaced and made sure no one was watching before whispering, despite the music being loud enough to cover our voices anyways, "Don't be mad. It's just that I'd always heard rumors from home about how this race brought people out of poverty, and even the runner ups were taken care of for life. I thought about you wanting your AmbularGo, and the medical expenses, and hating your job. It just all seemed so perfect."

I grimaced, not realizing how much I'd revealed to her about my financial situation, but mostly about my medical bills. She wasn't talking only about mine. My mom had been in and out of the hospital multiple times now with complications arising from the freak accident that left me paralyzed. She had been there with me, and we thought came out of it with no problems, at least none that they could have predicted.

"Ever think, maybe it was too perfect?" I couldn't stay angry with her, I never could, but this whole thing made me so nervous. It would have been great if we could get out of this with a ton of credits on hand, clear up the medical debt, and even get an upgrade to AmbularGo.

She sat on the ground of the glass cube and frowned. "I wanted to do something nice for you, and this is my thanks."

"Don't even start." I threw my hand up to stop her from continuing that line of reasoning. "Why are you in some weird consort cube?"

"Yah, umm. So, don't be mad, but technically speaking I didn't know about the rules about region selections, and bought our entries into this race off market. It's best if, you know," she only mouthed the rest of her thought while shaking her head, "we don't know each other."

She stood up seductively adding with a wink, "Also, win... so you can claim me as your bounty." Wiggling her booty at me, she blew me a kiss.

My cheeks flushed at her attention. I smiled at her and shook my head, teasing her back by grabbing the air kiss and pretending to place it in my nonexistent pocket. I patted it and acted like I'd save it for later.

"I'd do anything for you," I admitted. Then I remembered this was the first time I'd ever seen her in person. "You are more beautiful in person, by the way." I fiddled with my fingernails, and momentarily distracted myself with the food decorations.

She laughed, and it started off so smooth to my ears before a nervousness crept in at the end. "You too," she responded more shy than I'd ever heard from her. She was such an outgoing personality, it was strange hearing her sound so reserved.

I spun around in my chair giving her a show of my wheels, since I'd always had my video calls be from the waist up, she'd never seen me quite like this before. The fact that she smiled, and didn't give me that all knowing pity, and or awkwardness, I was expecting made me even more happy she was my best friend.

"It's stiff competition," I changed the subject feeling self-conscious about her telling me I was beautiful, even if it was only a reply to my compliment. It still made my insides buzz.

She surveyed the room and nodded. "But they don't hold a bolt compared to you. You're going to kick their asses and steal that AmbularGo right from those rich snobs' uppity nostrils." Kelly threw a fake punch in the air, and then did a dainty air slap.

I bit my lip, not so sure her enthusiasm was warranted. I'd already lost one drone today, but she didn't have to know that. I wanted to keep her spirits high.

If winning meant I could get her out of her debt to these mobsters, then that's what I was going to do. I couldn't trust whoever was going to win would be nice. The way she explained how the runners-up were treated didn't match the concern Mr. Azel was giving off. But he went from wanting me to win, to wanting me to lose at the flip of the proverbial Lord Prince Coin.

"Why'd you have to get involved with mobsters?" I sighed.

She raised an eyebrow. "They aren't mobsters. They're royalty where I'm from. Speaking of which, why were you being escorted by a regent? I may have been away from home for a hot micronum, but they aren't known for escorting pilots... plus, I didn't like how he was touching you." She pouted, and her tone got serious, "You didn't tell him who you are, did you?"

"Why?" I asked nervously, since he knew exactly who I was already.

"If you win, no one will be allowed to look into your data if you don't want them to, and you don't want them to. They can't figure out who you are. At all costs."

"Yah, okay." I waved her off.

"I'm serious, Pilot Sixteen." She didn't even use my name, "Your entry was purchased off market, and you aren't registered legally within the regions."

"You're talking nonsense. You talk as if this whole race is legal to begin with."

Kelly's voice hitched like she was about to cry. "That's the thing... it is. This is some modern-day gladiator shit, and it is completely legal where I'm from."

I hesitated before asking what I'd been putting off this whole conversation. "Where are you from?"

My skin tingled with the magic I felt in the air, and I didn't want my instincts to be right. I wanted to believe in science, in technology.

In anything else.

Nervously scanning around us again Kelly admitted, "Acatalec."

Chapter Fifteen

*Trust No One*

I recalled my time in Mr. Azel's library reading a book by that name: Acatalec. In it described different regions that surrounded one called Numa, but several pages were torn from the handwritten fantasy. And it had to be a fantasy, because what was described in the book was different fables from each region about seven monsters that held the power of a defeated deity that helped build the land. It read similarly to old poetry about an old civilization called Rome. They would talk about deities, and how they meddled with humans to create the land in such a poetic way that it was powerful magic. People turned into trees, and nymphs turned into echoes.

The story read:

*Acatalec was born from a woman called Nam, as strong as she was beautiful, wandering the worlds lonely and in search of love. In her travels she met a king named Marduk, that was just as strong as she. His strength and kindness over his people swayed her lonely heart. Marduk was a deity with many gifts, but when his sister Tiam came to visit, jealousy of the planet and the love of Nam led to a war that ravished the lands barren. Nam dove into her heart and pulled out seven keys that formed what are now the seven regions. From those keys a sword was crafted, imbued with a power that she'd found on different worlds to help restore Acatalec, and protect Marduk.*

*Without the keys Nam was weakened, and gave the sword, which was her very essence, to Marduk to protect the land. Sword in hand, Marduk betrayed Nam by holding her captive until Tiam's arrival with her army. Tiam revealed Marduk had no siblings. Using the sword, Tiam cut down the shocked Nam. Marduk nourished the land with Nam's blood, and from it a monster for each region was born with magic to protect the land Nam was now a part of, and they sought out vengeance for their mother.*

*Marduk and Tiam thought themselves safe and had a party to celebrate the conquering of Nam, as they wished to be the only deities to rule over humans, displaying the key sword for all the citizens to marvel at.*

*The regents born of Nam hid in plain sight, with their powers they were able to save Acatalec from the rule of Marduk and Tiam. Acatalec was free, and the regents continued to protect the land to this day with a Hand Rite Ceremony.*

That's all I could remember, and some of the story was missing about how the regents defeated Marduk, but I assumed that was part of the torn pages.

Every culture liked to embellish their history with a bit of flourish, so I was about to ask Kelly what else she knew about her home that I'd never heard of outside of a small leather book. I honestly had never heard the name or seen it on any map. I tried to connect to my contact for a location search, but it seemed that function was disabled while in this room. Hence why Kelly wasn't able to answer my calls earlier. How long had she been here? Before I could ask another person joined our conversation from behind.

"Taken an interest in the bounty?" A familiar feminine voice cracked.

"Bailey?"

"Shh, no names," she corrected, "You can call me Pilot Nine, Representative of the Regent of Priscus." She patted me harshly on the back before congratulating me, "I knew you'd make it. I had a good feeling about you," she boasted. Despite the very expensive party, she barely dressed up. Her dreadlocks were pulled back and she added a simple hair comb to elevate the ensemble. Aside from her usual dark makeup, she wore a long black dress with a deep cleavage cut, and a high slit up the skirt revealing leather pants underneath. She saw me assessing her and shrugged. "Regent told me I had to wear a dress, Cameron insisted on the cut, and I insisted on the pants," my eyes went to her shoes and I smiled approvingly, "and the boots." Combat boots with a dress might not have worked with anyone else, but they did for her.

Kelly tapped her foot impatiently waiting for her to be included in the conversation again. I gave her a cheeky smile before eagerly asking Bailey what I'd been dying to know since she left. Completely forgetting my guilt about getting her fired I asked anyway, "How did you do it?"

She crouched down to eye level, and wrapped her arm around my shoulders leaning in. "I'll tell you after I win." She wiggled her eyebrows and gave me a squeeze before smiling at Kelly. "Maybe I'll think about claiming you as my bounty, if you're nice to my friend here." Kelly merely scoffed at Bailey before narrowing her eyes at me. I tried to say sorry with my eyes, but still remembered that Kelly didn't want anyone to know that we knew each other.

"I'm still not caught up on the whole bounty, and race dynamics yet." I rolled away from Kelly to see the next display cube, the man inside bent down and winked at us. I didn't want Bailey to catch on that I had a preference for Kelly, or that I knew her outside of her cube environment. Mr. Azel's comments about not knowing Bailey or Cameron still ringing in my ears. I didn't know if I could trust her yet, but if I could, then maybe I could double my chances of winning by having her on my side.

"There's nothing to it really," Bailey shrugged it off before adding, "You're already a winner by being here. I've been helping all the diplomats get set up for the event but had to win my race to even get escorted here. All the pilots here today will be offered high paying jobs for the royal guard, or appointments with the regents, even if they lose. But winning," Bailey's eyes lit up, "now this year has a bigger vault than ever before. You get millions of credits added to your account, a bounty bonus, and the Lord Prince is going to be choosing a pilot for the Hand Rite Ceremony, which is basically like being inducted into royalty." It sounded suspiciously like some sort of arranged marriage, so I stared at her like she had grown another head. She laughed. "It's not the same thing as an abett bond. It's merely a position within the royal court to assist Prince Wyndall with his duties."

She was talking in riddles just like everyone else. It

was like everyone had a special language, or inside joke, I wasn't in on. "Abett? Royal what?"

"Your parents did you wrong. You must have grown up outside of Acatalec. Abetts are like mating bonds, and a Hand Rite Ceremony is merely a power bond. It allows for our abilities to be shared and assists the royal line to continue." She shrugged. "I suppose sometimes Hand Rites can turn into abett bonds, but I doubted the Prince was looking for that based on history. I certainly wouldn't be staying faithful to him in that way. Not my type." She winked at me, and I flushed.

Clearing my throat, I stupidly added, "Oh."

"I saw how you were devouring Bounty Number Five." She nudged me. "Cam is a bit of a stickler, so I'd have to convince her that she's our pick, but I'll see what I can do for you. She might be more into it if you tell her why you like her."

"I thought you said no names?" I whispered.

"She's kind of already known here, as her family is prominent in our region. She isn't here as a pilot, and those snobby brown nosers are not my biggest fans."

I couldn't recognize her in the crowd with the masks, and fancy clothes.

"I'd introduce you, but it'd be better if we stayed away. We are the entertainment for now, that is until I win and shove it in their faces. They'll happily let me bond with Cammie when I've powered up with royalty." Her eyes gleamed with a hint of revenge, and then glazed over with a heat that I could only assume was because she was thinking about Cameron. I felt a little naughty watching her expression like I was intruding on a private moment.

All in all, I was feeling a bit less nervous because of Bailey. She made me feel like this whole situation wasn't all bad. I'd happily let her win, as long as she was able to help Kelly. My stomach rolled at the thought, and instinct made me hesitate in my thoughts. How could I be so sure she would help Kelly if I let her win? Would I really risk Kelly's future on the chance, even if it was comforting to think Bailey would pull through for me? And after pausing that trust, I suddenly realized that trust made me completely gloss over what she was telling me.

She said they had powers, and my first thought was like magician magic, and then I relaxed a little thinking she had to have meant something like political power, similar to a standing within the ranks.

## Chapter Sixteen

*Powers*

"Now that we're out of earshot, I'll give you my secret to make the race more fun when we're out there." I listened closely to Bailey, eager to learn how she was able to upload her software into the system without being noticed. She rotated a small chip along her knuckles. It flipped one knuckle over the other, and she palmed it making it disappear and then made it float over her knuckles again for flourish.

"Stick one of these babies in your drone's back panel, and then link up. It creates a back door to the drone's software, so even though you aren't the authorized user, you'll be able to bypass the regulation settings, remove the chip when you're done, and no one is the wiser."

Baily flicked the chip in the air, and it landed on my lap. She winked, and I felt this overwhelming sense of gratefulness, and eagerness to plug it into a drone immediately to try it out. Holding the chip in my hand felt like a drug that I had to sneak away and use. I salivated, and greedily pocketed it without another thought. The urge repeated in my mind, need to use the chip, need to win no matter what, trust, trust, trust.

I blinked several times and pressed my palm into my chest like there was a tightness there that I needed to knead out. Bailey looked at me expectantly, and I realized I hadn't said thank you. "Uh," still dazed I forced out, "Thank you."

Her smile was big, and a dizziness came over me, an invisible gas rippled the air around her making it difficult to see and breath. "What are friends for?"

"Right… I've heard a few things about rules—"

"That's the best part. Anything is fair game. The only rules are in the selection process, and the use of regulation drones that are provided for us. Makes it interesting, doesn't it?" She patted her pant pocket to make me think about where I had put the chip in my own, and I found myself putting my own hand in my pocket to make sure the chip was still there. I had to feel it with my fingers, and I had to use it. Had to plug it into my drone as soon as I was able, as soon as I knew which drone was mine. Open the panel in the back of the drone, don't even have to get in it; it's located at the back of the drone, on the outside panel. Plug it in there, easier to remove it when I was done from the outside. From the outside, I repeated in my mind.

My neck was tense, and I cracked it from side to side to ease the tightness. I removed my hand from my pocket and flexed my fingers. My palms were sweaty, and I was feeling overheated.

"I think I need something to drink." I tried to clear my dry throat.

"Of course, I should get going anyways. They'll want to parade us around soon enough. See you out there." Bailey slipped into the crowd, and I went back to the drink fountain.

"Pilot. Pilot." Kelly tried to get my attention, and I

looked up from the floor, and then smiled at her. She was so very pretty, I could stare at her eyes for hours, and there were many nights that we hung out that I did. Such a dark sea green, so calming.

"Pilot," she repeated, and I blinked again to focus.

"Hi," I said absently.

"What did she say to you? Exact words," she demanded, and I was taken aback by her harsh tone. She'd never spoken to me like that before. I pouted, and she shook her head to repeat in a softer voice, "Exact words, tell me what she said to you."

"Anything is fair game, no rules," I paraphrased.

She nodded, "That's all?"

I tried to think of anything else she said to me, and then smiled to say, "She's going to win so she can get her girlfriend's parents approval to bond with her. Shove it in their faces, she said. Oh, and that she might be able to convince her to let her choose you as the bounty." I felt like a puppy needing praise for repeating my conversation. I thought about it further and felt more ridiculous at my behavior as the seconds ticked by before I scrunched my face up and groaned.

"You need to be careful about who you talk to here," Kelly warned. "It sounds like all she wanted was to influence you to be more of a risktaker during the race. No rules doesn't mean no risk. And too many risks during the race, can be dangerous. Stay away from representatives of Priscus, they are total mind freaks. Just fly and protect yourself. I know you'll win."

I nodded, steeling myself to win.

"Which region are you from?" I asked and she backed away from the cube like I had cut her. Hurt by her reaction, my stomach lurched before feeling a tingling sensation creep at my neck like someone was watching us.

"It's not polite to bring up region at a Peace Summit, unless they provide the information up front," Prince Wyndall said, and I could see Kelly bow to him. It was a good thing I didn't know too much about Kelly's past, because a question like that wouldn't make a stranger think we knew each other.

"I'm not accustomed to traditions as I," remembering what Bailey said about growing up outside the region I added, "wasn't brought up that way. You could say my mom just wasn't big on history lessons."

Amused, he seemed to be satisfied with my answer.

"I brought up the conversation about region, Lord Prince," Kelly added.

"Didn't realize it was a faux pas." I gave him the most innocent face I could muster.

"If you win," the Prince prospected, "has this bounty intrigued you enough to consider her?"

I tried to keep myself from barfing at the way he described my best friend like a trinket to be won. He may have been handsome, but I had to stretch my forehead muscles to prevent myself from scowling at him.

"Not to be ungrateful to the wide selection of bounty provided, but the whole bounty thing was never explained to me when I was selected for this race. You wouldn't mind pointing me in the right direction of who could give me more information?" I tried to act like a dimwit that needed his all mighty help. Most backward people, with twisted morals about people tended to have the same trait of self-righteousness, and dumb people that played into their opinions were usually a hit.

He raised an eyebrow at me, which was not what I expected from him. He nodded at Kelly before turning away from her and motioning for me to follow. So, I assumed he was going to lead me in the direction of someone to talk to, but instead he surprised me again. "I find the whole bounty to be distasteful, but it has been tradition since before my time, and most of the leaders here wouldn't hear of changing it since all of the bounties have signed consent to be included."

"It's consensual?" I couldn't keep the astonishment from my voice.

He nodded and then his voice became hushed, "Though, I do think some of them merely sign to pay off their debts. It is a handsomely rewarded job to be a bounty."

"I couldn't imagine." I feigned awe hoping he would continue to elaborate without me riddling him with questions. He could sense the curiosity in me and decided to indulge.

"Each bounty provides different services, we aren't barbarians. The bounties choose their specialties, and services they are willing to include with their time."

I breathed a sigh of relief, and the Lord Prince smiled at me, and I found him suddenly charming.

"Did you think we were still in the dark ages, Pilot Sixteen?"

"I didn't really know what to think Lord Prin—"

"Call me Wyndall," he insisted.

"Lord Wyndall."

He nodded, partially appeased by my adjustment, and waited to see if I would offer my name and, when I didn't, he continued, "Tell me, Pilot, how do you know Regent Azel?"

I gulped, feeling panic creep up my arms. This was just as bad as giving him my name, wasn't it?

"I stole his drone," I answered honestly, and the revelation made him laugh.

"I knew I liked you. I can imagine the look on his face when he realized there was nothing he could do since you were protected by the Court while racing." He took on an air of seriousness before adding, "Do not let him trick you into thinking you owe him for damages. Wouldn't want to see you in one of those bounty cubes in the future, now would we?"

I felt my stomach churn and my mouth hung open appalled by his suggestion. Lord Wyndall laughed before adding, "No, I wouldn't say so. Oh, it makes so much sense now!" He gesticulated his hands and gave me a big smile as his thoughts ran away with him, "The way he was possessively stalking you when you entered, I'd never seen anything like it in my life. He must be seething at the slight. Nobody here would dare steal from him with the influence he has. This is possibly the most entertaining news I'll hear this evening."

Thinking about how Mr. Azel was seething at me made my insides curdle. I was regretting not making it to the fountain of wine at this point.

"That's my job, isn't it," I said, annoyed, forgetting any employee decorum with how jovial he was acting over something I didn't feel good about. I was only here to entertain, that should have made me feel elated, considering I'd always wanted to be a performing pilot, but this wasn't the kind of performance I had anticipated.

Lord Wyndall, sensing my attitude, was unable to maintain his humor and who would've been able to; I was pretty transparent. "Among other things," he said seriously, "The races have celebrated the freedom of Acatalec since before there was a queen or king, when it was merely the people racing through the untamed forests because they could, and because it proved to themselves and others how powerful they were to make it through monsters and rough terrain with nothing but their own abilities." He regaled the history of the races to me with reverence, and I realized I had stepped on a sensitive subject that was important to him.

His mask made it difficult to see most of his expression, but for his square strong jaw line stern in his reproach. "Winning a test of wits and skill is only one of the races this event holds, and this year is more important than many before. Every citizen wishes to go down in history as becoming royalty and keeping our lands strong. You could become hope for our people in the coming days. This," he flourished at the people partying, "is just a show, but this," he placed his palm to his heart, and then crouched down to do the same to mine and my skin prickled feeling a wave of energy come off of him like a warming electrical current, "is the future of Acatalec's prosperity."

Breathless, I clamped my fist where his hand was, still reeling on the sensation he caused. The way he smoldered through that golden mask made my body melt feeling like he was still touching me before he said, "You are more than entertainment. Be proud to be here and prove to them and to yourself how powerful you are." He was like a life coach on drugs, and I wasn't going to lie… it felt amazing to be pumped up by the most powerful man in the room.

A man cleared his throat behind me, and Lord Wyndall adjusted himself lazily in response. "Cable," he gave a curt nod before amusement filled his eyes, "Never thought I would see the day that someone would decide to cross you and survive."

I saw my boss' face stiff as stone. He'd never told me his name was Cable, I mean why would he, when I was merely his employee, and one that stole from him at that. Sighing, I grabbed my pant legs under the shawl and gripped to prevent myself from looking up at him again. Staring down at my hands, I couldn't bear the way I imagined him running his eyes over me right now. Not after what Lord Wyndall said.

"She will do her duty for Acatalec, and nothing more," Mr. Azel growled causing a gleam in Lord Wyndall's eyes. I had a feeling there was something between them, and Lord Wyndall liked to press his buttons.

"I have high hopes for you." Lord Wyndall offered his hand to me and I reluctantly unfurled my grip on my pant leg to lift my hand. He bent down regally and lifted my hand to his lips pressing a soft kiss on my knuckles. The contact sent another wave of heat across my skin, and an unwelcome sigh left my gaping mouth. "Try not to let the other pilots get into your head too much." I followed the direction his eyes trailed off to, and in a half circle of people staring at us, was Bailey… and another familiar bounce of curls that had ran me off the road earlier today. She was okay, which sent mixed signals through me, one of relief and one of fear. Did she make it through, would I have to watch out for her during the upcoming race?

Without thinking I asked, "Who is that?" And my opponent glared at me before quickly returning attention to her current company.

"She's the next in line to take the regent position for her family," my boss answered.

"Yes, and probably getting an earful from her mother about losing to one of the wild cards in the race." Lord Wyndall smiled at me and then winked ignoring the scowls from my boss. I nodded, relieved that she was okay, and not going to be after me during the race to come.

I thought about my own mother and wished I could call her if only to hear one of her famous pep talks about how in my business it was my brains that counted, not where I came from, or how big my butt was. Every drone is just an ordinary combination of mechanics, she'd say, and it's you that makes it extra. I smiled knowing full well it was cheesy, but that's what made it work every time.

"She's very powerful—" my boss began before Lord Wyndall cut him off.

"Not in the race doesn't mean out of play. Revenge has been known to happen, but," seeing the horror on my face, he added, "You already defeated her once, what's another round really."

I was going to say, everything, because another round with her wouldn't be in a drone. I was defenseless outside of my comfort zone, who was I to prevent her from seeking her revenge before I even entered a drone. A sense of dread overcame me.

"Priscus selections are always known to make it to the finals, and manipulate their competition," my boss warned once we were out of earshot of Lord Wyndall, who had to make his rounds as host through the crowd of mingling dancers like a hot night club owner.

Chapter Seventeen

*The Diplomat*

"I'm told it's impolite to discuss regions during the races," I prompted Mr. Azel in hopes that he would fill in some more blanks I had about this whole situation.

He merely confirmed and moved on as quickly as possible from the subject. Not even a hint about what region even he was part of, not that the information was really helpful, considering I knew nothing about the regions to begin with, it would be just a name.

I heaved a frustrated sigh. "If this race is mostly a show of wits, then why are you data blocking me from having the best chance at surviving this whole thing?"

My boss resigned himself. "I'm trying to protect you."

"Or maybe you're just pissed off at me like Lord Wyndall implied." I jabbed at him.

"Is that what he said to you?" For a moment, the pristine stone of his features seemed to crack a bit.

"Keep me in the dark and let me lose to make up for going behind your back and stealing your office equipment."

He shook his head. "Those drones are more than 'office equipment' they are luxury transports, and," he breathed deep to restart and stop his ramp up, "I want to make sure that you can go back to your normal life after this race, Ms. Beryl. And the more you know about this place, and these people, the less likely that will be the case. I can't protect you if they find out who you are, and I can't protect you if—"

"Who am I to you?" I asked, my heart aching.

He hesitated before diplomatically responding, "You are my employee, and under my protection." He was a diplomat after all, some regent of Acatalec, and a big enough deal that he felt comfortable butting heads with the Lord Prince. Every other person in this room seemed to avoid any confrontation with him, but more than that they seemed to be smitten with him. Younger, older, men, women, everyone here was more than happy to cozy up to him and be in his good graces. One thing I did notice when I scanned the room, was that every pilot seemed to be surrounded by people fawning over them, they were celebrities at this event. I knew they were the pilots because my contact could do a basic link that showed me people's titles. Reading the data of Mr. Azel, it was empty, and so too was Lord Wyndall's. He was the Lord Prince, everyone knew who he was, but not even a simple scan of data was present while my contacts tried to link.

My boss peered at me for a moment and suddenly a data line emerged in my vision: Cable Azel, Regent of Tarquin, Champion of Acatalec.

I smiled at him, wondering what it meant to be a Champion of Acatalec. Which races did he participate in to get that title? A small quirk of his mouth let me know he was aware at what I was complimenting him for with a smile, I had a newfound awe of my boss. Then the data disappeared again. My heart warmed a little bit, knowing he gave me a little bit more information about himself. Even though it was such a small thing, knowing his name, and titles, I felt special since I figured his data was out of linking reach for a reason, but he allowed me to see it.

"Champion of what exactly?" I asked, intrigued.

He squared his shoulders as we approached the ornate drinking fountains. Cable plucked a glass flute from the table and filled it. In the same smooth motion, he offered it to me. "I wasn't always a regent," he began, "I was not born into a hereditary line of succession like most of the guests here. I competed in all the races, including this one, for years building a reputation until the regent before me, having no offspring to succeed her, stepped down and I took her place."

I looked at him with new eyes. This whole time I thought he was a pompous rich guy and, come to find out, he worked his way up to that level of asshole, where people kissed his perfectly sculpted muscles, because he earned it. He wasn't all that bad.

"I've heard of this reputation of yours," I teased.

Cable laughed, and I found myself smiling broader at the sound of it. "That particular reputation isn't from winning the previous races, though that added to it. My region is looked down upon by most of the elite here, and fear is a driving factor of that stigma."

"You're not that scary."

He leaned down to tap wine flutes with me. "Let's keep that between us." And I'd completely forgotten about why I'd found him annoying. He expertly avoided the most important question, how was keeping me in the dark protecting me?

"Mr. Azel—" I was going to repeat my question.

"Cable," his request was so silky, my mouth watered.

"Cable," I nearly purred before getting a hold of myself to ask, "Why don't you want me to win anymore?"

His eyes grew dark and possessive. "You can't bond with him."

Taken aback by Cable's sudden change in demeanor, I raised an eyebrow. "I wasn't planning on any weird bonding. Why didn't you bond with him when you became champion?"

He snarled at the idea. "Hand Rites weren't part of the races then, and if they were, I'd duel to force a pardon of duties."

"Isn't it some sort of honor or something?"

"There's a reason only the most powerful are offered a Hand Rite Ceremony, they are the most likely to survive it."

"Strong enough to duel, not enough to survive a bonding ceremony?" I tried to prevent myself from laughing.

He narrowed his eyes at me. "I would have been fine," he insisted, "but there have been many who have failed, and suffered the consequences. Hand Rites share one's power, and if one is not powerful enough they cannot handle the extra power boost from bonding with Wyndall. Also, I can't stand the guy, bonding with him disgusts me."

"Right," I said like I knew what he was talking about, "So, these powers?" I thought it odd the way everyone was talking about political power like it was some ancient right of grandeur.

"I've already said too much already. Just know that

if you win, you will be signing Lord Wyndall's death warrant," he seethed.

"Boss, I didn't know you cared so much," I joked.

"I will not allow it," he said in all seriousness, and I felt all tingly inside. He was frighteningly handsome when he tried to be all protective. Though I tried to hold back, I couldn't stop myself from feeling both happy that he would murder for me, but also upset that he thought I was too weak to duel for my pardon. I didn't care that I didn't know what a duel would entail, or that I was a bit at a disadvantage, or even that I didn't have any power to bond with to begin with. I mean, I was a nobody with no political advantage at all.

"Because I'm powerless?" I asked him through gritted teeth. That was always a trigger for my anger, I was not the sum of my legs, I was just as human as anyone else, and more than capable of destroying his or anyone else's ass for that matter.

"No," he said softly, as he watched me bite my lip. I could even feel my teeth start to make my tissue tender. Blood rushed to my face, and a drop of blood beaded up from the inside of my mouth. I eased up and licked my wound. Cable's eyes were animalistic, and I felt bad for losing my temper. He said gruffly before tearing his gaze from me, "There are some things that must remain the way they are for your protection."

"I can protect myself," I growled. "You said I could win, was that a lie?"

He ran his hand through his hair haphazardly. "Not a lie."

"Then what then? Does the duel involve legs?"

He smiled then, and my anger was more difficult to hang on to, and I wanted to hang on to it, because it was easier that way. "No, you don't need those to win a duel." The way he said you, had me wondering if others would have needed them, or if he meant the duel would be by drone and I could kick their asses in a race. He had a glimmer in those dark brown eyes.

"What's so funny?" I tried to remain serious.

"For a second there, I thought you wanted to bond with Lord Wyndall, but if you're prepared to duel then so am I." The way he said that left me confused, and he took the empty wine flute from me before I could damage it any further, a noticeable crack split down the glass, crystal, or whatever these rich flapping voyeurists used for their expensive party.

"What does that mean?"

"It means, I'll help you win." Those eyes darkened into something sinister, and I didn't know if I should be excited, or scared to join him on this hell ride.

Chapter Eighteen

*Even Me*

Cable bowed to me with a menacing gleam and left me alone at the beverage fountains. I rolled back over to Kelly, and she was impatiently pacing her display case waiting for me this whole time, a crazed look on her face.

"Are you okay? What did he say? Did he hurt you? When I get out of this cube, I swear…" she trailed off.

"I'm fine," I assured her.

"Stay away from him," Kelly was distraught, slamming her hands on the glass, "I may have grown up outside of Acatalec, but I know the stories of his kind."

"What kind is that?" I pressed.

Torn about answering she hesitated before saying, "Tarquins with power are dangerous, they've," she hushed her voice, "been known to kill people to live long lives, and gain power. The last regent lived for centuries before stepping down, and she's still alive in retirement now." I stared at her for a long time, unable to process her words. She saw the confusion on my face and clamped her hands over her mouth at the slip.

"Uh, it's just that um her spirit lives on, and—"

I held up my hand for her to stop.

"You said centuries…"

She nodded, squirming under my pointed stare.

"Are you high?"

Kelly fidgeted, holding her stomach while her gaze flitted from one end of the party to the other, making sure no one was listening, and I didn't have the heart to push back on her delusions about century old regents, so I played along to see what she had to say, "How is that possible? What exactly is this place? Who are these people?" I begged Kelly to tell me.

She gulped back her fear. "We aren't human... I'm so sorry Ty, it's just I really didn't think these races were that big of a deal, and thought we could score quick from it, and get the hell out of dodge. I messed up by bringing you into this, don't let anyone know you aren't from Acatalec, okay? I'll get in so much more trouble than being a bounty for some rich snob."

"Not human," I mouthed. My throat drying out quick.

"Please don't zone out on me, I'm still me, just different."

"So, Regent..." Cable...

"Everyone here, babe." She lowered her voice even further.

"Why am I here?"

"I thought it was just a drone race, and you are way better than anyone I've ever seen. You still are," she tried to hype me up, "You can win this."

"Lord Wyndall said that this whole race was to show how powerful someone is..."

She nodded solemnly.

"Not political power..."

Kelly bit her lip and shook her head to the negative.

"This seems like far more than a race." And I was

having trouble believing her about powers.

"I can help," she offered meekly.

"How?"

"I've been listening to people, and apparently the pilots get to choose a co-pilot. I can phase your drone to avoid small collisions, and possibly speed up your time by precious seconds…"

"Is that how you've won your other races?" I asked cautious and wondering if this was why she thought she won her other races. It didn't take me long in the illegal drone races to outrace her, and if she had the kind of power she said she did, then there should've been no way that I would have won at all against her.

She squirmed, which was unlike her. "Only when I was trying to win against you… but, look, you still beat me! That's how I know with my help we'll grab those credits and make like a fixer, disappear." She still wasn't letting up on the power thing; she believed what she was saying. I shook my head trying to wrap my mind around it.

I was still trying to process that my best friend just revealed that she had powers that apparently allowed her to manipulate matter for a few seconds. And even more intriguing, what was Cable capable of to win multiple races and earn a terrifying reputation, as well as a regent title? Did all of these quacks think they had superpowers?

"You better be right about this. I was told I'd have to duel someone at the end of this if I won just to get out of some bonding ritual. I have a feeling bonding with an alien wouldn't really be conductive to our disappearing act." I was planning on hightailing it out of here after anyways, but I was glad I wouldn't be alone, and I'd have to have a talk with her about her powers another time, when she wasn't so emotionally charged and vulnerable.

"Whoever you bond with would always know where you are, and it's a very personal decision," Kelly blushed at the idea before composing herself, "I've never heard of only a one-time race winner being asked to bond with anyone—"

Before she could continue her thought a link notification interrupted our conversation. There was no option of accepting the link, and if the look on Kelly's face was any indicator, it was that way for everyone in the room.

"It's another year of prosperity for Acatalec, and with it comes another year of races!" Lord Wyndall spoke to everyone. I spun around to find him in the middle of the room with a crowd forming around him. "It is with great pride that the regents and myself have come to an agreement to accept this year's winner to be selected for a Hand Rite Ceremony."

The entire room erupted into cheers, and excitement. And in the midst of the noise, Lord Wyndall rose up into the air to even more jubilation. I rubbed at my eyes and stared at him.

He was flying.

"For the Pride of Acatalec!" He roared.

"Num De RAL!" They chanted back.

I turned back to Kelly, who was becoming angrier by the second as she mouthed, "Shit."

He had to be wearing some sort of magnetism field to fly like that, but for the life of me I couldn't see where he would have hidden it inside his tightly fitted clothing.

"Enjoy the festivities, for tomorrow we race!"

Champagne flutes clanged, and the music took a turn for a techno club vibe as Lord Wyndall descended back to the ground. All the pomp and circumstance of the milling around to socialize broke, and the lights dimmed. All the cubes holding the bounties dropped to the floor and opened up allowing the people inside to be released into the frenzy.

Kelly took my hand and was about to drag me out of there, before she rapidly changed her tone and began to dance around me instead. Her butt wiggled down onto my leg, and my temperature spiked wishing I could feel sensations in my knees that were getting more action tonight than they had when I was eight and falling in the playground.

Lord Wyndall was watching us, and Kelly was making sure she was cooperating with the status quo. It was hard not to miss the encompassing presence of the man, he was both intimidating, but also unnaturally charming. It seemed like he was going to come this way and join us, but in the sea of mashing bodies I lost track of him.

Again, his voice boomed in my ears, "Tonight, we transcend!" All around me people lifted from the ground, and my hair was floating like the air was water. Kelly held on to my hand as she smiled from ear to ear.

Where were the devices? How did they plant one on me?

"My father told me stories about the parties at the royal port," she yelled over the music, she squeezed my hand to reassure me everything was fine, "I didn't believe him that one person could take over an entire room with their power."

"This is one person?" I asked noticing that I was losing control over my chair, because it was no longer attached to the ground.

Kelly nodded excited. "This is Prince Wyndall, the most powerful of Numa. He can make the air in the room like floating in water. It's how he can fly."

"Can you do that too?" I gripped her fingers so hard, feeling uneasy about my weird bobbing situation. Also, my whole bravado about thinking she was lying about powers was slowly fading the longer we both floated.

She laughed. "No, silly. I don't have anyone from Numa in my bloodline. Just relax." Kelly pulled herself towards me and tried to fiddle with my chair's straps.

"What are you doing?" I swatted at her, not that it mattered, she didn't have any access to unhook me from my chair anyways, but it tickled none the less.

"We're stuck here for now, might as well enjoy it. It's a party after all, we can strategize a way around avoiding a Hand Rite Ceremony tomorrow."

"Allow me," Cable's deep voice came around a pair of pulsating dancers. As soon as he said it, like before in his office, my chair unstrapped itself, and I marveled at how it slowly plopped back on the ground, and I stayed floating. Kelly grabbed my other hand and we rotated around, my shawl drifted away, and I desperately wanted to push at my dead legs to keep them from lifting up.

Kelly trailed from me to Cable, and back again. "We were just…"

"Allowing me a dance," Cable finished for her and Kelly grumbled before looking at me apologetically. She gently placed my hand in his, and he pulled me in giving me a spin before I collided into his chest.

"I'll be right over here if you need me," Kelly gave Cable one last glare before pretending to have fun dancing off to the side. It wasn't long before she disappeared into the masses, being dragging into the euphoria of the party. My chest tightened as she left and took away my excuse to pay attention to anywhere else but up into Cable's eyes. He was even more dangerous, and handsome up close.

"Where did you go?" I asked, letting my head rest on his chest so I didn't have to stare at him.

"Procuring some favors."

"Oh," I mumbled.

"Does that upset you?" He seemed concerned.

"No, just… if Lord Wyndall can do something like this, I'm not sure how a few favors are going to help me."

"Hmm," he paused before saying, "everyone no matter how powerful has a weakness."

With a gleam in my eye, I locked him in my sights. "Even you?"

"Even me," he agreed.

Chapter Nineteen

*Contract*

The wine from earlier was making the whole room seem ethereal. I wrapped my arms around Cable's neck and enjoyed the feeling of being weightless as he held me close.

I looked up into his eyes once more and my whole body hummed in response. His face was dangerously close to mine, and my lips lifted in anticipation for that tension growing between us to be released. We were adults. I was no longer an employee of Zeiten, though still technically employed by him. It seemed less wrong now than earlier today, now that I knew he was a part of a weird secret organization made him seem more approachable, and less able to be so high and mighty about my own poor choices in life.

I was a strong woman, and if I wanted something then why hold back? What was the worst that could happen? I talked myself up, convincing myself this was okay. That these feelings were okay.

"Will you kiss me?" I blurted out and my chest burned. The heat traveled up to the tips of my ears, and I bashfully turned away. It was the atmosphere of all the dancing, and the mood lighting that I blamed it on. I licked my lips not ashamed of being all right if he did kiss me, but more so if he didn't and I just put myself out there.

His eyes were dark, and a hunger seemed to brew there under his lashes. He scanned the area first, before growling, and pulling me down with him to the ground. At first, my skin tingled at his response, before I realized he was strapping me back into my chair, and my lips were still cold.

He had rejected me, and I was so repulsive that he groaned in disgust and had to remove me from the dance floor. I gritted my teeth in irritation, and any semblance of the happy buzz feeling I had was draining fast.

I yanked on his hand to bring him back to my eye level. "What's wrong with you?" Had I completely misinterpreted his reaction to me? Asking for a dance, pressing me close to his firm body, my head resting on his shoulder in a slow dance while the rest of the crowd raged to the techno beat, and the way he seemed to devour me with a single look?

"I'm not human," he bemoaned with a snarl. Deep down I knew that, I mean, even Kelly said everyone here wasn't, not that I really believed them, but I wasn't asking for anything more than a kiss. What harm could a simple kiss do?

"That's an understatement," I hissed back at him. He pushed my chair away from the gyrating bodies and I wailed for him to stop, "Wait, I can't leave without her."

He paused to consider this before calming himself to say, "She's contract bound to stay here until after the race. We," he emphasized, "are going back to the office until co-pilots are chosen, and drones are distributed tomorrow."

"I'm not going anywhere with you," I grumbled.

"You, like it or not, are contract bound to give me a certain number of hours every week, I specifically added this entire week to be double the amount of hours for this particular circumstance. Read your employment agreement you signed earlier this week again. I determine how you spend those working hours, and I'm deciding right now that you are on the clock and will come with me back to the office."

I fumed and searched the contract, scrolling on my contact lenses to find an article about hours, and he was right. I did sign that damn contract, and I didn't want to know what happened when you didn't follow a contract with someone as dangerous as him. What exactly happened to a human when they didn't follow a contract with an alien?

"Fine, but I better be getting a raise."

"I'll take it out of what you owe for the damaged drone," he responded flatly.

"Lord Wyndall said I was under race protections during said drones' damages."

"So he did, but that was after you had already signed an employment agreement with me, and the drone is company property." He pushed me towards the exit, and I quickly sped up so that I was rolling of my own volition. Kelly was prying herself through the crowd towards me, distraught by my abrupt departure.

He was unbelievable, going to work at what, ten at night? Did the man not sleep? Before, he made it to the doors, a soft wind whipped around us. And Cable growled before turning around to greet the emanating presence behind us.

"She has had too much wine," Cable defended his

early leave of the party to Lord Wyndall, who was now switching between us amused.

He gave me a once over. "She seems fully capable of completing her obligations to the court this evening."

"Obligations?" I didn't like the sound of that.

"You know well enough that no one from court will be summoning her now that they are all enamored with their current activities." Cable motioned to the chaos of bodies behind us. He wasn't wrong, I didn't think anyone except Kelly cared if I left or not.

Lord Wyndall offered his hand to me. "Would you do me the honor of a dance, Pilot?"

Cable scoffed and tried once more to interrupt. "She's already given you her obligatory introduction, or did I not let you speak with her earlier?" I suddenly felt particularly interested in taking Lord Wyndall's hand just then. He lost any semblance of right he thought he had with me when he turned me down earlier, and I had a feeling he didn't really have much of a choice if I accepted the invitation.

Which I did with a purposeful placement of my hand, giving Lord Wyndall's offering a small squeeze and displaying a winning smile in spite of Cable's objections.

"A dance sounds wonderful." I gave Cable a conspiratorial glance. Simply getting under his skin was a victory for me, and it didn't hurt that Lord Wyndall gave me a knowing grin sensing my intentions.

"I aim to please." Lord Wyndall ushered me away from Cable, and he seethed on the sidelines, obviously waiting for whatever dance we were going to have to be over so he could quickly pull me away to bring me back to my contracted work he so desperately needed me to complete right away. He probably just wanted me to wait in his office again, or in my very fancy new prison, as I liked to call it.

I was suddenly aware of Lord Wyndall's crisp blue eyes on me. Then he knelt down and asked with a charm that made me want to melt, "May I?" He gestured to the straps keeping me in my chair.

"Oh." I nodded and I was going to release the straps, but before I could they undid themselves, and I knew then that he could have done it without permission, but he had asked first. I immediately had a new appreciation for the Lord Prince, he may have been powerful, but he was also respectful. His large hands held me at my waist and the air around us became heavier, and by contrast we became lighter as he lifted me up.

With a twirl he pulled me into his muscular chest as we floated in the air like fairies. I let out a soft giggle I didn't know I was holding, and that brilliant smile of his made me feel giddy I almost forgot about the brooding man staring at us from the sidelines.

Lord Wyndall held me closer to him, and I gasped when his nose nuzzled into my hair.

"Tell me, Pilot, why did you come? I can tell it wasn't for the sake of Acatalec."

His question caught me off guard, and I didn't know how he would know that it wasn't, we had only just met. Did he find out I wasn't selected for the races, that Kelly bought my entry? I had to be diplomatic about my response.

"I didn't," I agreed with him, "I have other concerns."

"For him?" he asked, referring to Cable.

"No," I nearly laughed, "I didn't even know he was a regent until tonight." Then I pressed my lips closed regretting my lack of filter. No one was supposed to know I knew him outside of the races, I couldn't afford for them to know I wasn't from Acatalec.

"That's good. He isn't the type one should get to know," he warned before lightening the mood, "There aren't many that would go against his wishes, but twice now I've learned you've done so. You have guts, and I find it intriguing."

"Twice?" Those ocean eyes were smoldering, and my breath caught.

"You decided to dance with me." His voice was deep and commanding, and a thrill rippled down my arms.

I blushed, noticing Cable wasn't the only one watching us dance together. We were garnering a bit of attention, as a small girth circled around us. People had made sure to give the Lord Prince his space to dance.

"Uh, yah." I was about to admit I was using him to grind some salt into Cable's buttons because I had a feeling he didn't like Lord Wyndall, but I decided against it no matter how charming he was to me right now. "About that." I glanced around at our spectators.

Lord Wyndall made the air around us quiver, and the crowd seemed to deviate from their attention on us. He nodded at me, and whispered, "There aren't many things I have to myself with a position such as mine."

"That must be hard," I sympathized not knowing how I would be able to handle having so many people giving me the hawk eye all the time. I knew this room didn't begin to cover the amount of people that probably watched his every move.

"Sometimes," he admitted, "but I have an obligation to my people." He noticed me puckering at his use of obligations, that was always a trigger for me. I could already feel myself tighten and wish that I could punch Cable in the face for thinking he could oblige me to work this late at night after I was done rubbing this dance in his nose.

"If you were me, would you do differently?" he asked sincerely.

"Within reason," I said thoughtfully, "when it comes to your privacy you could just tell the court to shove it as long as you're doing right by the people you're protecting."

He laughed, his eyes shimmering in the low flashing lights of the fog filled room. "As long as I'm doing right by the people then my actions are agreeable to you then?" He searched my face for any tells of uncertainty.

"Within reason," I repeated, not fully understanding what he was trying to get out of my answer.

Lord Wyndall lowered his face close to mine and in a low seductive rumble asked, "What if what is right for the people takes away your own rights?"

I pressed my forehead against his, suddenly very interested in being an advocate for a man I didn't even know. "If you cannot protect your own rights, how are you supposed to protect the rights of your people? You are a Prince… do both."

He wrapped his arms around me and pulled me against his muscular chest, his forehead still pressed into mine as he leaned down. Lord Wyndall's hand trailed up my back and laced into my hair possessively.

His blue eyes intensified, and I didn't know if he was going to crush me or eat me. I had spoken without thought, and it was a constant battle within myself to keep my mouth shut.

"I will do both," he repeated and then in a low growl added, "with you."

I had no response.

My heart hammered in my chest, and I blinked several times not understanding what he meant by that, but the music transitioned through a few beats and obviously remixed into a new song thus ending our dance together. Our noses brushed against each other, and I felt heat in my stomach, and a soft tingle in my lips as they throbbed. I was so damned worked up that my body craved any attention it would get, and I flinched reprimanding myself for being so desperate. Lord Wyndall eased our bodies apart, and the moment didn't fizzle like I thought it would. Despite his hands on my arms, and a small chasm between us, there was this pull of electricity that seemed to nag at my insides wanting to close that distance again. Compensating for the tightness in my chest my lips parted. There wasn't enough oxygen and I needed to steal it from the only other source in the room. My whole body ached and was nearly going to grab the man's face and pull it towards me to put an end to this feeling. The way he drank me in and licked his lips was sending me closer to the edge.

I had to mentally flog myself, biting my lip to break the spell.

I could feel daggers being tossed at the back of my head by Cable, and Lord Wyndall eased me back down into my chair. He slowly clicked my straps into place and took my hand in his brushing those soft lips against my skin. I wiggled in my seat trying to get comfortable but knowing all was lost. I was a wreck, and this whole night just needed to be history. I'd embarrassed myself enough as it was.

"How was your obligatory dance?" Cable said, knowing how I felt about the word.

"Obligations and enjoyment are not exclusive, she can do both," Lord Wyndall remarked while giving my hand a squeeze before releasing me into Regent Azel's care. I shivered still feeling Lord Wyndall's energy all over me, and I didn't hate it.

I gave him a sly smile at his comment about doing both and added, "It is my right." I turned away from them both, and knowing Cable was only going to usher me out, I decided to do it of my own freewill. I had my pride, and it was my right to do so.

Chapter Twenty

*Leech*

We got into his fancy drone, and I glared in front of me. A strange sense of calmness came over me, and my head drooped until it lulled onto his shoulder. It was too much excitement for one day, with the adrenaline gone as much as I didn't want to admit it Cable made me feel safe, and I felt myself drifting asleep.

When I came to, the feeling of soft sheets greeted me. Rolling over I moaned and stretched, thinking of my chair, so it could come get me, only to hear a thud at the door. Now, much more alert I realized this was the bedroom I came across on the top floor of my boss' office. Throwing my legs over the side, I was grateful to see I was still wearing my slacks. Though the corset I had been wearing was lying on the plush lounger near the curtained windows. I squeaked, knowing I hadn't worn a bra, since that corset had built in support, and all I was wearing was a soft, over-sized cotton t-shirt. Bringing the material up to my nose, I inhaled the same scent of Cable. He had such a distinct smell, that I couldn't put my finger on, but whatever it was made me want to smother myself in it.

I convinced myself the only reason why I'd continue wearing his shirt, was because the corset was a bit fancy for outside of a party, and I had nothing better to wear, but I was struggling with the excuse because I wasn't sure if I'd want to take it off anyways.

It was driving me crazy that he had this effect on me when he flat out rejected me yesterday. It was almost eight in the morning, and I tried to get my chair to come to me again, and luckily the door wasn't actually closed all the way, so it finally rolled up to the side of the bed.

Inside the bathroom was a small display of feminine products, including a not too subtle anti-frizz conditioning spray, and a flat iron. I was almost going to storm out of the bathroom just in spite of him, but another part of me wanted to show him the version of myself he hadn't met yet and make him regret his missed opportunity. Because in my mind, I was done with him. I had to be.

I tamed this mop, and even applied some mascara. When I returned to the room, I finally noticed a sliver of clothing hidden beneath the flop of comforter and pillows that I flung off earlier. It was a beautiful cashmere sweater, and a flowing skirt that had to be designer, on the floor, at the foot of the bed, were a haphazardly tossed pair of beautiful kitten heels that must have dropped to the floor after tossing covers around.

Torn, I brought the collar of the shirt I was wearing up to my nose once more and scrunched up for one last whiff. I had to get over him and smelling like him wasn't going to help. Transferring to the bed, I pulled on the sweater, and excitedly found out the skirt was a wrap style, and I merely had to shimmy on top, and then wrap it, and tie it. I felt… pretty, and I wanted him to see how I felt. No, it didn't matter if he thought I was pretty, I tried to convince myself.

Reaching over my chair, hanging on with one arm, and steadying myself on the bed as well, I was able to pick up the shoes, and slip them on. I'd gotten used to being flexible, because I hated relying on others to get something for me. Shoving my black slacks into my chair's hidden compartment co-mingling with my joysticks, I expected Cable to be around the office, and planned on subtly passing by him to see his reaction, but he wasn't around. At this point I didn't care if I wasn't on time, so I helped myself to the expensive coffee in the front lounge area.

When I exited the elevator, it was like being struck by the uncomfortable stick, because as I passed by, everyone peered up from their desks. Instead of going back to minding their own business, they found it much more entertaining to gawk at me like I'd sprouted a third eye. I get it, I was late, but there was no reason to publicly shame me for it.

"Oh, look the little piggy decided to grace us with her presence." Jessi pushed up from her chair stalking over to me. She was ready to slice me with whatever was handy, and I always thought it was amazing how intimidating, despite how dainty and attractive, I ruefully admitted she was. Her endearment threw me, considering she was used to only badmouthing me about my wardrobe, or my work ethic. She seemed extra on fire today, and I could tell she wasn't finished.

"Had a good time squealing to management about how you couldn't even do your own job?"

I raised an eyebrow at her, confused. I wasn't sure where this one was going? Was she implying I told our boss about the report error? The wall still had her name on the pilot leader board, and no one else should have known about that except me, and her.

"Needed to let them know that an error couldn't possibly be your fault, because that would mean you'd have to be to work on time, and read a report?"

Nope, she was definitely talking about the drone error. I was already fired for the error, though she didn't know that. I did still come into the office and sit at that boring-ass cube.

"I'm not sure what you're rattling on about this time, I didn't—" I tried to defend overtop her tirade, until she cut me off with her head flying back in a laughter.

"Why didn't I see it before?" She pinched the fabric of my sweater like it was a rubber band, taking in my appearance.

"Didn't think you had it in you." I blushed at her accusation before she saw fit to continue, "You always did get special treatment, didn't you? Did you dress like a slob on purpose, so no one would find out that you don't actually know how to work?"

A growl that was becoming more common emanated from behind me, and my neck felt like it was on fire. I wanted to die right there, considering last night I had practically thrown myself at him and grabbed the back of his head like a hungry parasite.

His silky voice said in a charged but reserved way, "Ms. Felmon, if you feel you've been given too much of a workload, please see me in my office later and I'd be happy to adjust your circumstances further. As for you," I refused to turn around to face him, so he clarified, "Ms. Beryl, next time I ask you for a report on your work I expect you to include all contributing parties instead of claiming it as your own." He had basically vindicated me in front of the whole floor while at the same time chastising me. I could feel my embarrassment quickly turn into agitation, but he wasn't done.

"You'll see me after your morning duties to discuss distribution of your workload since you've seen fit to do my job for me. You'll be relieved of your training hours until further notice." I stole a peek behind me only to see him sweep around the room, creating a wave effect that had everyone turning away and diligently attending their interfaces.

Jessi pressed her lips together, and stomped back to her seat, those heels clacking purposefully. She gave me one last glare before reviewing her reports again.

He leaned over my interface, face so close his cheek brushed my hair, that hopefully didn't still smell like the perfumed anti-frizz spray, I'd rather he didn't know I'd used it even if it was obvious. Then he signed me in before disappearing down the hallway leaving the whole room feeling the tension lingering in the air.

"Is that where you go in the mornings?" My cube mate Kline asked and before I could answer he added, "Lately, you've been here way early, that I thought you were pulling double shifts this week."

"I uh," This week was an exception to my normal work hours, but I didn't feel like correcting him and having to explain more about our boss in the process, "I kind of owe the boss a bunch of extra hours." I smiled like I'd got caught in the cookie jar.

He nodded and grinned. "He's making you work off your earlier tardies, isn't he? I've heard he's a real work horse. I don't think I've ever seen him leave the building." This was the first time Kline has ever been so friendly with me, considering he was usually so far up Jessi's nose, he was sure to strike gold.

"I think I overstepped my allowances a few times." And the only step I could think of was when I ran my fingers through his hair, feeling the euphoria of floating, and asked him to kiss me. I was obviously only overwhelmed by my experiences, and probably imagined the whole evening. I mean today was Friday, and the actual day of the race. What happened yesterday was an overactive nightmare, like when they say you dream of crowds seeing you naked, just as embarrassing.

I'd get a notification today with coordinates, and like any other race, kick some butt, find Kelly flying beside me, and earn some credits. Though, that didn't account for why I'd woken up in Cable's penthouse offices on the top floor, unless I never really left them yesterday. That's right, I had fallen asleep in the library and none of this actually happened, I tried to convince myself.

The morning rolled by uncomfortably, with equal parts boredom, and equal parts scoffs and blazing stares from a pissed off Jessi. I couldn't take it anymore, I was minutes away from having to go up to Cable's office, and as much as she hated my guts, I was obviously not well with the dreams I'd been having lately and needed to resolve some issues. I made it up to her interface, and stopped to open my mouth, and felt a boulder lodge itself in my throat preventing me from saying what I went there to say.

Just in time to have her look up and jump back, because she had probably wanted to glare at me one more time, only to find me right in front of her. She quickly recovered and reclaiming her tough I'm going to murder you gaze she went off, "I don't care if he's into you or not, you're bad for him, and you need to back off."

That was the last thing I was expecting her to say. Taken a back I tried my best to recover. "Excuse me," was the best I could do.

"You heard me leech," she said seething between her teeth, showing off her canines. They flashed like sabers, when I blinked, they were gone. I thought she was going to eat me, and already knowing my imagination was prone to exaggerations I stared her down trying not to blink again. If I was hallucinating, my theory would be that if I focused on the scan in my contacts that the augmented overlay would prevent me from seeing something that wasn't there. I mean the scanners wouldn't lie to me about what was there, so I kept that scanner running, little green, and blue dots filled in Jessi's face. She was now completely filtered by my contact, and even though she looked the same, I knew now that what I was seeing would only be what the scanner would show me. This had to work.

"I didn't come over here to play a game of who can be the best mean girl," I gritted, forcing myself to stay calm and finish what I began. I could have started the conversation off better, it wasn't my intention to instigate her again, but it was difficult to break old habits, and if we were getting into it, she was just as touchy. Plus, she won the mean girl category hands down.

"You haven't seen me mean," she growled, and even though she was always on edge with me, this was a new level even for her. She at least kept a semblance of controlled attacks while at work, what exactly happened between her and Cable? She's not fired, or she wouldn't be here, but even that wasn't true. Since I was fired and still roaming the facility. Did he personally hire her too?

Holding my hands up in mock surrender, I had to get this over with already, "We can duel it out another time." I smiled to myself using my weird dream as inspiration for my current conversation. Dueling was on my mind, but hopefully she wouldn't take me up on the offer. "It's just that I came over here because I'm sorry that my existence on this Earth has upset you so much, and I kind of just wanted to know why, or at the very least clean up the issue so we can move on."

Her anger didn't seem to subside much, but enough for her to tell me, "You're right, your existence is an issue, but I can forgive it if you leave."

"Seriously? What did I do to you?" I snarled at her. She was getting on my last nerve, and I was losing my motivation to extend her any more neural paths for peace.

Seeing I wasn't leaving, and I could feel we were garnering more attention from the rest of the pilots the longer this dragged on, she huffed, "Look, you don't belong here. Why anyone saw fit to hire you in the first place is beyond me, but," she calmed herself while grooming her silky hair, "you are putting our boss in a tight spot with the," she paused and emphasized, "company." Though her involvement with Cable was beginning to feel more personal than anything to do with the company as she so eloquently put it. And I hated to admit it, but I was jealous of whatever implied closeness she was giving off.

Jessi had yet to actually explain anything, and I was quickly losing my patience. I tapped my fingers on the seat of my chair, and her eyes darted to the movement like they were worms to her bird of prey.

"I'm just here to earn my credits and move on. I mean, how many people are excited about staring at an interface all day?" I tried to bond with her on the common boringness of the job, but my comment only served to fire her up again. She stood up to tower over me, trying to intimidate me, and she didn't need to stand to accomplish that goal. Her eyes did that for her.

"This is a prestigious firm, and many people trained here go on to powerful positions with Re—" she stopped herself to say instead, "our boss' help. He will run more than this company one day. You're a power leech, and one day he's going to see that and peel your grimy manacles off and toss you into the swamps."

As scary as she was when she was angry, I just stared at her dumbstruck. She never really hated me at all. The realization washed over me that my dysfunction was that I, as she put it, existed at this firm. I should have been hurt she referred to me as some swamp creature, but her tirade merely put things into perspective. She was so obsessed about work that someone like me was the weakest link to the company's success and therefore her own.

I nodded at her and, not feeling angry at her anymore, I said, "Point taken."

I was everything she thought I was. Just there for a credit, and about to commit a crime using company property. My dream about taking the damaged drone to race was brilliant, but instead of having to rush to make sure it didn't disappear into the basement storage like last time, I'd hope I wouldn't actually be that pressed for time when the coordinates came in. I'd be out of Jessi's perfect hair in no time, if Kelly was right this race today would pay enough that I wouldn't have to stay here.

Jessi's anger seemed to fade into confusion, then just as quickly into suspicion, and I shrugged because it didn't matter anymore. I wouldn't be an issue for her, or for Mr. Azel much longer. A pang sparked through my chest. Pushing through the ache I felt, I rolled away trying to keep my face neutral. Cable had already turned me down, I'd crossed a line, and after this race even if I didn't win, I didn't think I could face seeing him every day.

Hopefully today was the last I'd see of him.

"Don't you think you're being a bit harsh Jess?" My cube mate Kline said as I passed by my interface to go to the elevator.

"You know as well as I do that she doesn't have license to be here," she hissed.

I turned around at that and saw all the pilots agree with her like I was an oddity. Always so focused on getting in, doing my job, and getting out I never really took the time to notice how they perceived me before. No, that was wrong. I noticed plenty, but I brushed it off because I always thought it was pity for the girl stuck in a chair. Every one of them never cared about the nasty comments Jessi would say every day, they put up with me… they agreed with her. A pilot next to me turned his face away when I met his gaze. Snubbed by the whole lot of them.

I got uncomfortably hot, and my sweater was

feeling like an itchy straight-jacket even though it was the finest, softest of wool. As much as I tried, I couldn't keep the hurt from my eyes. They didn't know me, not that I really tried to get to know them either, but the room held a new weight. I wanted to tell them all that I may not have had a fancy education, but I passed my qualifying tests for this job. I only needed a few more years of drone hours to get my commercial license, and I'd have a higher certification than any of them.

I opened my mouth to protest, but instead clenched my fists and used every last fiber of my patience to get to the elevator without rushing. I didn't want to lose any more dignity with anyone accusing me of running away.

# Chapter Twenty-One

## *Sabotage*

My face burned, and by the time I made it up to Cable's office, I was ready to explode. This whole company could just sink into hell and sizzle for all I cared. No one wanted me here, least of all Cable. Then my anger flushed, and I touched my lips, it was all a dream I told myself. I didn't actually embarrass myself in front of him… and I questioned how I knew his name then only to then see a frosted stenciling on the glass wall that said Mr. Cable Azel. I smiled to myself, of course I saw his name somewhere in this building multiple times probably over the years I'd been here.

I took a deep breath and unclenched my fists.

He motioned for me to meet him in the office. Scanning me up and down, his eyes narrowed, and it was not the expression I was hoping for when he saw me in the most presentable attire and grooming I'd attempted at work before.

"Are you feeling all right?" he asked.

"Uh, fine." Those eyes dug into me and I fumbled to give him more information. He had that kind of effect on me. "Must have not slept well." I had the most messed up dream, I wanted to share with him everything. Tell him the whole office hated me, I planned on stealing one of his drones for a race today, and that he was so attractive when he wasn't scowling.

"Right." He looked over his shoulder to where the bedroom was behind us, and I wanted to tell him it had nothing to do with the bed. It was the most comfortable mattress I'd ever been on, and then I questioned why I'd had to stay the night at work.

I cleared my throat. "Not that I'm not grateful for you saving my job or anything, but maybe I should head home sooner today. I don't think I should be falling asleep on the job again."

"Tyler," he warned and the way my name sounded on his tongue made me melt, "If you plan on stealing another one of our drones to try to get your friend out of bounty, you'll be disappointed to find that she won't try to escape with you."

"Excuse me?" I coughed. He was shattering my dream idea into a million tiny shards. And in the same moment I flushed realizing I had really hit on my boss, and he did really reject me. My best friend really was in trouble, and I had to win a drone race against powerful aliens to save her, and then win a duel to save myself. I sounded completely sane.

"Do not defy me again," he growled, "I've already made arrangements to help ensure your safety should you decide to be reasonable and throw the race. As for your job here, there are enough pilots to distribute the workload." He was one of those powerful aliens... I repeated to myself, but I still couldn't digest the information. This had to be my overactive imagination.

"I can't."

With my augmented scan still turned on, I was sure my contacts had a glitch because one moment he was sitting in his chair, and the next he was so close to my face I could feel his breath. I quickly turned off the scanner.

"You plan on winning?" he said in a chilling tone.

"I have to try, how can I let her be someone else's bounty?" I shivered at the thought. I didn't even know what she had agreed to as her available skills for service, it seemed suspiciously like being one of the creepy digital consorts with no freewill.

"Just her?" he asked, and I stared at him.

"Well, I'm not going to willingly let her become some sort of concubine." I redirected my earlier anger at him, "Aren't you some powerful regent or something, why do you vote to keep such a twisted tradition?"

His stature stiffened. "I don't," he said emotionless.

"Oh." I turned wanting to see anything other than his steely gaze.

"Though I don't agree with bounties, they are not unsimilar to employment contracts, just more difficult to void. Your friend would be fine without your help, though you on the other hand are taking a greater risk."

I sighed. "I don't think she's a normal bounty," I admitted.

He waited for me to explain, and I hesitated because I didn't know if I could trust him, but something about him overtook that concern. Kelly's warnings a mere blip on my radar. "I think she was forced into it." I may have wanted to tell him everything about why I thought she was in more danger than a normal bounty, but I held back. He was a regent, he could help me, but he could also stab me in the back. I had to be careful about how much I shared with him,

167

despite how much I wanted to melt into his embrace and give him anything he would ever ask of me.

It was messed up, but something about him was like experiencing magic itself. And now that I was trying to process that some magic was real… I probably didn't really feel this way for him at all, maybe that's just what his alien power was?

It had to be. I didn't want to think I acted like a love-struck monkey of my own volition.

"That's impossible." He disregarded my concern, and I fumed.

"You're impossible! I doubt very many of your bounties are valid contracts. Who in their right mind would volunteer for a job with such strict conditions?"

Out the glass window I took in the skyscrapers surrounding us, he shook his head like I was a child throwing a tantrum. "If the contract is impure then it isn't binding. Your friend could leave at any time."

"For such a powerful guy, you're numb sometimes, or you just don't care. You don't have to believe me, but she isn't there because she wants to be."

He merely nodded at me with an air of sadness about him, and pointed to the door, and I was glad to be dismissed. I didn't know how much more I could take, and I still was having trouble believing anything from the last twenty-four hours.

Why couldn't he understand that sometimes people can leave at any point, but at a cost higher than they were willing to pay? That was still against their will. It was still forced service. They held something over Kelly, they must have, because even if the bounty wasn't valid, even if she didn't want to be there, something prevented her from leaving… and it wasn't the bounty contract. I had to win... for her.

As the elevator scanned me the female A.I. said, "Your drone is ready Ms. Beryl." I still hated the way she said my last name, her 'r's sounded way too much like 'z's. The elevator went up instead of down, and it opened to the rooftop. A two-passenger warrior drone sat waiting on the landing pad, it definitely wasn't a luxury transport like the night before. It was one of those aerodynamic warrior military drones with the extra angled design, and sleek gliders. Even the rotating lifters had special guards on them to help prevent what had happened to that other drone during my first race. It would take a lot more impact to damage the lifter system with those, not impossible, but it would probably do just as much damage to the other drone.

My fingers itched to ride it.

A notification popped up on my contact, just a message: Please board your provided drones and meet at the provided coordinates.

It was a mass message probably sent to all of the pilots at once. And then I knew this drone was mine to fly. Within the excitement I felt this overwhelming need to examine every inch of the drone, just to be safe. I ran my fingers over the cold material, following it to the back paneling where its battery was held. This thing should have the top-of-the-line charger in it, and I had to see it. There was no timer clicking down on my contact, so I knew I still had time, but not much probably. Shifting the paneling away, so that I could see it, instead of running my fingers on the most expensive set up I'd ever laid eyes on my hand instinctively reached into my chair's hidden compartment.

I wasn't inside the drone, so I didn't have use of my joysticks, plus I could see when I approached that it was a fully stocked manual. My hand dug around and felt the slippery material of my pants I'd stuffed in there earlier. Inside my pant pocket a small chip could be felt in my grip.

Over and over in my mind, I could hear myself say, need to win, need to use the chip, need to have control. This was Kelly's future on the line, I couldn't leave anything to chance. Stack the code, insert a back door. I slipped the chip into the data core attached to the charger and secured the back panel in place.

Feeling sweaty and tired, I leaned my arm against the drone, wondering why I wasn't already inside to test the functions out. This was the fastest model available, and it was all mine.

Launching myself into the opened hatch, the compartment was a lot more snug than I was used to in a passenger drone. The coordinates popped up on to the interface after linking up, and I grabbed the joysticks excitedly.

Just because it was important that I won, didn't mean I couldn't have fun while I was at it. I could feel the force of the drone as I sped into the traffic and played around with the feel of the drone. The coordinates were out in the middle of nowhere, and with nowhere to land. When I arrived a link notification sounded.

"Hello Pilot Sixteen, please land and exit."

Below me was a forest, with a small clearing that could have fit the drone nicely. Wherever these coordinates were it was way too far from the city for me to make my way back without a drone, even with my chair's assistance. I had to be near a charging station to keep my chair active for extended amounts of time.

A beeping sound alarmed in my ears, and a warning light lit up my interface. One of the system scans kept on blinking like there was an error that it couldn't locate.

Without prompting the hatch lifted letting in the cool breeze.

"What is going on?"

The voice on the other link didn't respond to me, and continued speaking as if they didn't hear me, "You are to exit your drone within sixty seconds." I recognized the voice now as the one who escorted me away from the police after my first race.

Laughing, I thought he was joking. I was at least ten stories high in the air, and no sign of anyone else. It would only take a few seconds to land, and he did say land earlier, didn't he? So, I went to do so, only to have the drone stall.

"You are to exit your drone," he repeated, "forty seconds."

Again, I tried to lower the drone.

A countdown timer appeared on my interface, and an uneasiness grew in the pit of my stomach. Thirty seconds, and my drone still refused to lower to the available landing area below.

I noticed a pulley handle peeking out from under the seat next to me. Sure enough, leaning over I could feel a bag under the seat, and lucky for me the drone was so tight I didn't have to stretch much for it. It was a parachute. Scrambling I strapped it over myself, and knew I'd have to unstrap myself from the chair. It was much too heavy for such a relatively short jump. Normally too short for effective use, and too high not to use it.

Releasing my locking mechanism, I figured I could at least tell it to roll out after me and hope for the best. The interface blinked again, and finally the scan came back with a notification: Code Indigo, securing technology.

The countdown timer matched up with the time the race official had given me.

"You are to exit your drone. Automated course set to return in ten seconds."

"Shit!" It didn't seem like the official could hear me and wasn't aware of a code indigo either. Those kinds of codes weren't used in passenger drones, I'd only read about them for military, and the only thing I could think of was, BOOM, like my mind was trying to tell me that I'd seen the code before in my training and it wasn't good. That shit was for making sure their data wasn't stolen, by completely obliterating it. I didn't feel like blowing myself up today, and he seemed so certain that there wouldn't be any tampering with the official use drones for the race.

Except for me... the chip.

Five.

The hatch already lifted, and I was already unstrapped. I pulled my feet out of the stirrups.

Four.

Grabbing the handle on the lifted hatch I pulled myself up.

Three.

Breath.

Two.

Flinging myself out of the drone.

One.

Immediately, the wind whipped at my face making my eyes water. I patted the backpack trying to find the latch to release the parachute. Unable to control my legs to make this more graceful, I tried to lean my upper body forward into more of a dive and yanked on the strap.

I hadn't heard or felt any explosion yet, and I regretted jumping thinking I might have been merely spooked by the countdown. I didn't know for certain what a code indigo was, but with the countdown, the flashing red lights, and being prompted numerous times to exit the drone all collided together into panic.

Next, I was panicking about landing in a parachute without my wheels. Feeling frustrated I knew my chair was going to take some damage by flying out of drone after me, it was heavier than me, and without a device to slow its descent.

Then it hit me. A wave of heat on my back flying me outward from the drone.

Stunned I felt myself being whipped about, and hitting the top of a nearby branch, now clearly at the edge of the clearing merging into the forest canopy. The parachute billowed above me in deflated fury, the explosion damaging my safety net. My heart stopped in my chest, and I wanted to close my eyes so I didn't have to have my final moments of life filled with panic.

There was nothing I could do but feel the branches tear into my arms as I flailed. I kept whipping my head around to see the gray nylon float and catch on the branches with peeks of the blue sky, and green leaves meshing in a kaleidoscope around me. The clearing was out of sight now, and I wanted to be present for my last moments, so I forced myself to keep my eyes open even through the sting of harsh air, cutting wood, and the parachute yanking me.

A numbness came over me, and the shock prevented me from feeling anything more than the awareness that there was pressure in my ribcage as I bounced. Strange enough, if it wasn't for the colors of the forest, and the gray of the nylon, I would have sworn I was falling into the clouds.

The treetops were much too tall to survive, even with the parachute slowing me down. I only prayed that they caught and prevented that final plunge onto the hard ground.

I tried to keep my eyes open, for as long as possible, but my body was not my own anymore, and I braced for the shattering impact.

That's when the last thing I saw was his face. I knew he wasn't there, because he was wearing that mask from last night. And it was the face of someone I least expected. Lord Wyndall lifted the golden mask off his face, those blue eyes seemed to glow, warm and inviting like a summer breeze. I had forgotten Cable wasn't the only man I danced with, and when he leaned into me I had frozen, feeling self-conscious, before he had pulled away from me. His touch was gentle, and this time when my lips parted in invitation. In my mind I asked, "Will you kiss me?"

Without a word, he did.

And I was so happy, that just like that night...

The air felt heavier than me, and I floated.

Chapter Twenty-Two

*Pilot Seven*

When I came to, the sky was dark, and my contacts were cracked, making the moonlight striking through the sky like a massive red lightning storm on pause. Mixed with blood in my eye, it was difficult to see, but the contact screen flickered in and out with a message containing new coordinates, and a voice message that I couldn't even concentrate on.

Groaning I lifted my arm to take out the contacts, only to stop midway with a shriek. My vision blurred, and my body arched against itself trying to retract away from itself, only to feel even more sharp stabs of pain from the rest of my body. My arm hung at an awkward angle, bending at my forearm instead of my elbow. Discoloration bruised my skin, and a sick dark color let me know that if I moved just enough it would tear through the thin skin still hanging on, revealing the broken bone that bulged there. I felt twisted up in the parachute, but I was not dangling from the treetops like I thought I would…

And I was alive.

The gray nylon was torn and strewn above me in pieces. The longer I stayed still on my back, the more my shock was wearing off, and my body throbbed and ached.

My other arm moved, though painfully, and I took out the contacts since they were making me dizzy with all the flashing alerts.

Accepting the audio message, I found my NeuralGo still intact, sending a huge sigh of relief through me knowing that I didn't have to worry about brain damage.

"Pilot Sixteen, Welcome to the races." My official said in a very businesslike manner, his enthusiasm meter was as low as how I felt right then. "This year, due to the Hand Rite Ceremony, all pilots are to complete all the traditional race feats to insure only the most powerful will succeed. Your first race starts at the end of this message activating a timer with which you are required to make it to the next coordinates by. Only ten pilots will be allowed to continue past this point. In Acatalec we breath," he huffed and in a bored manner continued what sounded like a traditional cheer, "Num De Ral," but it fell flat from cheerful.

As soon as the message clicked, I heard, "Five num cycle."

I said, "Repeat."

It responded, "Four num cycle, and fifty-nine cores remaining."

It was counting down, in a very strange way, but the races didn't really matter anymore. There was no way I was going to make it on time to be within the top ten, not when I had no idea how long I was out for, and it was dark outside.

As much as I hated to admit it, I failed my best friend Kelly, and I would have to have someone come get me before I died out here.

Who was I going to call? I couldn't call my mom,

she wouldn't know where to find me and, honestly, I didn't want to have to admit to her that I was involved with some shady shit. I couldn't get Kelly, because if Cable was right about the bounty thing, she wouldn't be able to interfere during the race. So, I tried to see if I could call back the official, and if I really had to, Cable.

I didn't have my contacts in anymore, and my eyes hurt too much to even try. With my eyes closed I merely tried to locate the official via a link call. I kept hearing an error beep in my ear and didn't have to look to see that my contacts were probably popping up with distorted notifications telling me the I.D. was unknown or blocked.

Next was Cable, and though I didn't get the same error sound, it wasn't the sound I was hoping for. He was not accepting my link. I couldn't tell if it was a busy signal or disconnected, they both sounded too similar to each other, and usually people were able to read the difference on their connected lenses.

"Time," I requested.

"Four num cycle, and fifty-two cores remaining."

I sure as shit wasn't going to wait what appeared to be five hours on this cold ground for the officials to finally realize there was something wrong and come to my rescue. If anything, they seemed like the type that didn't care if I survived or not.

In a panic I finally said, "Call anyone in range."

My NeuralGo made a sound that almost made me weep. It was connecting.

"Don't tell me you're pissed," she said bored, "it's on tact to do what you have to do to win."

I hesitated, confused by what she was saying to me. The closest person within range to me that my

NeuralGo had access to was Bailey. She had given me her contact I.D. earlier this week, but I hadn't thought about it. My mind was too fuzzy to be thinking clearly, I just needed her to help me notify the officials that I needed help.

"I…"

"Look," Bailey groaned at me, "You're alive, so no hard feelings. All ten of the spots are already taken, and the time is up so, it was nice knowing you." She was about to end the link and I knew it.

"Wait!" I gritted my teeth, the realization catching up with me that the drone wasn't an accident, and she was responsible for it. At the same time according to her this phase of the race was over, but my timer was still running, and if five hours had already elapsed then why weren't the officials or someone searching for me?

"Can you at least send an official out to come get me?" I sounded pathetic, and I knew that. It was humiliating to ask for help from someone that was responsible for where I was crumpled to begin with.

She laughed like my request was a joke, and when I didn't say anything, she coughed on her own noises to say, "Wait? Are you being serious right now?"

"On second thought, you can go defrag yourself. Wouldn't be able to trust you to not try to finish the job."

Bailey laughed some more, and stopped enough to get a few words out, "Priceless. Look, I have nothing against you, and now that you're out of the races I don't care either way if you make it back to civilization, but I'll do you a solid."

"You'll have an official contact me?" I asked incredulous, it didn't seem like she was going to do anything to help me.

"No, don't be ridiculous."

I gritted my teeth, wanting to claw at her face and bulldoze her over like the scrap of junk she was.

"But," she continued, "I will tell you that I was paid to target you, and it was one less pilot to deal with in the races. Since Cam failed at taking you out before the official races began, it was a bonus to seek a bit of payback for my girl."

She paused to let me simmer and seethe in the knowledge before giving me what was probably her idea of a solid, "If I were you, I'd stay off the radar until the whole thing is over. And because I respect a pilot that can take a punch, I won't let anyone know that we linked up." In a cheery farewell she said, "Stay gone!" And the link was terminated.

Forgetting myself I slammed my fist into the ground, still clutching my contacts, and felt the force send sharp pain all through my body. My throat so dry and scratchy the scream that erupted rung silent, only the harsh air being pushed out of my lungs and nothing more.

I tried to contact Cable again, and nothing connected.

Then in a last stitch effort, I knew I'd get in trouble with the authorities if I tried to explain anything, but I called up emergency services.

Instead of connecting an automatic voice message was sent. I accepted it.

"Pilot, you have activated an invalid command during the race. If you would like to forfeit your entry, please remain where you are, and a drone will come retrieve you. If you would like to continue, please say, 'disregard'."

Despite what Bailey had said, I was still in the races, not that it mattered. I was in no condition to continue, but before the message ended, I heard a shout from behind me in the woods calling out, "Pilot Sixteen? Pilot Sixteen!" Her voice was like an angel's, and I thought for sure I was hallucinating.

Did the officials find me already? They were so fast.

"Ah, talec!" she swore, and for some reason even though I didn't know the word, her inflection made it sound like she was upset.

"Is it time?" I rasped, thinking I must have lost too much blood.

"Yah, sure," she said, "Don't move." I couldn't have done much of that anyways. Her shadow hovered over me, and the moonlight glowed between the treetops to settle around her shoulders like a ghost come to take me to my final destination.

"You officials are fast," I said before closing my eyes again.

"What?" She questioned, "The officials don't give a flying Goudo bark about us if we can't handle a race then we aren't fit to even think about a Hand Rite."

"I don't want a stupid ceremony," I mumbled.

"I know you don't, that's why I have to see what you're made of."

Now I was the one saying, "What?" I opened my eyes, only to squint at her because of the blood trickling from my forehead. Suddenly, I felt cold all over like I was being covered in a blanket of snow. It was soft and wet, making me shiver. The action alone should have made me cry out in pain, but I didn't.

I moaned instead. It was the strangest feeling I had ever had, and that was saying something since yesterday I was floating in a sea of dancers that weren't human. The woman's hands put pressure on my abdomen, and my back arched up to meet her like she was electricity, and I was floating in cold icy water. Her touch felt like she was reaching into my soul and massaging it back to life.

"We have to get you to the coordinates," she said like that answered my question, and explained everything that was happening.

"It's too late," I sighed feeling her move her hands to my legs. A tingling I hadn't experienced in years vibrated through my muscles.

"You took a nasty fall. I'd never had to work with this kind of damage before." And again I wanted to tell her that even that was too late to save. Even an AmbularGo wouldn't do more than send pulses, bringing the nerves that gave sensation back wasn't an option.

"Are you a doctor?" I asked her.

She laughed, and I grumbled not liking how often I was being made a fool, taken advantage of, and having just dealt with a lunatic who tried to kill me was making me adverse to the sound of any laughter as it pertained to me. It was difficult to scowl, when every time her hands touched me, my body responded with a wave of chilled euphoria. It was exactly as the old poets used to describe painful pleasure. If this was that, then I had definitely converted to BDSM.

"I'm Pilot Seven," she introduced herself.

"Are you waiting on the officials too?" I found myself feeling like I had taken some numbing drugs, and my whole body was cold, and without any pain. Which in turn had me feeling a bit more chatty, but still too out of it to even want to open my eyes again.

"Did you call them?"

"Tried, they didn't answer."

She sighed in relief.

"But I did get a message saying to wait for them if I wanted to."

Stopping her hands where they were, she lunged up to my face, and with her breath hot on my cheek she quickly said, "Cancel."

"They didn't use that word, they said I should say, 'disregard'. If I wanted to stay, that is. Which, how could I in the state I'm in?" And after I said it, she pushed up and continued doing whatever she was doing to my body, and I wasn't complaining.

Another audio message sounded, "Four num cycle, and forty-five cores remaining."

"When did you listen to your message?"

"Fifteen minutes ago, but I'm not sure the point of continuing the countdown when they already have ten pilots," I said slurring my words like a drunkard.

Lifting her hands from me, she said, "I think that's enough for now… plus, I wasn't expecting to exhaust myself this soon in the races."

"They already have ten pilots," I repeated and finally opened my eyes to find my vision wasn't as bad as earlier, but the shadows cast over her, all I could make out was that her hands were covered in a violet-white glow. Her figure fell backwards onto her elbows and she stared up at the sky with me.

"You think those ten are the ones moving on?" She didn't seem convinced.

"If they're already at the coordinates, and we aren't then stands to reason." I peeked over at her shadow and smiled. "Thank you for helping me, Pilot Seven."

"You can call me Rem." I could see her teeth from the moonlight, so I knew she smiled back. "We don't have much time to stay here, so you're going to have to get up soon."

"You're going to have to leave me here for the officials to find." My chair was probably a hunk of broken junk somewhere so she couldn't have known, but I was stuck here. I wasn't about to drag myself across the forest floor to who knew where.

"I didn't spend all of my power to fix you only to have you forfeit. Plus, you'll be waiting a long time for the officials to come get you. If your timer is still running then no one is coming for you."

The way she talked about the timers made me think that everyone's timer was different, and so I had to ask her, "How much time do you have?"

"I don't know yet," she said matter of fact, and it didn't make sense that she wouldn't know, but somehow I knew she was being truthful. And in that trust I had for her I thought about Bailey.

"What region are you from?" I had to ask, if she was from the same as Bailey, then I couldn't trust my own instincts. Kelly had said the Priscus region could trick your mind, and I realized firsthand what that was like but didn't think I would know if it happened again.

"No drinks first then?" She sighed. "I did just give your body a onceover, which can be very intimate." She paused to think about it and finally said, "Tullus, but I suppose I already gave that away when I touched you. So, there it is."

"Does everyone from Tullus feel like you when they touch someone?" I shivered, but it wasn't because she frightened me, it was because I could still feel my skin tingle from her touch.

"You're odd," she stated, waiting for me to tell her I was joking, but when I didn't respond, she couldn't take the silence, "It's rare to meet someone whose parents didn't send them to study our history, even if they did grow up on Earth. Especially, if you grew up with power to even enter the races."

By simply being part of these races, Rem assumed I was one of them, whoever them was. An alien from a place called Acatalec. And I certainly didn't have any power to win these races. If that's what it took my piloting skills weren't going to be enough, even without Bailey's betrayal.

"So, not everyone is born with power from Tullus?"

"No, in fact. If you had gone to our history class, you'd find that only a quarter of Acatalec is born with their region's specialty. Many of the telshures only bond with other telshures for this reason. Mating with someone with small to no power reduces your chance of having a child with your abilities. But," she added with a bit of pride, "sometimes two people with no power at all with a few recessive genes in them, can still produce a child with great power."

"I'm sorry, telshures?"

"The muckety mucks that own most of Acatalec's wealth. Those of "pure" bloodlines, keeping their power strong by mating with the strong."

"Awe." I got the impression she wasn't one of the telshures she was speaking about. "You know, genetically speaking, keeping 'pure' is actually counterproductive to strength of a person's genes."

"Yah, try to tell them that." Rem laughed, and I found myself liking her more the longer I talked with her. Her laugh didn't bother me anymore, it wasn't directed at me. "Many of the telshures aren't as powerful as they think, but they aren't inbreeding so they are more powerful than most. We can show them that power can be found anywhere... together if you like."

"I'm kind of stuck here, but I'll be your biggest cheerleader," I offered.

Rem sat up, and without warning, slapped me across the face.

Stunned, I cupped my sore cheek. Feeling a sharp pang of betrayal, I leapt up on instinct to fight her. She matched my pace and braced herself in the dirt to defend herself. Fists clenched at my sides, I felt tall, before my brain caught up with my body. My legs wobbled, and I swayed. Rem's arms reached out and I tried to swat at her only to fall into her. Holding on to her neck, she steadied my frame to her chest.

I whispered to her, "I think I'm dreaming again."

"I don't understand how you're still so unstable. I shot everything I had into you, you should be fine." She settled me back down onto the ground.

"Why did you hit me?" I pouted.

"You were annoying me. I didn't think you would give up so easily, but I also didn't realize you were so badly injured that you wouldn't be ready to leave yet."

I shook my head into her hair. "I'm sorry. I... I can't walk," I finally admitted to her.

"It's all right, you will soon enough. I can wait."

"No, you don't understand. I haven't been able to walk for twelve years, and my chair is destroyed."

She paused to consider this new information before she pulled back from me. Crouching in front of me she said, "There is nothing wrong with your legs, not anymore."

"What?" I didn't believe her. This was definitely a dream. I died when the drone blew up, and this was my subconscious living out my final wish before my neurons fired off their last spark of life.

"Well, it makes sense why I had to expend so much power now, but I'm not sure why you wouldn't just get that fixed a long time ago."

"What do you mean?"

"Any doctor in Acatalec would have been able to tell you that you had a neural block in place and could have easily had someone like me or even a specialist from Priscus fix you right up. Waiting so long was probably why it was so exhausting... and why you may need a little bit to get your bearings."

"I don't understand... how would I have a neural block?"

Rem sat back on the ground and leaned back to see the moon again before responding. "I could only speculate."

I waited, leaning in, and she groaned realizing I wanted her to do just that.

"Fine, any number of reasons, but there are plenty of people who could have done it to you on purpose. Those freaks from Tarquin could have glamoured you into forming the block yourself. It's easy enough to convince someone they can't use their legs, until they literally can't anymore, but the same could be said for the mind creeps of Priscus and they could do it in an instant. Or maybe, you were in some sort of accident, and some dumb human said you couldn't use them before you had a chance to heal properly, and wham you did it to yourself." Rem shrugged. "Who the talec knows?"

My mind was swirling with questions, and suddenly I wanted to know. No, I had to know if she was telling the truth. Was I cured? Did I not need an AmbularGo anymore? And more important, could I feel again?

Leaning in I held out my hands to Rem, and she reluctantly took them. I grabbed them firm before she could take them away and trying not to scare myself from never trying, I asked her to, "Help me."

Bracing herself she lifted, and I hung on tight.

"You need to help too you know." She groaned. "You're so heavy."

"Hey!" I said distracted, and under myself I could feel one of my legs twitch. "It's working. Pull harder!" Excited, I yanked up only to have her tumbling on top of me.

"Sheesh woman, ease up. If what you're saying is true, then it may take longer than we have for you to figure out how to use those things again."

"If I can use them at all then it doesn't matter." I flung my arms around her and gave her a huge bear hug. Even if this was my last dying dream, I hoped I stayed alive long enough to see the results, long enough to walk.

"Okay toppler, we can hug this out later. Right now, we have a time limit to get you to the coordinates and show those goudo bark eaters what you're made of." Rem lifted me up and with my arm over her shoulder began walking.

"I don't understand you, but I'm on board with the sentiment." I needed to show Bailey I wasn't one to be messed with, even if I didn't believe it myself yet.

"You really need a lesson in your history, but for now I'll tell you the bark of a goudo is the most putrid smelling thing on Acatalec, and probably isn't something you should say in fancy settings."

"I have a goudo bark eater I need to kick if my legs ever come back to me."

"That's the spirit!" she cheered.

Chapter Twenty-Three

*Not From Here*

Deceivingly strong, Rem hoisted me onto her back and carried me through the forest. The moonlight barely illuminated our way, and after some time I could hear her breath become ragged from the extra weight. I could tell she wouldn't stop. She was that determined to get us both to the coordinates for the race.

Feigning a groan, I fidgeted and felt her body quake under the displacement of my weight. My arms have built up quite the stamina having to rely on them most of my life, so I could have gone on without any issue, but I said, "I can't hang on much longer." Hoping, that she would give herself a break, if she didn't have to admit it was for herself.

"Right, you're still recovering." Rem eased me down at the base of a tree trunk and slumped next to me. Flexing my arms and stretching them out I purposefully made a wincing face that she probably couldn't see that well in the dark, but it made it easier to make the sounds associated with discomfort. In fact, after she did whatever her hands did to me, my body was feeling better than it ever had before.

"I just need a little rest." I tried to take on the responsibility for the break and her hands pulsed a faint violet white reaching out for me, much more dull than earlier. When they made contact, I could feel that cooling sensation and let out an unsolicited moan of pleasure feeling like I'd been freshly massaged at a spa parlor.

"I'm fine really," I assured her when I realized what she was doing, using more of her energy to help me recover my strength. She was already drained, and her hands seemed to sputter like a faulty filament in an old house.

"We have to make it there before your time exceeds some of the other pilots," she insisted, but as she rose again, she did it shaking under her own body weight. Leaning against the tree, she sighed.

"You should go without me."

"Can you try to stand again?" She sounded desperate, and I wanted to be able to walk again just to ease her exhaustion.

I pushed myself up along the trunk, trying to move my feet, but like before they wouldn't budge with my efforts. My hand lost grip on the bark, and the wedge of my feet in the ground slipped sending me back down to where I started. I wanted to cry, because she had given me so much hope that I could do what she wanted, that I could walk, and all I was feeling was numb.

Her hand cupped my shaking shoulder, and she soothed, "It's okay."

"I'm useless." My chest tightened, and I could feel the pressure of my own expectations shattering all around me.

"Why don't we focus on what you can do, instead of what you can't. What region are you from?"

I choked on a self-pitying whimper at her question. It was the one thing I was hoping no one would ask me.

I wasn't supposed to be here... I didn't have any powers. Answering as honestly as I could without giving away, I didn't belong I said, "I don't know about any of the regions, or what they can do, or why I'm even here. I-I d-don't know." I was close to breaking down all over again.

"Shh, you wouldn't be here unless one of the regents saw something in you. So, we'll just have to figure it out, preferably before you get to the next race. This is the easiest of the races, most pilots have already taken out someone else to make sure they are top ten and made quick work of getting to the coordinates for the second part of the races. But... you're going to need to dig deep and find out what someone saw in you to make it out of the next race. It relies heavily on your power, whereas this one is mostly strategy."

"I'm sorry, but I don't even understand why this race is in the woods, and why we aren't racing in our drones."

"Because they already know we can pilot a drone already. Now, they are testing us."

"Why are you helping me?"

"Because there are certain parts of the race that are easier with help, and as I said before, if I can beat out most of the pilots it would help my family. And maybe I can be the catalyst for people to understand power can come from any family, even a family from the outer rings of the regions. Or maybe, even from a wild card entry like you.

"You know," she continued, "the wild cards are Acatalecians from Earth, and they've never made it to even the first trek of the races, because most who grow up on Earth don't have any power. So, I guess what I'm trying to say is that I can relate, and we can show them we are better than they think. It just would have been nice if your parents hired a tutor, or the regent who picked you would have at least told you what region you were from…"

"I only know one regent personally," I said and couldn't help but turn away from her, even in the dark, hoping she couldn't see the blush creeping up my cheeks. Even thinking about him was a problem, and I had to get over it.

"Maybe they were the one that entered you in the race?" Rem sounded hopeful but added, "Though, that's not always the case, any one of the telshure could have seen something in you and recommended you. But, even so, which regent?"

"Tarquin."

"No shit!" she sputtered. "Uh, let's hope that's not where you're from. That region has kind of a reputation. But, honestly, if it is where you're from, I'm not sure how to figure out a way to see if you have that kind of power. I mean the only well-known things are not things you want to be doing anyway."

"What kind of things?" I was curious to know what Cable was capable of. The way Rem was talking was as if people from Tarquin were monsters.

"Scary shit. Their eyes are like looking into the depths of darkness when they use their power to make you feel things you wouldn't otherwise feel so that they can turn you into their slave. It's said they have ritual sacrifices regularly, and that one kiss from any one of them cursed with the power of Tarquin is deadly. Suck the life right out of you to preserve their own."

My heart sunk deeper into my stomach

remembering how Cable had refused to kiss me.

"Are you sure it isn't just a rumor to scare people away?" I asked more hoping for myself than actually defending the Tarquin region.

Rem shrugged. "I don't really care either way, but I'm not sure I want to test the theories out on you... just in case they are true."

"What kind of theories?" It worked out best for me if they weren't things she could test out, so I didn't have to put myself in a position where everyone found out I didn't belong. I was now regretting agreeing to go with her to the coordinates if the next part of the race would require I use abilities I didn't have. Bailey might have been doing me a favor by trying to kill me. I didn't really know what they would do if an outsider was found to know of their existence, and I didn't want to find out when Bailey could get away with murder and no one batted an eye.

"Well, you could try to make me feel something just by staring into my eyes... but that's a bit difficult in the dark if you've never done it before. Then again, have you had any instances in your life where someone's felt compelled to do things for you when they wouldn't normally? Or maybe, when you were hurt having a strange urge to eat someone to heal yourself? I'm not sure, Tarquin keeps a tight lip about what their powers actually let them do. Most people are too freaked out by them to really investigate, and maybe even if they did, they wouldn't be able to say. Either way, whatever your abilities, you must have used them at some point, because someone saw it to select you for the races."

"I think we should just assume they were mistaken

and try to focus on getting you through to the next race," I suggested.

"We'll figure it out, I promise you."

"It's all right, really." Both flattered and annoyed that she wouldn't let it go, I wasn't about to start mastering a power from another race out of thin air. I couldn't afford for her to find out I didn't belong here, dead men told no tales, and I'd already avoided death once today. That was enough for me.

If it wasn't haunting enough, Rem added, "Tarquins are a lot more dangerous than the Priscus, at least with the Priscus you know you're being influenced, and it gives you a chance to resist. A Tarquin makes you believe you want to do it, that it was your idea, and that's the scariest thing of all. If a Tarquin selected you for the wild card, you probably didn't have much choice in the matter, but," she saw the fear in my face, "don't worry, I'll make sure to give you a bit of juice to help defend yourself." Her hands gave a faint violet glow again.

"That can help?"

"It's a lot more difficult for a Tarquin to influence you when you're freshly touched by a Tullus. We aren't manipulated easily when our bodies are constantly hunting for something to mend, even the psyche."

Chapter Twenty-Four

*Weakness*

"Two num cycle, and twenty-four cores remaining," my timer replied after I prompted.

We were close to the coordinates, and I was pretty sure Rem was going to collapse from carrying my extra weight any second. With my partially shattered contacts in, I could see the marker coming up, we were actually going to make it before the timer ran out. Not completely sure how Rem was able to pull it off, but she was stronger than she looked.

"You better try to walk your fat ass the rest of the way there," Rem joked, at least I thought she was before she slid me off her back and I clung to her shoulders with my legs dangling to the side.

"You've been scrapping my legs up multiple times trying to get me to walk, haven't you given up already?" I groaned. My skirt was torn and tied around my legs like balloon pants, and my sweater wasn't any better off after the parachuting adventure. But this time I noticed something I hadn't the many other times Rem had flung me over to put weight on my legs; I felt the dampness of the ground on my feet. My kitten heel shoes were long gone, fallen off hours ago in my tumble down the trees.

Before Rem could say anything, the biggest smile

crossed my face, and I screamed.

"Are you hurt?" Rem immediately set me down and I landed with a thump, feeling a rock jab into my thigh. I screamed again, but it wasn't because I was in pain, though it did hurt, I was excited beyond words. Rem's hands faintly glowed again, but this time I noticed in the dark that the violet, white light was patchy, barely covering her hands.

Grabbing her wrists before they could make contact, not wanting her to waste her energy, I could tell she was already drained enough. It was noticing that my feet were bare. Knowing that I wasn't wearing any shoes and feeling the dirt beneath my toes.

I could feel it.

"I can feel my toes!"

"So you scream?" She groaned. "For talecs sake, I thought you were dying. Keep it in your pants, and let's get going." The glow in her hands puttered out, and she pressed them to either side of my cheeks. "If you can feel your toes, start walking on them, you freeloader."

Nodding with a new intensity I'd never experienced before, I grabbed her hands from my face and prepared to try again. She flung my arm over her shoulder and lifted. My legs twitched, and instead of being like gelatin they flexed, feeling firm and locked beneath me. I was standing. With help, but I was doing it.

"I can stand!" I screamed again in excitement.

"Yeesh, my ears are right here."

"Thank you," I gushed to her in a soft, hushed plea of gratitude. It was because of her. And even if this dream ended right here, I would be happy.

She shifted uncomfortable. "Just lead the rest of the

way."

I pointed with my free hand, it's just through there.

A gust of wind blew through our hair, and a large shadow loomed in front of us. It towered in the moonlight with darkness swirling around it. Rem froze and pulled me closer to her ready to make a dash through the final brush. And just as quickly, she gently pulled my arm away from her shoulder offering me up as sacrifice, and in a blur the shadow came upon us.

A low guttural growl vibrated in the darkness. Instead of feeling frightened I felt my palms grow sweaty, and my skin hum as the shadow lifted me into its arms. It had arms, and now that it was closer the moonlight reflected off the peaks and edges of a man. But he avoided my eyes, I'd know that smell anywhere. I nuzzled into the scent, because I didn't know when I'd get the opportunity again.

I could hear Rem's footsteps behind us, but she said nothing about the strange event. Cable carried me beyond the brush and to the coordinates, which was being used as a large gathering space, old stones were erected around the clearing. People danced around a fire that roared high and created beautiful moving shapes in the smoke and embers. I could almost make out a silhouette of a couple moving in the fire.

There were ten stones, and ten people in front of them. Cable held me firm to his chest, and his sharp features illuminated in the fire light, a handsome devil in his element. That's what he was, because every time I was close to him he toyed with my emotions. I wanted to have him and, in that moment, I frowned remembering what Rem had said about people from Tarquin. Their eyes made people feel things that made them lose themselves, and he was the regent of Tarquin, making him one of the most powerful of his region. What I was feeling wasn't real, it was just the effect his power had on me.

"She was supposed to protect you," he growled at me.

"Excuse me?"

"Only pilots are allowed during the first portion of the race, and she was supposed to protect you…" His chest heaved like he was going to turn into a dragon and light the whole dance on fire, along with everyone near it.

"I'm fine," I replied with less enthusiasm than I felt, still irritated that he was affecting my emotions, and in fact I was better than fine. I was a new me, I could feel my legs, and it was all thanks to Rem, who apparently wasn't helping me out of the goodness of her heart.

"You are covered in blood," he objected and proceeded to snarl. I should have been afraid of his reaction, or at least repelled by it, but I wasn't. The way his lips curved, only made me want him more that's how messed up being around him was.

"I'll have you know," I was overcompensating my irritation at liking him by shoving it in his face that if it wasn't for Rem, I'd probably be dead, "that was from nearly being blown up, and a bad parachuting incident that she had nothing to do with."

His grip on me squeezed and, with a tight jaw, he said, "Explain."

"If it wasn't for Rem I wouldn't be here."

He growled, and his eyes suddenly fell on me, and I knew that he wanted more information. Like always, I couldn't resist wanting to tell him everything. "Someone here wants me dead, or at least not in the race." I held back on who was responsible, because I had a feeling Cable wasn't the forgiving type, and Bailey wasn't the one who cared enough to lie about someone else hiring her to do it.

"I'll make sure no one will know who you are, and we will leave as soon as Lord Wyndall dismisses us. The five hours elapsed over three hours ago," he stated matter of fact. He was telling me what I already knew, the ten pilots were already chosen.

Rem finally walked up to us, and shakily asked Cable, "Is she... like you?"

His attention jerked to her direction like she was overstepping her bounds. I could feel the tension ripple through his muscles, he was still debating whether to believe she wasn't responsible for the blood covering my clothes. "You'll forget anything you saw her do, or the next conversation we have will be less than pleasant."

I looked from him to her, and back to Cable wondering what exactly he was saying.

Rem nodded, a mixture of fear and worry on her face before rushing to stand next to one of the rocks that were at least twenty feet tall.

"Why do I get the feeling you find a bit too much joy in firing everyone this week?"

"Not everyone," he corrected.

"Why would you make her think I'm from Tarquin?" Curiosity renewed in me.

"No one can know who you are," he repeated the same thing he said the night before like he had rehearsed this one answer and had no other to give me.

"Who am I to you?" And this conversation was beginning to feel all too familiar, the next step would be another rejection from him that would have me feeling like shit, and it was all because of his dumb power over me.

Except he didn't say the same thing this time. He said, "Weakness."

Chapter Twenty-Five

*Shattering*

Shattered couldn't begin to describe how I felt when Cable told me I was weakness. It was one of those words that cut deep into my core and hit all too close to the raw edges of myself. I loathed being considered weak. Whatever power he held over me with those dark eyes of his, it broke the same moment he said that word. My heart froze over, and I hardened myself to prove him and everyone else wrong.

Cable thought I was weak.

Jessi thought I was a leech.

Bailey tried to murder me.

And someone wanted me dead.

I wanted to prove to them all how wrong they were.

Then something snapped within me. A ripcord on something held back deep in my mind, the use of my legs weren't the only thing being held back by a neural block, and as the pieces broke away, I wondered why I never really thought about why I always felt so angry towards everyone. It was my body telling me something was wrong, upset that a part of itself was being held captive.

A dark film glossed over my eyes, and Cable squeezed to hold me tight against his chest before I stared him down. In a seductive growl I said, "Release me." And I felt his grip loosen before he closed his eyes to me and clung to me so hard, I could feel my skin bruising. When he opened his eyes again, they were terrifying like two swirling abysses sucking me in, but I was not afraid. A shiver ran down my spine, and I felt warm all over.

"You will behave yourself until we are dismissed." He gritted his teeth to control his breathing that became erratic, and deep. Cable's thumb stroked circles on my exposed thigh as I lay cradled in his arms and whatever anger I had felt moments before suddenly turned feral, and needy. I bit my lip to stop myself from making any embarrassing noises, and briefly regretted Rem healing my legs. If I couldn't feel it, I wouldn't have been so affected.

The instruments that filled the air were quiet making the sound of our heavy breath more pronounced. Thankful for the distraction, Lord Wyndall had the crowd hushed as well for him to speak, and presumably dismiss the failed pilots. Lord Wyndall floated in the air above the fire and sent a gust of wind simmering the flame to low embers. He was bare chested, skin glistening in the moonlight with the faint glow of the warm fire licking at his loose fitted silky pants. The fabric clung to his muscular thighs, and if it weren't for the shadows of the night, would have left nothing to the imagination. He was a wood nymph, a very strong, practically naked wood nymph. I shivered at the sight of him, and Cable's grip clenched pressing me into his firm chest.

The more I stared at Lord Wyndall, the more I thought about Cable's equally attractive bare chest when he came to train me in the mornings, before he'd pull over a simple shirt that shaped his body perfectly. Cable's sinewy forearms flexed under my weight, and I reluctantly was captured by his eyes, he was impossible to deny, and it maddened me.

"All results are finalized for the traditional forest run, paying homage to the beginning of the races, before the modern conveniences of today. We dance amid the stones, and fire as our ancestors did in celebration of the defeat of Marduk the betrayer of Lady Nam, who has gifted our lands with the regents of her power.

"It is with great pleasure that I present to you the ten pilots of Acatalec. Pilot Seven." Rem had come in first place?

"Pilot Nine." Bailey was second, and that didn't surprise me, but still made me fume.

"Pilot Four, Pilot Eleven, Pilot Twelve, Pilot Eight, Pilot Two, Pilot One," Lord Wyndall listed off the pilots, keeping their identities the same as they were from the first race to The Last Transport.

"Pilot Sixteen." I heard him say my pilot number, and I wasn't last, but I also made it to the final ten pilots, and I didn't know why. I was shocked and needed an explanation.

"...and Pilot Three. Would our pilots please stand next to a stone, and we will all offer our blessings upon you for the next tribute to our ancestors," Lord Wyndall finished.

"I don't understand," I mumbled.

"You were over two hours late," Cable mimicked my sentiments.

Rem took to the first stone and smiled at everyone

as the flame of the fire was stoked to a roar again lighting up her features that I hadn't really seen outside of the shadows before then. She was stunning, but she had arrived the same time as me how was she the first pilot?

"My countdown started as soon as I got the coordinates," I thought out loud.

Something must have clicked with him when I said that and he nodded. "She never opened her message."

I had newfound awe of Rem at how smart she was. This race wasn't just about speed, and power, but wits. She had the lowest time, because she never started her timer. She knew where to go because I had the coordinates. Taking a risk that she would find someone that could lead her where she needed to go, but I still didn't understand how she knew she shouldn't open it, why she shouldn't listen to the message?

He walked me up to the ninth stone, and the number made my eyes dart to the second stone, and she too did the same to me. Pilot Nine, Bailey, gave me the most wicked smile before shaking her head at me in mock sympathy. Her gleam told me without any words, you should have stayed in the forest. It was a lot safer there.

In the fire between us I could see my own reflection staring back at me, as if waiting for revenge. I didn't know then that my desire for revenge ran deeper than anyone could have fathomed, but I'd been wronged by Bailey, and I vowed that no one would get away with betraying me ever again. My reflection turned, and smiled back at her, and I knew she saw the same thing I did. Bailey sneered, and flicked her chin away, the trance broken all attention went back to Lord

Wyndall.

"In the Goddess we rise, in the Goddess we fall, with her blessing we join her. In her power we burn bright. For the Pride of Acatalec!"

"Num De RAL!" Everyone cheered and the fire roared to match their progression as the people dressed in thin gossamer fabrics that floated in the wind, billowing in the smoke of the fire, and others in nothing but scraps of fabric danced with wild rhythm. It was a stark contrast to Cable's formal business attire. The dancing guests of the party slid masks over their faces, each with a representation of mysterious animals or monsters. Some were strong, dangerous birds made of gold, others like ogres, some creatures I'd never seen before, ghostly angels, and others like onyx grim reapers. Their heads swung back to call out into the dark sky, reveling in the sounds of the drums and singing, then they'd bury their face down into their chests humming in low rumbles. I felt like I was part of a strange cult sacrifice ritual.

Among the sounds of the party, Lord Wyndall went up to Rem, and though I couldn't hear what they were saying, she looked to me before responding to him. He went to Bailey, and she too answered a question, before this continued down the line and he made his way towards me… and Cable. The air around me felt heavy, and by consequence made me feel lighter. Lord Wyndall's hand reached out for me, and upon taking his hand I lifted from Cable's arms, his grip on me clamped down before releasing me. With the air supporting me like I was nothing but dust, I stood only an inch from the ground. Lord Wyndall gave me the dignity of being on my own feet as he asked me a question.

"Who would you have be your assist in the races to come?"

I remembered Kelly telling me she could help me in the races, that there would be a co-pilot, and what she could do to help. Her ability could help shave seconds off my time, and avoid dangerous collisions, but that was assuming the upcoming race had anything to do with drones.

Lord Wyndall's blue eyes shone bright in the moonlight and the way they twinkled made me realize nothing in these races would be as they seemed. Even something as simple as walking through the forest and finding coordinates was seeped in layers of expectations that changed the course of the rankings. I was involved with a race where the rules were not spelled out, and I had a feeling the reason why there were only two extra pilots, other than the ten that were chosen were because the rest were hunted, never to arrive.

"Bounty five." I remembered Kelly's moniker.

Lord Wyndall ran his eyes over Cable and then back to me amused. Still holding my hand he bent down to give it a light peck. From under his lashes, he took me in and lingered on my hand. It was in this exchange that I had the time to notice the dried blood spidering along my skin from when I fell. Lord Wyndall followed my gaze all the way up my ripped sleeve before whispering in the wind, "Another victory I see, Pilot Sixteen."

"Lord Wyndall, don't you have other pilots to greet?" Cable prompted a swift end to the abnormal amount of attention. And I was thankful because he wasn't the only one noticing the longer Lord Wyndall stayed with me, including the courtesy of using his ability to let me stand, and bowing to me. It was making me uncomfortable the more people stopped to watch.

"I do have one more to greet, don't I." Lord Wyndall acknowledged and released my hand. Righting himself he walked over to the last pilot and I remained floating, with my toes curling into the dirt, and my heels lowering to the ground. It felt good to stand, almost on my own.

In a blink, Cable was at my side again and slid his arm around my waist to support me when the air became lighter than me again, but it didn't. I waited for it, the moment where I'd collapse into his embrace, only to search for Lord Wyndall in the crowd wondering when he would take his ability away from me. It was generous of him to give this to me, but I would be a fool to think he'd waste his time on me for long. To avoid being humiliated, I wrapped my arms around Cable's neck.

"Let's get this over with," I grumbled, hating to have to rely on him.

"You'll have to continue the races now," he explained, "Are you sure about your assist?"

"I couldn't have chosen you, could I?" I mocked him, but he merely answered in a calm and business-like manner.

"No, regents are unable to interfere with the races directly." It wasn't lost on me that he said directly.

"Then, there you have it. What other choice would I have had."

"Any one of my pilots would have assisted you."

He'd lost his mind. "Yah, I'm sure any pilot here

would be happy to help someone else win." That's exactly why some of them had bruises and blood splatters like they'd been in a fight just to be here.

"No, not any pilot. My pilots. They value their rank within Tarquin far more than bonding with the likes of him." There was bad blood between Cable and Lord Wyndall, and the way he referenced him, it was clear there was a history.

"With the way all of the pilots, including your pilots, are looking at me, I don't trust any of them to have my best interests at heart."

"It isn't about what's in their hearts, they will do as they are told," he growled, and I sensed a crack in his cold calculating bravado. Cable was affected by me being in these races, and I didn't know why. Was he so bored and entitled that he thought it would be fun to toy with a powerless Earthling for a change in pace? I was feeling resentful at him using me, and in that moment was when my body felt anything but light and I slumped into his chest with the weight of gravity pulling my useless legs.

Cable transitioned my weight seamlessly, with deft movements he swept me into his arms. His dark eyes darted to the pilots a few stones away from us, and their eyes reflected back at us with a glimmer before giving a small bow of the head. They must have been what he called his pilots, because they immediately left their posts, disappearing, and reappearing in front of us so fast my eyes couldn't even process it. Like all those times I could blink, and he'd be gone, they were just like him.

"Shard," he addressed one of the pilots. She was tall, slender, and the night only served to highlight how gorgeous she was. The angled cheekbones, and the way she held herself spoke of a strong warrior, a striking viper. Her eyes were hazel gray, in contrast to Cable's brooding brown. "Make sure to assist Pilot Sixteen if she needs it."

She scoffed like I was an insect. "She only made it because everyone had already thought they secured their positions." She sniffed me and grimaced. "She's a liability, the others will target us."

Cable tensed up, his whole presence swelled, and the shadows gravitated towards him. As if the room were smaller making him seem larger, and by contrast Shard and the other pilot seemed to shrink.

Shard growled at him. "Xio will not be pleased. There are more important things on the line besides your guilty conscience."

"You will hold your tongue," Cable seethed. What did he have to feel guilty about? Shard bowed her head to him, but slightly sideways so that she could still glare at him from under her long lashes in a sort of defiance.

"So be it," she gave in and yanked on my hand before I could protest. Pulling it from around Cable's neck she held it out before her and sunk her teeth into the thenar meat of my palm below my thumb. I would have screamed, but it happened so fast that by the time my mind caught up it no longer hurt. Shock, silenced me, and she flung my hand back at me, and licked her lips.

He nodded to her like what she did was normal, and he'd wanted her to bite me like an animal and lick the blood from her prey.

"She'll be able to find you now," he told me as if that explained everything, and made it okay. Coming to my senses I turned my face from him refusing to meet his eyes. I relied on him too much, but that didn't mean I had to make it pleasant for him. Wiggling, I tried to make the hold on me as uncomfortable as possible for him but based on the lack of response from him I served to only make things more uncomfortable for myself.

Chapter Twenty-Six

*Don't Hold Back*

"Let the pilot breathe, Regent Azel." Lord Wyndall approached us before we could leave the celebrations after our forest trek. "If I didn't know any better, I'd say you were claiming this wild card for yourself instead of for the people."

"She isn't yours," Cable said with an undertone.

"No." He smiled mischievously despite my obvious scowl at being referenced as an object. "Not anyone's as far as I can tell. Such is the state of a wild card." And I was beginning to like Lord Wyndall more and more, if only because he gave me a small bit of dignity in all of this chaos. With his ability he had allowed me to dance, to stand, and without his ability allowed me a small bit of space for myself. I was no one's'. I managed myself just fine before all of this mess. Lord Wyndall's comment seemed to ruffle Cable's hard scale exterior, and I rather liked it. Served him right for thinking I wasn't enough, that I needed a babysitter, and that I wasn't good enough on my own.

"May I have a moment without your escort, Pilot?" Lord Wyndall asked me directly, ignoring the overbearing suit that held me in his arms. There was this tug within myself that rejected the idea of leaving Cable, my fingers clutched to the hairs at the back of his head, weaving into the softness of him. The contact gave me a high, and it was because of that feeling that I forced myself to remove my hand from holding on to him. The mere act of reaching out to Lord Wyndall took all of my strength, and I pushed past the emptiness I felt as the space between our bodies expanded.

Weakness overcame me and I had to see Cable's face, and he refused to meet my gaze. Those steely orbs focused only on Lord Wyndall, and they swirled with power as the fire flickered in them, highlighting the amber in his brown eyes that were almost black in the evening. That intensity promising to consume any and all in its path.

I already felt like melting, before Lord Wyndall grabbed my hand breaking the spell. Whatever hold Cable had on me, it was strong… and I had to resist it, but the closer I got to Lord Wyndall that same intensity returned but in the opposite direction. An electricity buzzed through the hand Lord Wyndall held, and my pulse quickened.

"Regent Azel, I do believe you have other obligations this evening." His voice was smooth and hinting a bit of triumph making me squirm at being between them. Cable's hand on my thigh as he held me was hot on my skin and left a burning trail up to my torso as he lowered me gently. My toes eased on to the ground, curling into the dirt. I loved the feeling of the soft granules rubbing against my skin. It didn't matter to me that my legs were splattered with mud, and my feet were covered to the point of blending in with the shadows. I could feel the softness of dirt, and the sharpness of the rocks scattered within threatening to break through my sensitive layers. I felt giddy, before I traveled up from my feet to the amused stare of Lord Wyndall.

Every inch of me was in disarray. What was once an expensive, elegant outfit this morning clung to me in tatters. The fabric marred with grime and blood. Now, that I felt exposed standing with the help of Lord Wyndall's ability my giddiness faded. He must have been thinking what a mess I was to boldly smile at myself, but it wasn't my appearance that I was proud of, it was all the little sensations coming back to my numb limbs. From the touch of Cable's hands on my thighs as I lay cradled in his arms not moments ago, to the grit between my toes that I hadn't felt since I was a child.

How could my own mind be responsible for keeping all of this from me?

Lord Wyndall continued to hold my hand, and as he moved forward, I ungracefully stumbled forward with him. I clamped down on his hand harder than I intended to keep myself steady, stiffening my arm, and leaning into him. His chest was bare, and even though he shimmered in the dim light, he wasn't sweaty. Flinching, I tried to pull back, but he held me close, mischief in his eyes at the opportunity to rile up the Regent of Tarquin, I guessed.

Cable was irritated by anything Lord Wyndall did, and at the moment it was that he wasn't in control of his employee anymore. Why they got under each other's skin, I didn't know, but I was the pawn they used to torture each other with for now. I could sense that at least, and part of me was smug about causing this reaction in Cable as payback for thinking I was weak and making me feel foolish for falling victim to his abilities. He knew that his eyes sent shocks of feelings into his victims, and yet he had the nerve to reject me like a piece of garbage. Served him right to feel a little bit of agitation. I wasn't at all remorseful at utilizing Lord Wyndall to sense the shadows around us grow, and fume because things weren't going according to whatever plans he had for his toy pilot.

I was not his toy.

"Thank you for helping me walk," I tried to break the awkward silence.

"The pleasure is all mine." Lord Wyndall directed me away from the fire, and the gyrating dancers.

"I mean it though. How you make the air feel heavier than me is..." I didn't know what I wanted to say, only that I was grateful. "Thank you," I repeated.

He stopped walking then, curiosity evident in his raised brow, before regally giving a tilt of his chin in acknowledgment. "I've taken you aside to make sure you understand something. As a wild card, I'm aware that your parents probably didn't instill in you the same teachings as they would have growing up in Acatalec."

I wasn't sure where he was going with this, but I nodded at him, because I craved more information about the situation I was in, but also I didn't want to say anything that would give away that I didn't belong here. I waited for him to speak again, hoping my silence would be enough for him to continue.

"You barely made it into this round." He seemed disappointed before his voice lowered. "It is important that you take these races seriously." It was then that I felt chastised, and my neck burned like I was getting in trouble with the host, and just as important, the prince of these aliens.

"I did come here to win," I choked out, and it wasn't a lie. It was my intention coming to this race to win, get some credits, and save my best friend from destitution. However, that intention had quickly changed to ensuring no one found out I was human, staying alive, and hopefully along the way retribution towards the ones that attempted to take my life.

He smiled a broad dazzling smile that would have made any of his subjects swoon and squeezed my hand. "That's good to hear," he said lightly and then stared at me with those intensely blue eyes, "If you throw these races intentionally, and hold back your power then I'd be forced to test your abilities myself in a duel."

Pressing my lips into a thin line, I narrowed my eyes trying to prevent myself from showing him that his words frightened me. If I hung on to my anger at being called out for squeezing by in these races by hanging on to other's help, I thought I'd be able to get through this conversation without giving myself away. I had no idea what he would do to me if he found out I wasn't one of his subjects, but now I knew what he would do to me if I didn't make it through the next round of races. He thought I was throwing the race, and he would duel me personally if I lost the next.

I would have responded to him, to tell him I had no intention of dueling him, but if I did win the races that statement would have been a lie. I couldn't bond with him… I had no power to give. I would duel him, and lose, rather than expose how human I was. Gripping his arm for more support and adjusting myself I thought I distracted him from my lack of response. He was indeed distracted, but as I followed his gaze it landed on my torn sweater, where my chest pressed up against his powerful bare bicep. I hadn't realized how much of the fabric the branches tore away from me, and I was feeling especially exposed. I turned away from him refusing to let myself think on it further.

Lord Wyndall's next words were laced with a feral undertone, and my insides squirmed. "Do not hold back." He cleared his throat. "I will not bond with second best, and one way or another I will draw the power out of you. Regent Azel cannot keep you to himself when the future of our kind is in the wind. Do I make myself clear?"

I knew he wasn't going to let me leave this conversation without an answer, and my heart was hammering in my ribcage at just how clear he was making things. He thought I had power because Cable was trying to protect me, and because of his and Lord Wyndall's feud I was in greater danger than I could have imagined.

"Crystal," I growled at him.

Lord Wyndall gave a feigned pout. "Do not be angry with me. I have a duty to my people, and I'd like for us to be friendly when you join me for the Hand Rite Ceremony."

"I doubt threatening a person is really the best way to remain friendly, but your point has been made, Lord Prince," I prodded, and it only served to make him smirk.

"Wyndall," he corrected.

"Lord Wyndall."

"When we are to be bonded, I'd prefer you call me by my given name, dear. And it would be only proper for me to call you by yours." He was prompting me for my name, and my eyes darted around panicked, trying to find Cable in the crowd. Maybe even Kelly, if she were here, she'd know what to say. She always knew what to say.

"Lord Prince," I reverted back to his formal title, pressing my luck but trying to ease it back by giving him my best smile, the one Kelly would say makes her hot under the collar when I was contemplating dating at some point. My eyes smoldered, and I could feel that same intense darkness in them fueled by my irritation at being dictated to. "Wouldn't want to spoil the surprise when I win this race," I bluffed my confidence.

His eyes matched my heat, and his chest muscles heaved. I'd have to thank Kelly later for trying to teach me how to be seductive with only a glance, though if I were being honest, I thought I was going to fail at it miserably, especially with how much I felt like choking him with the nails I was currently digging into his arm muscles to keep standing.

"I look forward to it," his voice vibrated with power. "As a parting gift I will warn you about your race escort. He has gained his position in this court through brute force, and many have gone back to the land at his hands in his pursuit. The power you hold, do not fool yourself in thinking he would be so kind as to bond with you to share it," he paused and his blue eyes heated, "he will merely take it for himself, as he has done before."

I shivered at his words, and the picture of the Regent of Tarquin filled in with even more darkness than there was before. He said it himself… he was not human.

"Isn't that your intention?" I spoke boldly and narrowed my eyes at him.

He gave me a charming smile. "There is a distinct difference, Pilot. I will not force you."

## Chapter Twenty-Seven

*The Assist*

Sitting me down on a flat rock on the outskirts of the festivities Lord Wyndall left me to be a gracious host, mingling with his citizens. Grateful that he wasn't going to grill me further about my name or my absent powers, I searched the crowd. I knew I shouldn't, but when I couldn't spot him, I felt a sudden onset of loneliness in the open air. Cable was gone. I should have been happy that he wasn't smothering me with his controlling nature, but I wasn't. Part of me wanted to fight with him, because even that was better than nothing, better than accepting that he didn't want me.

Closing my eyes and groaning into the moon above me, I swore under my breath. Why did he make me want him? Was this all a ploy to trick Lord Wyndall into thinking I was powerful, and embarrass him publicly when he tried to bond with a human? He knew where I came from, that I wasn't from Acatalec. But he didn't stop me from joining the races. He could have… but he didn't.

I remembered that night, and how the elevator was conveniently left open for me to leave his office. The scanner still glowing green as if malfunctioning, though I suspected on purpose, to allow me to escape. He was nowhere to be found… because he had already left to dress into a fancy tuxedo and waited for me to arrive at his lawyer's office.

He knew, I seethed.

This was all his fault.

Completely ignoring the fact that Kelly needed me to help her, and she had no idea what she was signing us up for. We were always taking a chance every time we signed up for an illegal race. I huffed, irritated that I was even beginning to make excuses for him. Sure, I had my own part to play in this mess, but he knew better... and did nothing.

No, worse than nothing... he cleared the way. Training me, leaving the door wide open, and the final puzzle clicked when I thought about the drone I used to get there. Why didn't I think about how odd it was that the drone hadn't been serviced by the engineering floor yet? It was conveniently next in line to be serviced, when it was a basic hardware scan job, and those were usually first in the queue. It had been days since I sent that drone down for service.

It shouldn't have been there...

Practically waiting for me.

It was waiting for me, I postulated.

I had fooled myself into thinking he was trying to protect me, even for his own gain, but still protecting me. I was wrong. He wanted me to join this race, and it was because of him that I'd almost been killed twice, and I had to know more. Did he manipulate Kelly as well? Does he know who she is to me? Was he the reason why she was a bounty, why she was so scared when she saw him? He didn't seem sympathetic when I explained that she was there against her will.

Clenching my fist, I knew I may not have had any

abilities myself, but if Rem had taught me anything it was that wits and partnerships were just as powerful as holding power yourself.

Now, not only was I rejected by a backstabbing boss, but his antics had a very powerful man fooled into thinking I could help his people, and he wasn't going to back down until he knew for sure that I had nothing to offer. And damn me to the bone, there was something about Wyndall that was charming, if not simply overwhelming my common sense. He could do both, I smiled to myself, fulfill his obligations and protect his own rights. Power didn't have to be mine to be used for my benefit, I would also do both.

"Don't get too comfortable," an unknown man's voice said from beside me. I glanced over to see he wasn't wearing the odd clothing that the rest of the people at the party were donning. He was in street clothes, like he was caught off guard to come here, like one of the pilots, but not one that was standing with me in the continuing ten.

He was one of the pilots bumped from his placement… because of me.

"I'm not all too comfortable to begin with," I admitted but couldn't keep the venom out of my voice from discovering how much Cable was pretending to be innocent in all of this.

He seemed to take in my appearance and lifted a brow at me. "You got a bit messy for a simple jaunt through the woods."

"Speak for yourself." I eyed him down. He wasn't one to talk considering the state of his own attire. Admittedly, his clothes were in much better shape, but still covered in blood. Part of me tensed up as I tried to find where the blood came from and found no signs of it being his own.

He watched me assess him and smiled knowing full well the conclusions I was coming to, and not denying any of it.

"Some of us sacrifice ourselves to clear the competition. They don't deserve to move on if they can't win a duel. You, on the other hand," he sniffed the air before continuing, "didn't win yours... now did you." It wasn't a question. Somehow, he knew I was covered in my own blood.

"But somehow you find yourself here, and not even as the tenth pilot, but the ninth." Pondering this for a while, I stewed in the baking silence not wanting to say or do anything to set him off. He seemed on the edge of sanity itself, and he fixated into the flickering bonfire in the distance.

"You were the ninth pilot," I inferred from his tone.

"And now it is you. Caught me off guard, didn't think there were any left out there worth finding after the timer neared its remaining seconds."

"You were correct the first time." Stroking his ego and insulting myself at the same time seemed like the best course of action considering the chills that were coming off of him. I was wrong.

Hissing under his breath he said, "Look at me when you dare to mock me, I am the son of the Velyre House of Romun, heir to the regency. Do not slight my courtesy I've extended towards you, who have claimed a spot rightfully my own." His features shifted in the darkness, morphing his face into something sinister and scary.

I met his gaze and held it like you would a snake. Don't make any sudden movements, try to muster as much intensity as I could back at him so, like any other animal, he would be fooled into thinking I was not worth the fight. Prey on equal footing as the predator.

"You can have it," I said offhanded. I didn't want this anyways, but then remembered what the prince had threatened me with if I didn't succeed. "But I'm kind of in a bind if the Lord Prince doesn't see me perform with great power this next round, he will personally see to it that I duel him." My eyes still on him I felt my heart race as I risked another comment, "I'd rather not duel anyone, if I don't have to." The words seemed to linger in the air like heavy humidity clogging up my lungs. A softness overcame the Romun pilot, and his eyes gleamed.

"You have piqued my interest." His features twisted like a messed up watercolor painting drowned in acid. "I will dismiss my revenge if you appoint me as your assist. The name is Achon, and it would be my pleasure to ensure we both catch the Prince's eye." His teeth shined in the moonlight, and as I blinked it was my own green eyes that stared back at me. His blonde hair grew and fell in locks morphing into a well-groomed version of myself, even the hair changed color with a shift of the shadows. Achon was the exact image of me. My mouth was slack, and he let his lips part, but the way he did it was more sensual than I believed my own face was capable of. I was in shock, but he was obviously mocking me with a twisted, practically illegal, sultriness of my own features. He had taken liberties with his disguise. There was no possible way I could achieve that same effect.

Not skipping a beat, I closed my mouth and stilled my heart to process that the power of Romun was dangerous.

"Is this how you cleared the competition?" I had to avert focus away from my body double, before I let myself think that maybe I did die in the fall from the drone earlier.

"Everyone tries to team up in some way or another... and when they do, they are the most vulnerable," as his words continued, they became more feminine and sounded like I was going nuts... talking to myself.

"They thought you were someone they could trust," I surmised.

"They never really trusted them to begin with, if they did, I'd have to work twice as hard." Achon was not someone I wanted to mess with, but for some reason he wanted me to have him as my assist. I didn't see any way of convincing him otherwise, and I didn't trust him to assist anything other than his own agenda, whatever that might have been. If what he was saying was true, then trust was the last thing I could give him, because that's exactly how he got rid of his competition.

He stood up, and I shook my head. "No one will believe you're me if you walk around like that."

"You think so?" Achon challenged.

"I can't walk."

"So you say, but do they know that? Or is it all just an act to put them off guard?" He didn't stay to let me finish, and he gracefully swished my hips back and forth to taunt me as he left with my face... and a better version of my body if that ass was anything to judge by.

I feigned gagging realizing I was complimenting my own ass.

I watched as Achon went up to the Lord Prince, whispered in his ear, and then disappeared into the crowd, probably taking on another face.

It was then that I knew he had changed my assist whether I liked it or not. And I wasn't going to test the prince's patience with me by approaching him again, I wouldn't have as easy a time disappearing into the crowd as Achon had.

Instead of leaving me alone, he returned, with what I assumed was his original face, but I couldn't be sure of that, or anything for that matter.

"Have fun pretending to be me?" I said with absolutely no enthusiasm.

"It wasn't that hard, I just had to sound like a petulant child begging daddy to be a good boy and grant all my wishes," he mocked and made a whining sound before his provocations made me growl involuntarily. "Calm down byzer. We will win this thing even if I have to drag you there by your bra straps."

"Excuse me?" I had no idea what byzer meant, but it didn't sound endearing, and he didn't give me an opening to ask.

"There isn't much else to hang on to." He snubbed me with an exaggerated flick of his eyes down his nose at me and pinched the fabric of my sweater. At his touch another chunk of my top tore away from my shoulder, leaving me with a flopping rag dangling off my wrist. I was practically sleeveless at this point, so I ripped it the rest of the way off and threw it in the dirt.

"You don't have to duel," he repeated my own

words back to me in my voice and then back to his own he added, "not if I'm the one to duel them for you. And after I win, I can reveal myself, bond with the Prince, and you can do whatever it is that your kind do."

"One condition," I said boldly.

He raised an eyebrow at me.

"You give me your bounty claim, and we both leave without anyone coming after us."

He smiled. "What do I need of another bounty? The Prince's power is all I care about. And you and whichever bounties you want are free to disappear."

That was easy, I thought to myself, and I thought about how I was supposed to disappear and get away from Cable at the same time without credits, so I swallowed as much courage as I could and added, "And the credits."

He waved me off like he didn't care about the credits, he was an heir to the Romun regency, so credits probably weren't much of an issue for him. "It's a small sum. Just keep your mouth shut and tell no one that we are working together."

"Deal." I quickly agreed before he had a chance to change his mind. I didn't know how I'd gotten away with it, but somehow I was able to get exactly what I wanted. A way out of this whole mess, with Kelly, no one finding out I'm a fraud, and a chance to disappear.

"Doesn't the Prince already know we're working together?" I asked concerned about his plan to be me.

"It's a possibility that he may suspect it at some point, but that's why we must work together, and convince him until the very end. I will reveal myself, the whole court will gasp in surprise and excitement that it was a Romun the whole time that wins the races.

It will be a testament to my abilities to pull off such a feat, and the court will accept my right to bond with the Lord Prince."

I was briefly feeling sorry for Lord Wyndall, at how the whole court, and the races viewed his bond as a prize and nothing more. I knew Bailey talked about how there were two different bonds, and this one was purely for power sharing, but the way Cable said it was an intimate exchange had me searching the crowd for Wyndall, newfound pity weighing heavy in my gut. He may have been the most powerful in the court, but he was also the most imprisoned by the traditions of his people.

It wasn't Wyndall's choice who he bonded with, it was decided by a race. I felt bad for trying to trick him, but not so bad that I wouldn't do it. He had threatened me first with a duel, and I wondered why he did it? Why would he want someone like me to show him what I was made of, if I didn't want to be there, if I didn't want to bond with him. Him of all people should understand what it was like to be a victim of other's decisions.

"Isn't bonding an intimate thing?" Guilt was plastered all over my face and I scanned Achon trying to find some semblance of that same emotion on him as well. I found none.

"I'm the heir of the Romun Regency. I'd be a catch for the Prince, he'll learn to enjoy it."

I narrowed my eyes at him. This power bond sounded a whole lot more intense with the way he said that than I previously thought. "Learn to enjoy it?" It felt awfully dirty to talk about it like that.

"Well, I'm not going to force an abett bond on him,

if that's what you're implying. Though, in the future I wouldn't take it off the table after seeing how tasty he is outside of a normal court setting." He licked his lips and motioned towards the festivities where Lord Wyndall leaned against one of the stones with the firelight rolling over his bare chest. A sadness shown on his features staring out over his people, or maybe that was just the new lens I put on him after realizing what he was being forced to do after these races with whoever won. "Wouldn't you agree?"

"Sure, tasty," I answered him absently.

"Don't be so sour," he hardened and defended himself from what semblance of guilt might have rubbed off on him, "He can choose whoever he wants for an abett, that is one thing the court doesn't have a say in his royalty's life."

"How decent of them," I grumbled.

"Don't worry about what you won't be around for. Stick to the deal, I'll worry about the Lord Prince."

"Will you?" I wondered if he actually would worry about him.

Achon groaned, and patted my shoulder like it was a spider, and this was the most awkward thing to try to empathize with someone. "I promise you, I will not force myself on him. What better bond could he ask for, I can be anyone for him. He will be in experienced hands," he saw me glaring into the fire and he added, "if he chooses to be."

"Whatever, it's none of my business, and he's not much better than you anyways. You've both threatened me to a duel this evening."

"There you go luv, just keep reminding yourself of that until we win, and you can scurry yourself back into the dirty hole you crawled out of safe and sound, not a duel in sight."

Chapter Twenty-Eight

*Stakes*

Through the throng of bodies reveling in the moonlight, Lord Wyndall caught me watching him. He shifted, letting the shadows consume him, and he disappeared. Achon tore off his bloodied shirt and went to join the half-naked dancers as his last hoorah before claiming his rightful place with royalty, as he explained. I thought I had finally been released from any more social expectations, only to be disappointed.

I could see Rem making her way through the crowd into the shadows where I sat observing the scene.

"Hey." she lifted her hand in a shy embarrassed way, and I ignored her.

"Look, don't be like that," she grumbled.

"Don't be like what? How am I supposed to be? You weren't helping me, you were helping yourself. You relied on my coordinates to get here, and even if I looked past that you were following orders given to you by him." I didn't even want to say his name anymore, even the sound of it on my lips made me ache and wonder where he was. I'd unconsciously searched for him throughout the night. I felt betrayed by Rem, because during the few hours that we spent together, we bonded, we struggled, and I thought we came out the other side... as friends.

"Woman," she huffed, "you…" Her hand seemed to reach out for me and then drew back in a fist. "He isn't someone you want to cross, okay." She shivered.

Keeping my chin solid, I tilted my head away from her, it was the best snub I could do given my circumstances, not being able to move from this spot.

"Real mature. Being first has its advantages in the next race, and sure I used you to make it happen, but you'd be dead if I didn't. If he didn't tell me to find you, I would have just used someone else, and you'd be dead.

"Don't you get it? You'd. Be. Dead. So, get over yourself, and…" She slid her eyes over me, up and down. "Steal someone's clothes and get ready."

If I was being honest with myself, I wasn't angry with her, only hurt. But, in all my stubborn glory, I would still make her squirm for as long as I could under my icy glare.

"It's already begun." Rem surveyed the party, and nothing seemed different upon first glance. "The other pilots will realize it soon enough, and we need to leave while we still have the advantage. I've already given you more time than I should have to let you cool off."

"How can I trust you?"

"Don't then, it doesn't matter. You're my assist, whether you like it or not. I'm first pilot now, and no one can contest my claim."

"Why?" It didn't make sense. She had any pick at her disposal, and she wasted it on me. Seeing my incredulity, she smiled. "You could have had anyone…"

"Because I made a promise, and I've never broken one of those yet. I'll help you figure out your shit, and I trust you. That's a rare commodity here, so quit stalling and let's go before we lose our edge."

"Why did Lord Wyndall even ask me who my assist would be if you already named me?"

She shook her head letting her braid fall over her shoulder. Those violet eyes searched my face. "The races are never the same, that's why you have to follow your instinct. Answer your own question." Rem waited, but I could see her patience falter as she dug her boot into the ground in an antsy motion.

"I don't know."

"First thing that comes to your mind," she insisted, "It's your question, and it means you think there's merit to knowing why. Tell us why it's important."

"I, uh... I think we should bring my assist with us," I answered quick, and searched the crowd for the shirtless Achon, but I wasn't sure why I even tried considering he could be anyone.

Rem nodded. "You think because I chose you, we also get who you chose. They better be here now, because if not they aren't going to make it."

"They're here." I cringed at my own words, because my original request was for Kelly, and she was nowhere in the crowd. If she were, she'd have come up to me as soon as she saw me. But she didn't, so I knew she was still back at The Last Transport.

"This is your one chance to leave, I won't force you to come with me," Rem offered.

"I don't think they'd let me leave, even if I wanted to."

"You can, this is your chance. Right now, here. If you head east through the forest, there's all the drones from the telshure, they love their privacy, none of them will allow someone to track you. You could leave."

"Why are you saying this?" I asked seeing the desperation in her eyes, she felt like she needed me, but still offered me a way out. She would have been better off without me, I was a liability.

"I know you don't want to be here, and that something else other than winning has brought you to this race, but this is your only chance to back out. I hope you don't, but I'd understand if you did. You won't be able to leave the races until they are finished if you come with me. Will you come with me?"

"I told you before, and I'll tell you again. I don't care if I win, but I do care that I can trust someone that does will let me choose a bounty for myself."

"I didn't ask before, but why is the bounty so important to you that you won't leave now that you can?"

"Someone tried to kill me, and since I'm an unknown here, they know me," and it wasn't until Rem had asked that question that I truly put the pieces together, "they know her, and she isn't safe if they win, if they get her bounty... I don't think she'd survive." My heart sank as I said the words out loud, the ones my instinct knew before I did, the ones that I didn't want to say... because that made it more real. More true. More dangerous.

And I knew...

I couldn't leave.

And I knew...

I had to win.

Rem shouldn't have trusted me.

Because I'd do anything now that I had accepted the stakes.

"The bounty is yours," she agreed and offered her hand to me.

I was too focused on the panic setting in my bones that I took it without thinking. And with muddied thoughts, I pulled. Lifting myself up... I stood.

"About time." Rem released my hand, but I didn't waver.

"How is this possible?" I searched for Lord Wyndall, or for the crowd floating in the air to explain how I was able to stand. I bent my knees, though shaky, I still maintained my balance.

"All you needed was a strong enough reason to stop thinking about how and accept that it is. Whoever the bounty is, she must be important." Rem bit her lip, averting her interest on a particular spot off in the distance instead. She cleared her throat and offered her hand again. "We need to go."

"I don't know how to find my assist... they are kind of hard to pinpoint." Which was putting it mildly, since Achon could be anyone.

"But you think we need them." Rem's eye twitched, and she groaned, "Fine, meet me at the stones. You have two minutes, before I grab you and go."

I nodded and didn't even know if two minutes would have been enough time for me to walk to the stones with how awkward I was. My feet slid across the dirt, unable to chance lifting them and falling flat on my face. For high society, all of the people dancing seemed awfully intimate like I should be averting my eyes to what was surely going to turn into some sort of orgy scene.

Under my breath I kept whispering the name,

"Achon?" hoping that as I was passing through the writhing bodies that one of them would pull themselves from their activities and come to me. That was, in hindsight, a silly idea, considering that he thought I was something that slithered out of a dirt hole and he was better than me. Why he would have pulled himself away from whoever he was dancing with, to have a chat with me was unknown, and low on his priority list.

My two minutes were up and leaving without Achon would mean, when they caught up with us, that it would not be a happy reunion. I wasn't even sure that since Achon wasn't part of the ten pilots that he would even be able to come with without joining us now.

I didn't need to call Achon's name to finally spot him… or her. It was obvious, once I paid attention. She wore one of the gossamer gowns, stolen from someone else at the dance, and didn't even clean the blood off our face. Convenient, that they also got bloody during the forest run, because the blood, black on her skin, or our skin, made it like we were part of the night, shimmering in the moonlight. On her, it didn't come off as deranged, like it surely did on me, Achon looked playful.

And that mischievous grin plastered on her face was directed at the host of the party. Lord Wyndall pulled her close, his muscular arms wrapped around her waist… and they danced. I shouldn't have been surprised. It was our plan for him to be me. But something came over me seeing him use my face in such a way, in such a setting, and being better at being me… than me.

I was jealous.

The large fire roared, and the wind picked up

around me pulling the smoke and heat in my direction. Lord Wyndall following the smoke met my eyes. His hands dropped from the impostor he danced with, and recognition crossed his face. I knew darkness covered me, the smoke billowing around my body, but I did not choke on its fumes.

Movement caught my attention to the side of Lord Wyndall, and I could see Rem grab Achon's arm and drag her away before the prince could object. But I knew he wouldn't object, not now that his attention was on me. He glided through the crowd, using his ability to gracefully move without walking.

I watched as Achon followed Rem out of curiosity, but those eyes, my eyes, darted to me smiling before they both disappeared, jumping into the fire. Too upset, and irrational about not setting ground rules for using my face. I didn't bat a lash at their sudden exit into the fire. They didn't scream, didn't sizzle, and were gone without a trace. No one noticed, no one took heed of the two lost pilots who were no longer at the party, but I knew... and I would follow them.

Moving closer to the fire, I hesitated as the heat hit me, and it was enough of a window for Lord Wyndall to reach me. His firm hands wrapped around me and pulled me to him. The smoke still covering us, the wind still turned in our direction, part of me knew no one could see us. No one would object to it, even if they did... he was the Lord Prince of Acatalec. Still, my earlier anger surfaced, and I glared at him for doing it. I didn't care who he was.

"Is this your way of punishing me for making my intentions clear?" Lord Wyndall's voice was cold and a stark contrast to the heat blaring in front of us. His chest heaved against my back as he held himself from whatever punishment he thought I deserved for deceiving him. It didn't matter that it wasn't me, but it wouldn't be the last time I would do it either.

My legs were still not ready to resist him, and the yank of pulling me into him had already set me off balance. I relied on that same treacherous arm wrapped around my stomach to keep me held against him, it was the only thing keeping me standing. He knew it, and his possessive grasp tightened.

"From what I just saw, our earlier discussion didn't begin to clear up any of your intentions."

"How do you not know? From the moment I saw you, I knew."

Finding my footing I attempted to wiggle free from him, but he kept his grip firm and his breath hot on my neck.

"He knows, and you will not survive him," he continued.

"You're all nut jobs," I growled.

Lord Wyndall finally laughed, and his arm loosened, but didn't release me. With my back pressed against his torso, his head lowered into my wild hair.

"My whole life has been for my people," he whispered into my ear, "I will not force you to understand reason, but it is too much to ask me to leave you alone. The courts be damned, for once I will pursue my own ends," he released me, and I stumbled hearing his last words before the fire consumed me, "and one day perhaps you'll let me."

Chapter Twenty-Nine

*Gateway*

"For Talec's sake, why didn't you say your assist was a Romun? You think I like surprises? Well, I don't!" Rem rambled as she swayed her hips back and forth mesmerizing our third into a trance. She pointed at Achon with disgust and slapped them.

"Take that face off, you high-born piece of goudo bark."

Achon seemed to only accept the high-born part, and glossed over the insult before letting what I assumed was their original face twist into place. They'd thought it was entertaining to keep Rem's face as they helped steady me to walk.

The bonfire felt like my insides were being ripped apart and put back together. When I finally opened my eyes, Achon was dragging me by the leg across the ground like a rag doll. Wherever we were, it didn't feel like we were in Seattle anymore, or even Washington for that matter. The air was warm, and we were somewhere sandy. I sputtered feeling the gravellyness of it in my mouth and closed my eyes as soon as it kicked up into my face with every one of Achon's steps.

They stopped when I fidgeted on the ground, and then Rem went into her tirade about dragging the wrong person with her. As far as I could see there were mounds of sand. Achon didn't care that they were dragging me around by a foot and seemed more concerned that they had to touch something so dirty to begin with, but they didn't have time to waste.

My mouth still dry, I observed both of my companions hoping one of them brought water with them, but neither of them were prepared to enter a desert. If walking wasn't difficult enough on solid ground, we sank into it with every move.

"Where are we?" I croaked.

"Unfortunately, it looks like we're in the Servun Region," Rem answered, but that didn't do me any good.

Achon added, "Worst possible region to start in."

"Why's that?"

Achon merely glanced around himself and nodded to the surroundings. We were in the desert, unprepared, with no food or water, and horrible clothing. Even Rem, who was a badass in her leather bodysuit, still would have been just as uncomfortable had she been wearing shreds like I was. I was feeling the whip of sand rubbing my skin raw, and it didn't help that I was barefoot trudging through clinging to Achon's shoulders.

"Other than the obvious," I added.

"They are cut off from any hubs, so," Rem tried to explain, "they are a byzer bunch of tribalists… with a feral attitude towards outsiders."

"And command of a horde of rockjaws," Achon added with distaste, "Ugly beasts."

Rem shook her head. "The rockjaws are the least of our worries, most of the tribe's hunters are just as deadly. Plus, they don't give a flying Numa's ass about the races, and we'll be treated like anyone else who is trespassing."

"What exactly is a byzer, or a rockjaw? And a Numa's ass?" I hated having to ask, but I wanted to know what I had to keep an eye out for, and this was the second time I'd heard the word byzer, not knowing what it meant. Though, it wouldn't have mattered considering out here it was us… or them. So, pretty much anything that broke up the monotony of the desert sand probably wasn't friendly after listening to them explain it all.

"Rockjaws are sightless mongrels with chompers that can crush you like a marshmallow," Rem offered before pointing to the rising sun, and noticing it wasn't the only sun in the sky. There was already one above us, and now another peeking beyond the horizon. "Oh, and byzer is a small beast in the forest that stays in groups of no less than twenty, and attacks anything that comes within a five-foot radius of its burrow, they have no forethought about what it is, it could be a twig, it could be an animal ten times their size, they don't think about it, which makes them one of the wilder creatures on Acatalec. It's also what we call anything that is wild and acts first without thinking."

"We need to hurry, before we're noticed."

"What about the Numa's ass?"

Achon cracked up and nearly dropped me at my question. "Finely sculpted buns of perfection is what that is, and if you hadn't interrupted earlier, I could have gotten a piece of it before the night was out."

I glared at him, remembering him taking my face, and rubbing my body all over Wyndall. Achon could feel the tension and shrugged.

"Numa is the region the Lord Prince is from, and where the main port is. Powerful people from Numa fly around, you see their asses in the air," she groaned, "it ruins it if I have to explain."

"Oh." I calmed down realizing it wasn't a comment about Wyndall specifically. Achon was merely trying to ruffle me.

"Before we get our next linked instructions," Achon sobered up from his humor, "We split as soon as the assist is over." His eyes didn't leave Rem's, but he squeezed me to himself as if telling me, but not you we have a deal.

"You can do whatever you like," Rem agreed, and it wasn't lost on me how she punctuated the 'you' in her statement. Neither of them planned on letting me go, and I honestly didn't understand why. It was all helpful to utilize their abilities, but I was nothing but an extra person for them to watch after, slowing them down.

"Stop!" I tried to dig my feet into the sand preventing Achon from dragging me any farther. It had nothing to do with their bickering. The same kind of instinct I got when piloting a drone came over me, my skin tingling, and it wasn't from the sand burn itching my calves, or the chaffing of my arm rubbing over Achon's shoulder every time we took another step.

They both looked at me, Rem with concern searching my face for answers, and Achon with annoyance, he was already putting up with his maximum patience by practically carrying me.

Rem guided, "Just speak, don't think."

"Something is wrong." When Cameron tried to

push me into a building, she came out of nowhere. This felt the same, like I should be swerving out of the way, but we had nowhere to go. Every direction spanned out as far as you could see... waves of sand.

"Talec," Rem swore.

"We should leave her here, so we can jump them," Achon suggested while swinging my legs up and preparing to run.

"They'll never believe I traveled alone, jackass," Rem fumed.

"Fine." Achon dropped me in a heap and slid down the sand to our right. Disappearing, like he was the sand himself, he ditched us.

"Stay calm, don't move," Rem offered and held her hand up as if warning me not to try to get up.

And then I saw them. They were fast in surrounding us, and they all wore tan face coverings to protect them from the sand. Tan and cream loose-fitted pants, with brown leather straps holding it all together, and keeping the sand at bay. They were assassins with mud plastered around their eyes, and those eyes were so hungry and yellow like an animals. One of the figures stood straighter than the others crouching around us, and with a wave of their hand they clicked their tongue as if using another language.

Behind them mounds of sand shifted, and actual animals surfaced with their eyes closed. They hunched over with arms as long as their large body. Their legs were short with a wide stance which were more to balance them than transport them. Their claws came out of the sand, black daggers slicing up from their knuckles, and they used their arms like an orangutan, completely ignoring the use of their legs, and they were fast. In seconds they were in front of us, never once opening the slits I believed were their eyes. They were the rockjaws, I was sure of it, and the way their mouths made this grinding sound didn't make me eager to experience why they were named that.

I stayed still, and the rockjaws mashed their large maws in the air, as if trying to find us, but even so continued to keep their eyes shut.

The leader stepped forward, and finally spoke, "State your business." Those yellow eyes took in my tattered clothes, and Rem's dominatrix outfit before the woman grunted for us to explain, and explain quickly.

"Passing through, take us to the borders and we will not return." Rem held up her hands to show she was unarmed. Then the leader watched me, wanting me to contribute to the story. I knew my appearance was dismal, I already felt grimy, and gross, covered in dirt, sweat, blood, and getting sand in areas I didn't even want to think about.

I saw the assessment in her eyes, and I didn't know why I said it, but I did, and there was no taking it back.

"Training."

That answer seemed to satisfy her, and a twinkle of excitement could be seen in her fierce eyes. She pulled her hood over her face and clicked her tongue once more. She didn't say anything more, and the leader walked away, the rockjaws delving into the sand once more to follow her. Her wrist flicked up in the air in a twirling motion, like she was saying, round em up. Rem lifted her arms up in preparation, as a group of them closed in for one of them to pick her up like a sack of potatoes.

I could hear Rem grumble, "Couldn't let them

think we're just travelers could you, no," she bemoaned, "had to let them know we were some sort of warriors that needed to be taken back to the tribe. Just another ordinary Saturday."

One of the warriors of the tribe nudged me with their foot and jutted their chin up. When I didn't move, they did the same action again, and I knew they wanted me to stand. It was much more difficult to meet their request when the sand sunk down with every movement. Struggling to get my legs to function, I decided to do things the way I always had before this whole ordeal. My arms were strong, and like the rockjaws I pulled myself forward using only my upper body with my hips digging into the sand, and my knees barely assisting behind me.

The warriors were obviously not impressed, or a patient bunch. One grabbed my arm and pulled me to my feet in a single swift action. The other warriors watched him as he launched me over his shoulder mimicking Rem's pleasant encounter. I too was now a sack of vegetables. And over a few more mounds of sand, a small tent village appeared below the next dune. It disappeared in the sand and sunk deep making me wonder how it survived not being consumed by a windstorm.

I could hear the warrior holding me whisper, "They want you to prove your strength to them."

It was Achon. He had turned into one of the warriors, and I again found myself being threatened with a duel.

Chapter Thirty

*Switch*

What seemed like days went by where multiple suns rose beyond the horizon, and yet the night never came. I was beyond tired and keeping my eyes open was becoming harder each time they blinked. Every time my lids fell, it took twice as long to pry them open once again.

Achon had left me, and Rem was tied to a similar post as mine, but down a few tents. Facing out of the tent, at least I got to watch the sun come up, over and over again. How many suns did this place have? When would these people sleep?

The same woman from before cast the only shadow I'd seen the whole day since I was tied up here. The whole tent was layered with heavy rugs, and she threw back her hood and pulled down her face covering to crouch. Meeting me at eye level, Trasa kneeled before me taking me in her sights, those yellow eyes mellowing in understanding.

"I see the strength in your shoulders, the weight of the world sits on you." She clamped down on one of my shoulders and pressed down making me feel as if I would crumble. She'd made her point, I was not a warrior, and the time spent waiting had taken its toll on me.

"Our people know of the stories the spires tell. They do like to talk, but people don't go to them for conversation. They do not listen to the spires," she rambled on, and she pinched my chin between her strong fingers and lifted my weary eyes to meet hers.

"We listen," she continued then tossed my head to the side, letting it roll atop my shoulders, "We will listen." She closed her eyes then and waited for me to do the same. When I didn't, her gloved hands gripped my face again. With her thumbs she eased my eyelids shut, and I didn't know if I had the strength to open them again without the same assistance.

"We will listen," she repeated.

Unable to lift my head, or open my eyes again her hands left me, and even though her boots walked along the carpets soundless, I knew she was gone. Her powerful presence was no longer stifling the air.

Next thing I knew I felt hands untying me, and two people lifting me from under my arms, dragging me deeper into the tent, behind the curtains I'd been staring at over my shoulders for hours before.

The sound of my clothes ripping from my body, gave me one last shot of adrenaline to open my eyes. One warrior was tearing up the slit of my skirt to rip it from my hips. I tried to wiggle away from them, only to have the other one removing the final vestiges of cloth from my damaged sweater. Pushing back my exhaustion I flung my arms at them both, and I felt my foot make contact with the one in front of me.

Groaning, the warrior grabbed my ankle firmly, and with their other hand splashed water warmed from the sun outside over my dirty legs. In a swift motion they took a cloth and yanked at my leg once more to

246

stop my fatigued attempts at escape to scrub at my feet.

They were cleaning me.

"I can do that myself," I screamed.

"This one is not a warrior," he mumbled, and I became even more embarrassed that a man was seeing me in only my underwear. I tried to cover myself as best I could with my arms. The other holding me up by the armpits, while the other cleaned my feet. He lifted one foot for the other warrior to assess.

"Delicate," the other agreed with him. I saw all the painful wounds from walking in the forest and red rashes from the sand as he cleaned off the dirt and blood.

"Should we tell Trasa?"

"She wouldn't hear of it."

It was then the warrior directed their eyes to me and said, "We will prepare you for your service to Nam. If you are strong you will survive, and we will escort you to wherever you need to go."

The one holding me up clucked their tongue before correcting their partner, "All those who defeat their pleogite will be treated as guests, and we will be at their disposal for whatever we can provide for them. Should you fail, we will do our best to honor your bravery and escort you outside of our territory, and we ask that you respect our borders and never return again."

"Pleogite?"

They clinked their tongues again and then the one squeezing water on my legs said, "Other warrior." I believed he was simplifying the meaning for me, and it meant something more than that, but it was enough.

"I can prepare myself." I reached to grab the damp cloth as it made its way up my thigh. Stopping it before it went any higher, and before any other bits of my dignity could be taken from me.

The warriors bowed their head, and the one holding me up by my underarms warned, "You have five cores to clean, and dress." He motioned to the large bucket beside us, and folded clothes on a bench next to it, before reaching into the back of his pants and throwing his washcloth into the bucket for my use.

"We will finish the job, if you cannot." The other released my foot and shook his head at the sight of my delicate feet, as he put it.

"Not even a warrior," he said with pitied concern, "Show us your bravery, and I will see what I can do to end the service before the rockjaws join."

"Do not promise her such a thing, only they can show us what to listen for."

"Those feet have never seen battle," he urged his partner to reconsider.

"It is not our call." He glared at me. "You have five cores." They both let the curtains close behind them, and I was left with my bucket. I took the dirty rag from my feet and used that first to get as much off as possible, then the clean rag to do a rinse. Knowing my hair was equally gross, I dunked my hair into the bucket, and scrubbed at that too. There wasn't a towel to dry off with, but with the weather I figured I'd dry off soon enough. Scooting over to the stool, I pulled over the shirt, and shimmied my way into the pants, then used a few of the leather ties through the hoops sewn into the fabric.

I ran out of time, and the warriors came back in to assist me with the rest of the ties around the ankles, under the knees, at the waist, wrists, elbows, under the bust, and around the neck. There was a brown leather corset that laced up and acted like a sort of armor. As well as leather forearm bracers, and they stopped before slipping on the leather knee high lace up boots of the same material.

With delicate hands the warrior applied a salve to my feet and wrapped them up. By the end of it I appeared just like them, and the taller one grunted in approval once he finished braiding my hair away from my face. I regretted having my hair layered recently, because strands were already falling out of place.

I was ready for their battle on the outside, but inside I was screaming.

They pointed to the cushions on the floor and left the room again. Crawling over to the inviting surface, I only made it so far as to place my head on the first cushion my hands grabbed before passing out. I don't know how long I slept, but it was still daylight out, and I wouldn't have believed any of it happened if it weren't for Achon staring at me when I woke. He was also wearing the same thing I was.

"We're about to make our debut in this hovel." He tossed a hood at me.

Groaning I turned my face into the pillows, wishing for this whole thing to be a nightmare.

"Unless you'd like to get your hands dirty again, I'd suggest you put that on, and take me to the cult circle they're forming out there."

Shaking the grogginess from my neck, I pulled the hood over me, and adjusted the mask over my mouth so only my eyes were showing.

"You're really going to go through with this?" I nodded to the curtain.

"You don't know me, but tricks are not the only thing up my sleeve." Achon's face twisted and reappeared as my own. My reflection staring back at me. The only way it was going to work is if I walked out of here. I gritted my teeth and pushed myself up, my legs wobbled, and Achon was about to catch me before I held up my hands to tell the other me to wait.

Something about having yourself look back at you with mocking eyes made me push myself to believe I could do this. I had to do this. And I did. I walked, slowly, but I did it by myself. Reaching the curtain was the easy part, Achon offered her arm to me, and wrapped it around my waist as if she were using me for support only giving an illusion that the jagged movements were hers, and not my own. No one was on the other side of the curtain waiting for us, it gave me time to adjust more and be less awkward. The tent was wide open, the sun still in the sky with the two other warriors I'd met earlier on either side of the entrance.

Chapter Thirty-One

*Last Words*

There's always a price to pay for letting others hold
what should have been yours to carry. If I'd known that
she was waiting for me, I'd like to think I would have
done things a little differently. Outside, the Servun
village was gathered around, too many for me to see
what was hidden beyond their bodies, but my own
shivered at the sight. There was danger, and I lowered
my hood to hide my eyes from it.

The two warriors grabbed Achon from me, and as
they walked the crowd separated making a path to the
battle they so desperately wanted. I knew he was
strong, and I knew he'd done things… terrible things to
make it to this point. Covered in multiple pilot's blood,
and not an ounce of remorse from him as he took on
another's face and danced in the firelight. He was just
as dangerous as whatever it was that they wanted him to
fight, but when I was around him, I never got the
feeling that I was getting now.

Something had changed in the air, and I couldn't
stand back like Achon wanted me to. I had to get closer,
I had to see. Before the crowds closed the gap
completely, I eased my way forward as if I was
supposed to escort them, but before the end, I veered
off to disappear into the people dressed exactly like me.

Sand gusted up, and as it settled her figure emerged staring down my doppelgänger. Her dreads were perfectly swept up in a ponytail, she lazily leaned her weight on one leg, and she was wearing a black armor-plated bodysuit with her platform boots. It was very similar to the outfit Rem was wearing, but with black armor that made her appear to be a samurai.

"I'll speak up this time, since you're hard of hearing," Bailey goaded Achon.

He didn't say anything, not wanting to betray the facade by saying something that would make her think he wasn't who he appeared to be.

"I came here just for you, and I've already seen what happens to someone who fails in this village, so I don't have much of a choice but to finish what I started. Don't make this harder on yourself, okay."

Achon's eyes got dark, and they swirled with black ink. My heart was about to leap out of my ribcage thinking he was blowing his cover with her, she'd know it wasn't me. That was possible, but Bailey didn't bat an eyelash. She smiled, and threw her head back laughing.

"I think you need to trust me." Bailey slinked forward, her hips swaying in a seductive rhythm as she stared Achon down. Her eyes seemed to vibrate, and I felt my chest tighten. She wasn't looking at me, but even staring at her eyes from here made me sway to the same rhythm of her hips. A warmth rushed through me, and I needed to walk closer to her. I made it to the very front of circle, and at the cusp of stepping into the ring, I stopped myself.

I wanted to go to her, and I wanted her to show me her... knife. I didn't see her holding a knife, but I knew she had one. My lungs wanted to burst into screams, letting Achon know that she was going to stab him. He was stronger than I gave him credit for, stronger than me.

He pretended to succumb to her ability and walked forward. He reached out, and in a swift movement grabbed her wrist and twisted it back into her own throat. Bailey screeched in fury before a knife shot out from her wrist and she barely pulled away to have it slice down on Achon's palm. Using my own face, he gave a twisted sneer and licked the blood off the injured hand. I recoiled seeing myself do something that could only be described as demonic.

But again, Bailey didn't seem phased by the odd things Achon was doing with my appearance. Achon stared her down, and they both stalked around the circle calculating their next moves.

"Before I end our fun little chat, I wanted to let you know that you can thank the Regent of Tarquin for our kismet meeting today." She blew Achon a kiss. "If it wasn't for him, I wouldn't have been able to find you. You know how benefactors are, they don't like it when a job goes unfinished."

Everything in me quaked, and the sand rolled beneath the open circle. She thought she had already won against me, and she was telling me who was trying to kill me. Her benefactor. Bailey told me she didn't care either way, but someone wanted me dead. She was telling me now, that it was Cable, and I kept shaking my head not wanting to believe what she was saying.

But the pieces slid into place so neat and tidy. Cable let me join the races, pretending he didn't want me there. He made sure I had a drone. The drone that

took me to the forest was waiting for me on the roof of
his company's building after we spoke. That drone
blew up. Lord Wyndall warned me about how
dangerous he was. He made sure his pilots could track
me. I searched the crowd, and sure enough I saw those
black eyes on the other side of the crowd, Shard. She
stood there on the sidelines, watching a version of me
against Bailey and did nothing.

My fists balled up, nails digging into my palm. I
didn't understand why he would do this to me, a
nobody. What was I to him?

In my stunned revelation I'd missed a crucial part
of the fight, and Bailey had somehow gained the upper
hand on Achon. He held out his hands grasping the
blade of her knife, blood trickling down his arms tie-
dyeing the sleeves under the bracers. Bailey stared him
down, those vibrating eyes working their way into his
psyche. Even from here I could feel my body grow
limp, and this sensation of needing to relax. I had to
relax, let my muscles loosen. I shivered realizing that
any slack in Achon's efforts would mean being impaled
by Bailey's knife.

I couldn't let him die because of me. This was my
fate, not his. I tried to take a step forward, but my legs
buckled feeling much too rubbery to move. In the front
row, on my knees I watched as the knife plunged into
Achon's chest little by little. That sinister gleam in
Bailey's eyes as she finished her job of killing me, but
it was Achon, and he still held my face instead of
letting her know she had the wrong person. For
someone able to massacre a few pilots to win a race, he
had earned more than my trust in those moments as he
steeled himself to make sure Bailey never knew her

mistake.

Bailey backed away leaving the knife where it was. "Any last requests before I let the rockjaws finish with dessert?" She hovered over him with blood spitting from my own mouth.

"See you at the finish line," he said before he closed our eyes, and his hair blew across his face. I gasped from where I knelt, appalled at myself for what I'd let happen.

The rockjaws rustled under the sand, and their large mongrel bodies surfaced within the circle. One next to Bailey sniffed the air around her, and then ignored her as she stood very still. The crowd clucked their tongues at the rockjaw's response, and all three of the rockjaws that emerged slowly made their way to Achon's body. Bailey waved to the crowd, thinking the noises they were making were a sort of applause, and she exited the circle unimpeded.

I darted my focus over to where Shard used to stand, and she was gone. Bailey was out of sight, disappearing into the crowd, and off to claim her royal bond with Lord Wyndall at the expense of what she thought was my life.

I wouldn't let the rockjaws have him. His features started to shift, and I knew he didn't have much time. His body grew in size, no longer trapped in my small frame. Without Bailey's mind games to contend with I found my legs were stronger than they had ever been. Rushing out into the middle of the ring, the rockjaw's attention moved to the sounds of my steps and their maws mashed, and their claws dug at the ground.

No longer approaching Achon's still body, they were fast, and surrounded me instead. An awful screeching sound came from their opened jaws full of rows of razored teeth. The slits where their eyes should be opened, and what was there couldn't be referred to as eyes, but as black holes that whorled and made you question your sanity. I stared back into those orbs and felt myself grow dizzy, until the screeching stopped and all I could hear were my own screams hollowing out into a silent breath.

In one swift movement the closest rockjaw was inches from my face, and it stopped with its claws digging into the sand at my feet like it had hit a wall between us.

The slits closed once more, and it snapped its teeth at me a few times before it sunk into the sand leaving me be. I collapsed where I stood just moments before, angling to the side to find Achon's chest rising and falling.

He was still alive.

Without being given even a moment of relief, I felt a sharp pressure in my leg as the rockjaw's claws pierced my flesh and dragged me under the sand.

Chapter Thirty-Two

*Under the Sand*

The longest breath is also the shortest when you have no control over its comings and goings. I closed my eyes, focusing on the pain pulsing through my leg to tell me I was still alive. Sand flowed across my body filling up every crevasse, the force of the pull watering my eyes because I couldn't seal them firm enough. Everything burned. My skin heated from the friction of quickly burrowing in the ground. I didn't dare open my eyes, though they were raw enough that it felt like I already had, entering a world of blind turbulence.

Time was innumerable, I couldn't tell you how long I'd been under only that my lungs were on their last holding pattern. Deflating as slowly as I could manage. An excruciating fire as my breath seeped out from my nose, it couldn't be stopped. Sand rushed and stung making my body fight to blow it out. I tried not to. I tried to hold it in. Keep air in my lungs.

But like all things, control was only an illusion.

I had none.

With one last uncontrolled huff through my nose, the sand dislodged, and for only a moment my body seemed to slow taking in the last vestiges of time that it had before it did what it always did when it needed to breath.

Weightlessness took over me. I felt lighter, and part of me accepted once again that this was my end. I imagined the sand swirled around me, a vortex seeking to consume my final breath, because there wouldn't be a next, this was my final destination. I felt cold, despite the heat of the burns on my skin.

Then without any thought, my mouth gasped letting my lungs open up to suck in whatever it could. Surrounded by sand, my lungs filled.

One big gulp.

The kind your body takes when it has nothing else to lose.

Wide open.

And to my surprise, the only salt I tasted was from my own lips. I opened my eyes, and it was like waking up in an hourglass, as if time had frozen and I was in a pocket of sand beneath the ground. I touched the sand, and it moved between my fingers. Time had not stopped, at least it didn't seem that way. I felt a pull from the pocket I rested in, my hand suctioned to the sand, and I pulled it away and let it suction to my palm again.

There was airflow. The sand was moving from the air circulating from where I was, to wherever the air was. I took another breath, and I coughed from the granules still lingering there, but it was fresh.

My legs were still submerged in the sand, the bubble only surrounding my upper body, and I was still moving. As the sand suggested, when I plunged my fingers into the sides, the sand rushed around them. The claws still dug into my leg, I knew that, but I couldn't feel the pain. A soft throb radiated up my leg, and I couldn't move it.

In dreams, until you realized you were dreaming nothing was as it seemed. And I thought to myself, if this was my last dream, why waste it drifting? I imagined the beast that had taken my leg was my betrayer. Those dark chocolate eyes whispering deceitful fantasies within their depths, tricking me into feeling there was something warm beneath the ice.

My fists clenched, and I didn't know it then, but that's when I accepted that I was strong. That I was nobody's weakness. That I would crush the ones who hurt me. Punching through the sand I dug for the claw embedded in my tissue. The rockjaw's hand felt like solid stone, and it didn't worry about me grabbing at it, because it was used to being nearly indestructible. My nails were no match for its thick, hard shell for skin, but I wasn't trying to scratch it.

Clamping around what I imagined was its wrist or forearm, as I couldn't see beyond the sandy wall of my air bubble, I yanked. Not caring about my mangled leg, it was dead to me for too long to care that its claws would shred them if not handled properly. Calling out into the deafening enclosure, my screams echoed in my skull as the claws tore through fresh tendons and muscle. I bit down feeling as if my teeth could shatter willing myself to finish the job.

With another swift draw towards myself the movement of the rockjaw stopped, and its claw was in my hand twitching with meaty flesh hanging from its black daggers. Its mongrel face tore through my bubble with sand pouring out of its opened maw, sharp teeth exposed and ready to masticate its prey.

Hollowed slits where its eyes should be opened into empty sockets of swirling darkness, and anger filled me.

"Not this time," I said through gritted teeth. Meeting its stare, the intensity of everything I was boiled up sending a fire in my belly that rose and burned.

"Take me back!" I growled at it, and its eyes snapped closed.

Hanging on to its limp arm, we turned, and sped through the sands up to the surface. It listened to me. I didn't know why, but it did, and that was when I questioned everything. Rem's words came back to haunt me, have you had any instances in your life where someone felt compelled to do things for you when they wouldn't normally?

*Tarquins are a lot more dangerous than the Priscus, at least with the Priscus you know you're being influenced, and it gives you a chance to resist. A Tarquin makes you believe you want to do it, that it was your idea, and that's the scariest thing of all.*

My heart sank, and I knew my eyes really did appear as haunted as how Achon revealed. Bailey didn't flinch at all from the abyss within my eyes.

I was a Tarquin.

I was taking away people's freewill.

Why else would Achon risk his life? Why else would Rem, as a stranger, expend most of her energy to heal me? Why else was Cable trying to kill me?

I was dangerous.

Clutching tighter on the rockjaw's arm, I could feel its tough skin bend to my will, and I felt the tornado build within me. All they had to do was train me, guide me, tell me who I was, and all of this madness could have been avoided. I would show them what true danger was. I would show them the monster they feared, free Kelly, and then when my revenge was complete, I'd disappear never to harm anyone else. I wouldn't let myself take anyone else's freedom.

I was fire, I was raw, and I wouldn't listen to any other solutions. I didn't care about winning the race... I cared about finding Cameron, Bailey, Shard, and Cable. Making them understand what it felt like to be hunted.

The surface of the sand burst open for the rockjaw, and I tossed its limp arm arching into the air. My body was light, and though the sand was no longer surrounding me the bubble around me stayed. Invisible to everyone else, but I knew it was there, and lifted me before popping.

Crumpling to the soft sand, my awareness of my mangled leg finally surfaced in my mind. I peered down, and my left leg was grotesque leaking blood in a pool around me. Clucking sounds vibrated through the air. Many hands, more than one person could offer, cradled my body, and carried me to someplace soft. Coldness shivered through my body, and warm liquid dabbed at my face.

"Delicate warrior," one of the voices murmured.

"We have listened," the leader, Trasa, agreed.

"You're all crazy as ass crack on a *worbler*." I could hear Rem swearing, she sounded tired. My awareness trickled away, feeling the burning revenge working its way through my bones. I would never wake the same.

Chapter Thirty-Three

*Delicate Warrior*

I should have stayed buried in the sand with the rockjaws, my bones decorating their dwelling, because then in my last moments I could truly believe this was all in my imagination. That I had dreamed this epic adventure to another world before I died that first day crashing into a building after Cameron veered me off course. Everything after that could have been written off as the last firing neurons entertaining themselves until the light faded. Time moved differently for a mind dreaming, days could seamlessly pass in a matter of minutes, because I would have no concept of time before I faded.

A cold hand wrapped around my own, rubbing with their thumb in a light massage. I could believe it was my mother, as I lay on a hospital bed before they pulled the plug. No one would be hurt, except for me. Bailey could still be an interesting girl that I wanted to get to know, she had a wild side, and we could have been good friends if only I had more time. Kelly could be broke from entering us into an illegal race, but otherwise not in danger. Cable could still be the man with sad eyes that I could've one day opened up to see what kind of electricity we could've created one day.

I'd never have met Rem, Achon, Shard, or

Wyndall.

A world without Acatalec.

A world where I was human.

But I didn't stay in the sand.

And it wasn't my mother rubbing my hand.

"I don't even know her name..." Rem sobbed, "How am I supposed to wake the unstable sleeping beauty if I don't know what to call her?"

"Call her what the rest of us do, Pilot," Achon added, though he sounded rough.

"Her name is Delicate Warrior," one of the Servun warriors offered.

"What I wouldn't give to smear your face in bark," Rem's voice ticked in agitation, "We already know what you psychos think of her."

"Now, be nice to the psychos, they're giving us the royal treatment now that we're associated with their Delicate One."

"Delicate Warrior," he corrected.

"Yah, whatever, just keep packing the salve on, and massaging that disgustingly awesome gunk into my body," Achon sounded gruff, but amused.

"I'm no one's delicate anything," I finally added, though I had tried to speak normally, my voice was barely above a whisper.

"You tell 'em, dark goddess," Achon cheered, obviously not in his right mind.

"She's awake!" Rem screamed, and the hold on my hand grew tighter.

Opening my eyes, Rem was hovering over me, and though her face was filled with relief I had to turn away from her. My head rolling to the other side, I was ashamed of what I had done to both of them.

Everything they had been through was my fault. I didn't deserve her worry. And she did something only Rem could do and get away with.

She slapped me across the face, I didn't even flinch feeling I had deserved it this time. And somehow her outburst had made it easier for me to look at her.

"How dare you make me think you died!"

"Achon? Is he okay?"

"I've already done what I can for him, and the people here have been dotting on him like he's some sort of prince since you rose from the dead."

"I'm heir to the Romun Regency," Achon bellowed like it made sense that they would be tending to his every beck and call. I turned my head to see that he was lying down on a cushioned surface on the floor with two Servun tribe members rubbing him down with a mud paste. I had a blanket over me, and my next concern after knowing everyone was safe was seeing the damage on my leg. About to lift the blanket, Rem's hand stopped me.

Shaking her head, she warned, "I'm tapped out, and it isn't pretty."

Through the curtains of the tent, Trasa, leader of the tribe, entered. The warriors at the entrance guarding us bowed to her, and then she bowed to me.

"Delicate Warrior, it is important that you listen as we have listened. The Spires have told us of one who carries the whole of power.

"Though there are many in Acatalec that mate across regions, their children take after only one parent. You have been born whole, not half of your lineage. Most will covet your power, but none more than an old enemy that will seek to absorb all. If you fall victim to this power, Acatalec will fall with you.

"Understand Delicate Warrior, that you are in danger should you leave here. Our tribe is yours. We will protect you with our lives," Trasa finished, and she knelt down at my feet. Taken aback, I stared at her and for a brief moment thought about what it would be like to abandon everything and stay.

"Look here Sand Lady, we are thankful for your uh, well your recent, hospitality, but we are definitely not staying here." Rem glanced at me and then back to Trasa then back to me to confirm, "Right? You're not considering this, right?"

I shook my head, Kelly wasn't safe. My attempted killer knew my life, knew who I was, and Kelly would be next. There's no way Kelly would agree to coming back here to live out the rest of her life. We would have to find new jobs, have new identities, and move out of state. As much as I wanted revenge, I needed to make sure Kelly was safe more.

"You're very generous, but I won't be letting anyone risk their lives for me again. I'm going to disappear, and I've been seen here already."

Trasa nodded her understanding and said, "It had to be offered. I've already prepared our packs to escort you to the safest portal."

"You knew I'd say no?"

"The spires told me you would be a strong warrior, none of my warriors would wish to lay down their arms when a battle was beyond the horizon. We will ready ourselves to join you when you have need of us."

"I don't understand. You didn't say anything about a battle before?"

"Don't listen to her. She's obviously cracked,"

Rem offered, "Plus, you're not going anywhere right now, none of us are ready to travel."

"You will leave tonight, your friends will stay," she said then noticing my panicked eyes dart from Rem to Achon she added, "When they are ready, they will be escorted to wherever they need to go by our finest warriors." She tried to ease my worry, but all she did was confuse me more. I stared at the blankets covering my legs, which Rem said I shouldn't even look at, and wondered how she thought I was ready to leave tonight?

"She's in no condition—" Rem was cut off by the commanding resolve of the village's chief.

"The portal is old, and will not carry three," Trasa explained, "your friends will be escorted to the nearest portal in Numa. You should not travel by monitored portals, you will travel with me and leave alone, or we will not leave at all."

"Woah, stalkerish much," Rem objected. She tossed my hand from hers and gesticulated. "Look Sand Lady, I am not leaving her," she took me in warily, and in a hush hush aside she added, "You got your spires, I've got mine own reasons, so let's all just hover on this a moment."

Trasa ignored Rem and motioned for the warrior guard to handle things if necessary. Peering at Rem closely, I knew she was in no shape to be fighting anyone. We would do as Trasa asked, because it wasn't unreasonable, and well, there wasn't much of a choice. We would all be given leave of the village tribe, it just wouldn't be together.

"Okay," I agreed, and the guard stepped back before starting a fight with Rem, who was close to exploding if he did.

"You can't be serious," Rem bent over to whisper, "You trust these backwards nuts?"

"Not any more than I should trust Achon, and he risked his life for me."

"Not for you," Achon grumbled, "I just didn't like the way that mind twister thought she'd already won, and I gained a secret pleasure in knowing I wasn't you, but she thought I was. So, don't go thinking I've gone all soft."

I smiled despite myself, not realizing how much I'd attached myself to them. They didn't even realize that the trust they held in me was fabricated. I'd manipulated them, and they were better off without me.

"I'll go," I repeated, "I need to get to Kelly before Bailey does."

"Kelly?" Rem thought about the name, and I realized I had done so well not saying anyone's name until now, and then it clicked for her, "Right, the bounty you wanted."

"That's why you wanted the bounty?" Achon asked.

"He knows?" Rem looked at me, hurt.

"He's my assist, and we had a deal that no matter what I would get the bounty."

Rem asked quietly, "This Kelly is that important to you, that you'd betray me to increase your chances of saving her?"

I couldn't take those violet eyes searching my face for an answer I couldn't give her.

"Well, look at you." Achon added sulfur to the wound. "I was obviously the better choice to win."

"Don't be stupid, you were already bumped out of

the race once," Rem fumed.

"She's the reason I'm here, and she's the reason I'm leaving," I admitted, half expecting Rem to turn and slap me again, but she didn't. Rem merely nodded, and Trasa, leader of the Servun tribe, was waiting patiently leaning against the wall as we hashed things out.

"Look, I get it. I already betrayed your trust before we even met, but we're even now okay. So, you're going to need this." Grabbing my hand, she slipped something in my palm before closing my fingers over it and squeezing. Whatever it was, it was small.

When she released me, I opened my hand to see a pair of contact lenses. I looked up at her. "What is this for?" These were obviously hers, and she'd be giving up a lot to give them to me, her race wasn't over.

"I've added a program into them that decrypts location blockers, so they know every location they've ever been... It's also how I tracked you in the forest. Though, the big explosion did make it easier, since pinpointing small locations isn't really the intent of the software."

"Does that mean—"

"Yah, you can find the coordinates to The Last Transport with those... also me if you wanted to find me again sometime, you know... if you wanted to." She fiddled with her fingers nervous, and her lashes fluttered waiting for my reply. I didn't know what to say, because it was one of the nicest things anyone had ever done for me. My heart ached, wanting her feelings for our friendship to be real, because they felt real to me.

I nodded, my lip quivering with emotion. Grabbing

the contacts, I immediately put them on. It was then that I knew, I really did trust her. Linking up to the contacts, they connected to my NeuralGo and booted up. These were better than anything I knew was on the market, and I wondered if these were even from Seattle, or were these from Acatalec?

She saw the awe in my face and answered, "My family runs a small business in Oregon, repairing odds and ends. Engineering stuff, those were built by my mother. Not on the market at all, she'd never sell them, it's why our family gets hired for odd jobs," she hinted to the job she took from Cable, and she bit the inside of her cheek.

"It's okay," and I actually meant it this time, "thank you."

Trasa was done letting us have our moments together, because after that she stood and towered over us. "Nothing said here, should leave here," she waited for all of us to give her our attention then continued, "To the world of Acatalec the Delicate Warrior must be considered dead, or this will not be the last attempt on her life. It is why you leave separately. It is why you will not speak of this day, and why you must not try to find her again."

She waited for some sort of acknowledgment, and when she received none, she repeated in a booming voice that commanded the tent, "She is dead."

"Yah, okay, she is dead," Rem repeated.

Trasa took in the sight of Achon still being pampered by the warriors, and at her glare, the warriors stopped what they were doing and Achon's attention was lulled over to her. "Delicate who?" That answer seemed to be enough for her, and she nodded.

"I will grab our supplies and return for you." Trasa motioned to the room, and all the warriors left the tent, leaving the three of us alone for our final goodbyes.

Achon groaned as he adjusted to a sitting position. The mud caked where he had been stabbed, I couldn't help the shame I felt when staring at him, and he noticed.

"It missed my heart, and Twinkle Hands was able to mend my lung, but the rest of my tissue, well whatever this gunk is seems to numb it enough," Achon explained.

"You shouldn't have been put in that situation," I lamented.

His eyes seemed to take on a sinister vibe as he leaned back against some propped up pillows. "It won't be the only position I find myself in with your skin."

"What?"

"Well, you see we've already came up with a plan without your psychotic groupies, and honestly, it'll probably work better without you anyways."

"I'm going to be you, and be Twinkle Hand's assist, we're going to win this damned race, and claim what's mine."

"What's ours," Rem amended.

Achon scoffed, and his teeth clenched at the tightening of his chest.

"You're still going to try to win the race?"

"I have my reasons."

"She's got some sort of family obligation," Achon fake heaved, and regretted it the moment he did clutching at his chest again.

"You'd have better luck without my face, and you heard Trasa, if I'm not considered dead, you're not safe."

"That's the beauty of it," Rem explained, "We can still say you died here, that when Achon was stabbed that was you, and he took your place in the race being my assist. We can all pretend to be shocked when he reveals himself, and everyone can then look back at whatever drone footage there was to confirm your death."

"They're recording everything?"

"Well, not exactly. We left so fast that the drones didn't get a chance to follow us, but two did follow Bailey, and one stayed behind in the village waiting for us. The psychos don't like being watched, so as soon as Bailey left her drone went with, and the one that tried to stay behind got destroyed.

"I can guarantee more drones are waiting outside the village. We have to leave together, as you they'll think you came back from the dead, and then boom, when Achon reveals himself, they'll understand your death was real, and we'll win by freaking everyone out about your indestructibility."

"Many of the pilots will be too afraid to touch me, because the last thing they saw before the drone above us got destroyed, were the rockjaws surrounding me with a dagger in my heart."

"Whatever person truly wants you dead won't have a chance to try again, before he reveals he isn't you, plus, if someone does, he'll just change back and reveal a little sooner. We won't be in any more danger than what we signed up for originally."

I didn't like the plan, but when Trasa came back in I asked her, "How are we going to avoid the drones recording the race?"

She smiled and, behind her, a rockjaw grunted, flaring the curtains around its sandy head. I understood why only I was going with her, and not my friends. We were traveling under the sand.

"Not going to happen," I protested, "That thing isn't going to drag me around like a rag again." I growled at it, and the beast stumbled backwards between the curtain once more as if it understood my displeasure with it.

The leader clucked her tongue and the beast still remained where it was, not listening to her. She shook her head.

"Ride on them." She clucked her tongue again, and the rockjaw reluctantly eased forward on its large stone like orangutan arms. It's skin flaps on its shoulders flared and created a small pocket behind them that you could theoretically hunch down blocking the sand from berating your face as it traveled.

"Under the sand…" I cringed.

"The rockjaws have been making rounds every cycle in different directions. The surveyor drones won't be able to tell the difference between us, and a regular round of rockjaws with the sand cover."

"Is that how your villages have avoided having parleys anywhere else outside of Numa?" Rem asked.

"Servun doesn't serve the courts, we serve the land, and our queen," she explained, not answering directly.

"The queen died two decades ago," Rem countered.

Looking at me, Trasa asked a simple question, "How old are you, Delicate Warrior?"

I coughed and refused to answer. I didn't like what

she was insinuating.

Rem and Achon both stared at me. Achon insisted, "How many zeniths are you?"

"She grew up on Earth," Rem corrected Achon, "years, How many years?" Now all of them were waiting for me to answer. I pressed my lips into a thin line and turned my head.

"Twenty," I whispered.

"No shit…" Rem was in awe like that explained everything.

"She doesn't look anything like her," Achon debated, and I agreed with him even though I had no idea what the queen looked like.

"She isn't the queen," Trasa confirmed and sensing the next question she added, "nor is she her daughter." I sighed a heaping pile of relief so big that I probably wouldn't have been able to move at all with the weight of it. This was exactly what I needed to hear. Wasn't it enough that I had to eventually confront my mom about who my real dad was?

My ribcage tightened at the thought of how my dad left us, and I always knew it was because of me, and now I had proof. I wasn't his real daughter, though he still made sure to have dinner with me every second Sunday of the month. I ached, and I wanted my mom to tell me I was wrong, that I should be going to my dad and asking him why he didn't tell me about Acatalec? Or, what if it was mom? What if she was Acatalecian and didn't say anything? One day I'd have to ask her and try not to sound insane when I did it.

"I'm not a queen, that's been established, now can we move on?" I choked out, and then Trasa motioned her head to the rockjaw behind her. It was time. I threw the blanket from my legs. Rem gasped, obviously upset about it. I laughed. I still had my leg. It wasn't a filleted piece of meat.

Rem stared down at my leg in horror, and I wiggled my toes realizing there was nothing wrong with my legs at all. She was just upset I had a huge, deformed scar ripping through my skin from my calf all the way up my thigh where the pants were tied off like shorts on that one leg. It was a badge of honor, a reminder of what I'd been through. I was a warrior who had defeated a rockjaw. Well, fended one off anyway.

Rem finally spoke, "I didn't have enough left in me to heal it all the way, you can blame him," she motioned to Achon. "The psycho sand people used their mud on you for the rest of it. You'll be scarred for life," she gasped like it was the end of the world to have such a huge mark.

"I was already scarred for life," I assured her, "At least this way I'll know it wasn't a dream."

"The num cycle is approaching," Trasa prompted, and I had to say goodbye.

Achon gave a dismissive wave, and Rem clamped onto my shoulders from behind to give me a hug. "See you on the other side."

"She's supposed to be dead," Achon reminded her.

"You're dead," she spat back at him before squeezing me and whispering in my ear, "my parents can help you start a new life." She backed away from me, and pointed to her eyes then to me, signaling to the contacts that I wore. And despite knowing that it was best to cut all ties, I knew I would trust her. I would take her up on her offer of a new life.

Chapter Thirty-Four

*Portal*

Leaving the two people who hadn't done anything but help me, against their own better judgment, I followed Trasa into the front of the tent. The front flap of the entrance hung down, though I could see the suns were gone, and the day had turned to night by the shadows that peaked from the crevasses. The tent glowed in torch light, and the leader grabbed hold of the edge of one of the layered carpets. Flinging the heavy rug from the floor, she exposed the sand beneath us.

The first rockjaw leapt onto the sand and began sinking down. She stepped onto the thick hunched lower leg of the beast, and gracefully mounted its large torso. Its shoulders flared, and she ducked her head behind the shield, with her arm bracers clinking into the hard folds of its back. She held on.

She motioned to the other rockjaw in wait and the last thing she said was, "Hold your breath." Then the sand swallowed them, disappearing. I had my chance then to refuse to follow. Simply walk out of the tent, follow with Rem and Achon, but I didn't.

My rockjaw positioned itself on the sand and waited for me. I followed the same steps I'd seen Trasa do, and as my bracers tapped against the creature's skin they latched on automatically. Not trusting the contraptions completely, I also dug my fingers into the fold as extra grip. Its shoulders flared, and I ducked my head behind its skin before the sand consumed us.

Entering the sand, I closed my eyes, and with the help of the shoulder flap, I didn't have to feel the lashing of the sand on my face, and the hood did a good job of keeping any backlash from pelting me from the sides. I also noticed that the skin acted like an air bubble of sorts while we moved, and even though Trasa had said to hold my breath, I found that involuntarily my nose was still inhaling, despite my best efforts. About to be forced to take a large breath whether I wanted to or not, the rockjaw surfaced in a plume of sand cascading every which way, and I took another breath, watching as I was part of a horde of dark shadowy billows of sand before plunging back into the sand once more.

After several rounds, the shock faded, and I got into a comfortable rhythm of breathing when the rockjaw surfaced. We traveled like that for quite some time, but I realized it would have been near impossible for any drones to tell I was riding one of these creatures. With the darkness, and the sand cover I was just another rockjaw moving about the sand dunes with its buddies.

Until that last jump out of the sand when we didn't descend beneath the surface again, there were only the two of us. The rest of the group had veered off the course, leaving us alone sometime under the sand.

"We're here," she explained as the sand settled, and I could finally see the moons in the night sky, there were three of them close together, and they gave a soft glow to our surroundings, much more than one moon would on Earth. It was beautiful.

"Three moons…"

"Unfortunately, only three. Why, is a story for another time. We must go, the rockjaws stop here. Just beyond this hill is a rock formation our people call the Beltur Ob, it was used a long time ago as a portal before it was forgotten, left to the Servun to protect for a time such as this. The court knows nothing of this place."

I wanted to ask why, but the seriousness in her features told me she wouldn't be explaining anything right now. We walked in silence through a crack in what was larger than a mere rock formation, it was as big as a skyscraper in the Seattle skyline. Wandering through the tunnels, I could see how something like this could be forgotten, it was a maze that we barely fit through, let alone to know where we were going before feeling like we were going to be crushed. Then it opened up into a small cavern where a small, rusted drone sat.

I pointed at it, and she nodded.

"Are you telling me your portal is actually a drone?"

"No, it is the stone behind it, but only that drone can take you through unharmed. The exit is much too high that, should you go without it, you'd not survive. It is some mountain range called Rainier."

"That thing has to be one of the first models ever created." I was in shock that the piece of junk would even still be functional. Rust and sand caked on its decrepit form like a second skin. Its lift system only had eight over-sized propellers with no guards and no rotating system for ease of maneuvering. It was such a large and bulky system and such a small haul space, that it would barely even fit me. I was the only one traveling in that old technology.

"It's been here for ages unable to leave Beltur Ob except through the portal. You'll find the same amount of days has passed on Earth as it has here, though you've noticed our days are much longer. Be quick to grab your friend and leave, there is more time here than on Earth. Good luck Delicate Warrior, do not fall victim to the one that seeks your power," she struggled to lift the hatch manually on the drone, it's rubber worse for wear in its stay here, "For the Pride of Acatalec."

And remembering what they said at the parties I smiled at her and offered, "Num De Ral," in a muted farewell. It was full of all the things I didn't have time to say, and all of the emotions I couldn't relay. I was on a time crunch to grab Kelly, and leave before anyone knew I was still alive, or at least before anyone could see I wasn't with Rem as her assist.

She nodded and planted a fist over her heart and then slammed the hatch back down. My NeuralGo was useless to connect to the drone, and there were no manual joysticks, old-school wheels for navigation, or anything to grab onto. There was a simple screen from the two-thousands that crackled to a very pathetic excuse for a life when I touched it. The screen was cracked, and flickered, but allowed for an input of a destination in the navigation system. It didn't even use coordinates. It used an address like the lost days of postal services.

Rem's contacts allowed me to find her previous

locations, and thankfully had access to a search system even in Acatalec to shoot the coordinates through an old converter for what would have been an address. I manually entered the address into the screen, and its propellers sputtered, kicking up the sand and dirt around us.

At least I thought there was an us, before I realized Trasa was already gone, slipped away through the cracks in the wall. As the system searched for access to a satellite system that didn't exist on Acatalec it bumped into the ceiling of the enclosure trying to achieve its preferred altitude. It bounced around, obviously whatever collision avoidance program it had was broken, or nonexistent to begin with considering how old it was.

Hitting the rocks at just the right angle, or the wrong one depending on how you saw it, it bounced backwards, and disappeared into the wall covered in tribal markings. In seconds, the flickering screen flashed red with an alert that said, error, altitude breach. The propellers seized up, and the defunct drone descended in an awkward top heavy kind of way, where I could see my death from above me, instead of below me. I pressed my arms into the cracked glass roof of the drone, it was that small that even my elbows could take on some of my weight. The fissure on the glass expanded and webbed out.

My temples pounding with the added pressure, I saw a cliff side that was about to crush this contraption, and on instinct I pushed out my hand to brace myself, and the wind picked up and the course of the drone swayed, missing the jagged rocks by inches. I hitched my breath, and before I could swear my ghost would haunt Trasa for the rest of her life, the system reached its preferred altitude, and its propellers spurred to right itself. Clenching my shirt around my neck, I lifted the fabric up for its intended use as a face mask and took long deep breaths to calm my nerves.

The drone was finally connecting to an old satellite system and routing its course. I slumped in my chair and watched as it increased in speed and plateaued at sixty miles per hour. This was the slowest drone in existence. Suddenly a timer appeared on the screen with an estimated time of arrival. Just under an hour.

The drone had a solar panel jerry rigged to it, I knew this, because it was now hanging by a few wires on my right. I checked the battery life on this thing, and it estimated it had two hours before it died, but I wouldn't bet my life the programming was accurate, so I only hoped that that solar panel stayed attached just in case it pulled anything that would reduce the time it had to function.

Chapter Thirty-Five

*At His Command*

The flight there was relatively boring, since it was dark out, and according to my contacts, ten p.m. by the time we reached the address and the drone automatically lowered, but thankfully it had enough sensors to know when it was met with solid ground, the ground being close enough to the landing pad of The Last Transport. I recognized the glass doors that were back lit by the inside tropical rain forest feel. There was no one at the door guarding it; why would they need to, since they would normally be able to sense a drone coming in. Suddenly, I was grateful that this hunk of junk was so old.

Silently, I thanked Rem for her lenses.

Then I tried to open the hatch to get out, and realized it wasn't budging. I had to kick the glass out of the top of the drone, most of the work was already done for me since it was so badly damaged. That thing would barely be able to carry the weight of both Kelly and me. Plus, I had no idea how long its battery was going to last, especially in the dark.

I took a deep breath and steeled myself for going into The Last Transport. The door scanned me and popped open like it was expecting my arrival. Though, I didn't see any survey drones blinking lights in the sky for them to have known I was coming.

"Welcome Pilot One," the automatic A.I. greeted. I wondered if our pilot names were updated since the last race, and it was scanning my contact lenses for an ID. Rem was the first pilot from the forest.

I walked down the corridor, and the walls transitioned from the forest to footage of the races from different surveyor drones, like a viewing gallery. One in particular caught my attention, as it replayed my final moments in the Servun village. It appeared so much more gruesome than being there in person. The cameras really zoomed in hardcore to capture all the facial expressions and spanned out from my doppelgänger to Bailey, and then her finishing blow of stabbing me in the heart.

The commentary scroll at the bottom of the screen capturing Bailey's last words through a lip reading programming to Achon, as he wore my face, "I'll give — your regards." Though her face buried into my ear so no one would know what name she gave, but I knew who she meant. I hadn't been close enough to know she even said anything in those last moments.

How did she know hearing his name as a final farewell would add so much salt to the wound? I supposed it would have been obvious if she saw him reject me at the dance. The rockjaws closed in from all sides, and Bailey ran off to be the first one to the finish line, wherever that was. Then the screen crackled and cut out, only to be replaced with a host narrator giving final thoughts on the last moments of Pilot Sixteen, and the rising star of Priscus Pilot Nine. I forced myself to continue down the hall, not wanting to read what the captions were saying about my death.

The open doors to the ballroom showed me that no one was present, or celebrating here at the moment, so I continued down the corridor to the elevator at the end. Just like the previous door, it opened for me, and the A.I. offered, "Please select a floor…" among the options popping up on my contacts was Bounty Lodging, and I selected it.

So far, this rescue was going much too smoothly, and the longer I went without seeing anyone, the more nervous I became before the elevator chimed, and opened to the floor above where Bounty Lodging should be. I selected the option again, and the doors remained open. I exited, and noticed this floor was labeled, Destination Suite.

The whole floor was covered in the drone footage for the races, and I lowered my hood over my face as a lady dressed in her finest jewelry and gown shuffled past me into the elevator, not even bothering to look at me before saying, "Do be a dear and tell the curators to switch up the footage on screen sixteen, I think everyone would like to keep their stomachs about them for the Prince's upcoming toast."

"Of course." I bowed to her, and the elevator doors closed.

Sticking to the edges of the party, I searched for Kelly, or perhaps a stairwell to go down a floor. But then I spotted her, and I was thankful the elevator didn't have access to her living quarters. She was wearing the finest beaded dress that fit her like it was made to follow each and every one of her curves. Floor length, with a high slit up her thigh, and her hair was perfectly formed, not a curl out of place, her dark skin flawless and glowing. I almost had to slap myself to stop from staring and find a way to make my way to her without too much attention, but I didn't have to when I saw the smeared mascara across her cheeks. She'd been crying, and based on the shine, she still was. Her arms were locked in place, as her shoulder shook, and she held herself up on the small table where people set their drinks.

Next to her was the man of the hour with his hand outstretched to comfort her. He was dressed in all black, and his blue eyes were set on a single screen as it repeated the scene I had just watched in the hallway. Why would they torture themselves having that replay over and over again, how many times since it'd happened. And I caught myself realizing Trasa's words, on Earth it probably was happening to them right now, even with the hour delay in traveling here. They probably only saw the replay a handful of times. It was fresh. I'd have to ask someone later about how the time differences worked, but it wouldn't matter if I left quickly.

I needed Kelly to move her hands. I needed her to see me, but I couldn't afford to pull back my hood, or draw attention to myself more than I already was by being under dressed. I was filthy, and with every step leaving a small trickle of sand in my wake as it jostled loose from whatever crease it got itself into.

She lifted her face and went straight to staring at the stern, dreamy face of Wyndall, and then wilting into his arms as he caught her. He was angry, but was gentle with her, and I wondered how Kelly was going to explain why she was so upset about the death of a wild card pilot, when no one else in the room seemed to care one way or the other.

I had to get closer, but something came over me as I watched him hold her. Jealousy. My eyes throbbed, and the same feeling came over me as that night Achon stole my face without talking to me about it. I didn't know why, but I clenched my fists, and a wind gusted through the room picking up skirts and tossing manicured hair. People made small sounds of surprise and all eyes turned to Lord Wyndall for answers.

The only pair of eyes not on him, was his own blue orbs staring back at my black ones. He smiled across the room, and I growled under my breath. No one had noticed me, but him, but he was enough to screw my plans. He turned away from me, and I went back to the elevator.

Another gust of wind swept through the room, but more direct, less chaotic, and the room filled with guests floating through the space cheering the display of power by their Lord Prince. Kelly finally removed her face from his chest, sniffling and wiping her eyes, confused, but without a word he set her down. She mumbled something, where I could only see her lips move. He bent down to her and patted her hands before dismissing himself.

The elevator refused to open, and I wondered why such a large place only had one entrance. He worked his way through the room, and I knew he was coming for me, but he hadn't announced me to everyone here, so I didn't know his intentions. Undeterred by his charm, Kelly proceeded to follow him, and I was thankful, because worst case scenario I would drag her ass with me and try to knock out the Prince of Acatalec in the elevator.

I realized he was much bigger than me, but I had

already convinced multiple people to do things they didn't want to do up until this point without trying, so I figured it'd be the perfect time to use my Tarquin powers on purpose, instead of by accident.

Trying to casually stand in wait for the elevator, he stood by my side pretending he didn't know who I was.

"Tyler," he greeted me casually, and I was caught off guard by his use of my name, so I met those intense blue eyes, my hood falling back from my head.

"How?"

"Ty?" Kelly's voice quaked, barely audible behind me.

"Don't look back," Wyndall warned, and Kelly pressed up against my back wrapping her arms around my waist.

"Tell me I'm not dreaming," she choked.

"I'm not leaving here without her," I said firmly to Lord Wyndall.

"Nor should you," he agreed, shocking me again.

"We are leaving here," I specified, just in case he meant neither of us would be leaving.

"Of course," he said while walking into the elevator with us following behind him. He selected an unlabeled floor that wasn't even an option when I had entered earlier.

"Why is he being so agreeable?" I asked Kelly. She squeezed me into her as hard as she could, and before answering me finally realized that I could walk.

"How are you walking? I almost didn't know it was you? You were dead! How is this possible?" She flooded me with questions, and I sighed not wanting to get into everything right then.

"You have earned your bounty, I wouldn't deny

you what is rightfully yours," Lord Wyndall answered.

"I don't understand." I twisted around to give Kelly a hug, so that she would stop hanging on me and pinching to make sure I was real. I gave her a look that said this wasn't the time and glared at Lord Wyndall to explain himself.

"All the clues given to the pilots, though you left before receiving them, were to lead them to the coordinates of The Last Transport. It's the first time in history that we've used this place as part of the races. Fitting, since it is also the first time the races have been used to find someone for the Hand Rite Ceremony. Where we start is where we end."

"No one can know that I was here." I stood my ground and faced him, trying to keep the fear out of my voice.

"You wish for no one to know that you finished the race first?"

"I wish for no one to know that I'm still alive," I corrected.

He smiled at me, and it was a regal smile that if it were any other time would have been endearing, but right now when our fates were in his hands it was unnerving. "On one condition."

He turned to me then and, ignoring our company, made the air around us heavy. My body lifted and pushed into his chest, and his hand scooped me up with ease. Those eyes blazed with that same passion I'd seen in them before. My breath caught, and I found myself melting into his warmth unexpectedly.

I gave him a breathy, "What condition?"

"That when I find you, and I will," he assured, "you will fulfill your obligation to me and our people."

His head leaned down, and the tip of his nose nuzzled the side of my cheek before his lips grazed the bottom of my own. Taunting me, my whole body seemed to vibrate in response to him. A soft hum coursing through my blood and he pulled away enough for me to catch my senses.

"Obligation?" He knew how I felt about that word.

"You will be mine, Tyler Beryl," his eyes were the hottest kind of fire, and he noticed my muscles tensing at his proposal, "but I will not force you. When we meet again, I'll make sure you beg me to bond with you as punishment for making me wait." My whole body visibly shivered at his proclamation, and I could hear Kelly make a disgruntled sound beside us.

I finally noticed the elevator door had already opened, for how long I didn't know, but I cleared my throat and watched the door again to redirect that intensity anywhere else but on me. I could already feel the sand caught between my thighs chaff and rub the more I could feel his hips grinding into me. I didn't want to think about what he meant by finding me again, or why he made my body betray my mind so fast. He was from Numa, and everyone knew his powers were controlling the wind, so he couldn't possibly be controlling my mind, but it wandered all over his muscular body. He had to release me before I made a fool of myself.

My insides squirmed, and I knew my eyes turned dark with emotion staring into his blue pools. I quickly closed my eyes, not wanting him to fall victim to the needs coursing through me. I would ask him something, and he would be forced to do it thinking he wanted to. Gasping, his hands roamed up my back, and I couldn't help but wonder if he was in the wrong place at the wrong time the night I had asked Cable to kiss me.

Was he acting this way because I manipulated his feelings when I had wanted so much for Cable to like me? He was there when I was with Cable. And guilt washed through me, cooling me off faster than an ice bath. I had done this to him, these were not his feelings for me. They were mine reflected back at me. I bit my lip and struggled to free myself. I couldn't do this to him, no matter what my body was doing in response to him.

He made me tingle in ways I never thought possible. I had to make it stop before I couldn't let him go.

"Do not be ashamed," Wyndall whispered to me, "Every inch of you is perfect." He had thought I retreated from him because I was ashamed of my eyes, of what I was, of being a Tarquin. And he'd be right, in a sense, because of what I was I could never be sure that anything he felt for me was real. He deserved better than that. His large hand came up to cup my cheek, and I leaned into it for the first and what should be the last time.

"Your Breath of Numa only speaks to me, Tyler Beryl," his voice was husky and layered in need. He was speaking about the wind that Numa controlled.

"I'm Tarquin," I corrected him.

"You are both," he insisted before easing us back to the ground and let me join Kelly outside the elevator. Kelly grabbed my hand and pulled me next to her possessively, before assessing Wyndall with new eyes.

"You didn't tell me you wanted her," Kelly admonished him.

"You didn't ask." He gave her a devilish grin.

"I didn't think I had to, I thought she died." She motioned between them. "We thought she died. There was an understanding, I was mourning," she tried to make sense of it, and narrowed her eyes at him while clinging to my arm. I smiled at her and kissed her forehead.

"I'm not dead," I assured her. When I looked up again, I could see Wyndall's eyes narrow, and twitch at the affection I was giving her. Kelly bristled with her hips shimmying.

"You won't find us," she huffed at him. What was she thinking, goading him when he was letting us leave? I gave her a stern squeeze to tell her to ease up.

Wyndall laughed darkly and shifted his eyes to me giving me all sorts of lovely goosebumps, with the way he gobbled me up, that I had to look away. "Do you wish to make me change my mind? Torture me further, and I'll see to it that she never leaves my side."

Kelly quickly pivoted to have a gap between us but continued to hold my hand. Wyndall groaned, running his hand through the hair at the back of his head.

"Leave before I change my mind."

"You know someone is trying to kill me," it wasn't a question, my instinct was telling me that's why he was helping us.

"I could protect you," he offered.

I smiled at him knowing he meant it, and he probably could. He was powerful enough, but he couldn't be everywhere, as evidence of the last few attempts on my life, and I couldn't be at his side every moment. It wouldn't be right for me to ask that of him. He had his people to take care of; I was only one person.

"I know."

He knew at least one of the reasons why I couldn't stay with him, and that was enough for him to let me go. I didn't know I could make someone care that much about me with merely a look. I had to be careful in the future when my emotions ran high, but before I went, I had to ask him a question. I had to know that he would be okay when I left.

"How long does it take before someone is themselves again after being glamored by a Tarquin?"

Kelly took me in and then Lord Wyndall before responding, "Depends on the person, but the longest anyone has ever been under the influence without being glamoured again was a few days."

"If there is even a small part of the person that wants the same thing as the glamour's intention, then that person would have done it regardless, even if not quite so fast as a glamour would allow. Even then it would fade after a week, and whatever was there to begin with would still be there after." It was as if he knew exactly why I was asking and tried to say it was not affecting him. Did he know that I had glamoured him unknowingly? Does he think he wanted it? Will he still think that way in a week? All these questions and more whipped through me, and he countered even that.

"When I return for you, you will have no excuses to ignore me," he growled.

"If you return for me," I amended.

He was on me so fast, I felt the wind pick up my hair. Those blue eyes blazing down at me. His large body towering over me. His hands gently cupped my face, and I let out an involuntary sigh feeling my blood rush to my center. How did he make me feel this way?

"You displease me with your doubts. I chose you, even if you had lost the race, I would have forced you to duel me so all could see your worth, and still I would choose you then." He nuzzled the top of my head with his nose. "Much of my choices in life are for my people, rarely do I choose something for me, and only me."

Kelly cleared her throat.

"You're smothering her, big guy." She pulled me back with the hand she still held.

My face flushed at the contact, and how his presence consumed me. I licked my lips at how dry my mouth was, and the need pulsated through my body the closer he got to me. I didn't understand it, all I knew was that I was hungry for everything he was offering me. Warm air swirled around me, and he smiled, a wolf's grin, knowing exactly how he tortured me. Somehow, I knew the way the hairs on his arm moved like the wind was touching him, that it was because of me. And the tingling on my lips was a targeted hit with him teasing me with all the things he could do with his precision.

"I choose you Tyler Beryl, and you may not accept it yet, but you have chosen me too. This is not the end. I will find you."

Kelly dragged me backwards, as I continued to stare at him in awe. He was so brazen, dominating, and possessive, but he was also letting me go. A big smile formed on my face. I couldn't help it.

Before I turned around to follow Kelly to the drone sitting in the private hangar I whispered into the wind.

"Find me." Too soft for anyone to hear, not even

Kelly, but the way his face darkened seductively, I knew he heard me.

The wind was at his command.

## Chapter Thirty-Six

*Control the Sky*

First thing they teach you in training after safety was being aware of your surroundings. Scan all traffic and anticipate problems before they can't be avoided. But I wasn't focused and too much had happened to get back to basics. Kelly ripped her dress up the other side of her beautiful dress, to have two slits for ease of movement. She jumped into the pilot seat, and I was too dazed to object. The drone was top of the line, everything you could possibly ask for was included, and everything you didn't even think you needed, but now that you knew it existed would rather never live without.

Wyndall stood in the distance like a regal statue watching us leave with his personal drone. The glass windows were built like a garage and rolled up into the ceiling, giving us a direct leave from the building into the night. My heart ached watching him turn into a small dot in the distance, back-lit by the room's illumination.

I knew I told him to find me, but I also knew I couldn't let him. We'd have to ditch this drone and pick up another one that couldn't be traced back to us. We had to do this the right way, under the radar, where not even he could find us.

"Ty?"

I grunted.

"I'm sorry," she finally said before explaining, "I didn't realize you were from Acatalec, and I shouldn't have put you in that position. I should have realized the race was too good to be true."

"Why did you sign the bounty contract?" I asked absently, not even really worried about the answer anymore, since I had her, and we were leaving.

She cracked her neck and pulled the drone off to the side, down an alley between the buildings to hover. I knew we should have kept going. I knew we didn't have time to chat. We would have had all the time in the world to chat when we started our new lives together, but Kelly stopped, and I let her because I wanted to know the truth.

"I bought the entries for the wild cards from a family that didn't want the court to know their kids inherited any abilities from them. They are Numplums, Acatalecs without powers, and have been allowed to stay on Earth without any restrictions.

"If their kids joined the races, they said they'd have to register them, and their lives would forever be changed. They don't know about Acatalec, and they wanted to keep it that way, since their power is negligible, and wouldn't cause any real trouble on Earth."

"Instead, it's our lives that are forever changed," I tried to keep the accusation out of my tone.

"I know, but I didn't think you had any power, and that it was just a simple drone race. What harm could winning some credits do?"

I was about to tell her just how much harm, and

everything we would be giving up for just a race, but she stopped me before I could.

"I know, you practically died before my eyes," her voice shook as she tried to keep herself from crying again at the thought of it, "The official knew I didn't qualify for the wild card entry, because I was born on Acatalec. If I didn't fulfill my duty as a bounty for the cost of losing a pilot, he'd make sure to find out who my entry was meant for, insure they also paid their dues to the court for illegal activity, and bring up my actions to the court to remove my access to Earth.

"If he looked into where the entry came from, he'd find out there were two entries, and find out who else was not supposed to be at the race. Now, knowing what you are... you would also be restricted from Earth for however long the court deemed fit. I couldn't let that happen. I had to stay, I had to sign the bounty. For that family, for you, and for me." She buried her face in her hands and crumbled at the helm.

"You understand, don't you? Can you ever forgive me?" She wiped at her smeared mascara.

I sighed and helped her collapse in the backseat. Kelly was in no condition to continue piloting, but no one really had to pilot it anyway. She was only manually piloting because we didn't have a destination to go yet, and I didn't want to enter one so there wasn't a log of previous routes in the programming that I'd have to clear. I ran my hands over her hair and rubbed my fingers into her scalp to soothe her.

Finally, her sobs eased, and I knew she was close to sleep. Slipping her head onto the seat instead of my lap, I moved into the pilot's chair to get us somewhere safe.

We were only around the block from The Last Transport, and as soon as I moved out of the alleyway, my instincts ran hot. Like the time Cameron came out of nowhere and guided me off the streets and into a building. Or when we were surrounded by the Servun tribe. All the hairs on my arm stood on edge, and my blood pounded in my ears.

I lifted into drone airspace and pulled up the overlay on the contacts to see the traffic, but none of that would show me a drone with their collision software turned off.

A link request activated through my NeuralGo, and the name that popped up made my teeth grit: Bailey. I was so caught up with everything I hadn't even thought to remove her contact. I would have to completely wipe my system to make sure this could never happen again.

The link ended, and a voice message played, "I know you're close, or have you forgotten that Shard has your blood lingering in her system? It's not an exact science, but I know your general direction, and I'm coming. I just thought I'd make it more fun, by giving you a heads up. You have thirty seconds before I find you."

"Kelly, wake up!" I immediately plugged in a random coordinate into the system, and put the drone on auto control, because if she really was after us the worst thing I could do was speed up and try to outpace her. I'd stick out like a sore thumb, I had to play normal drone, and pray she was too focused on finding the outlier speeding in the dark, that she misses the fact that this drone was a one of a kind.

Damn this personal drone, and all of its cool upgrades.

"What's going on?" Kelly mumbled, and maybe things would have been different if I had let her sleep, but I didn't.

"It's Bailey." I held onto the command sticks with a death grip, hoping I wouldn't have to use them, but being prepared if I did. I'd find out in the next thirty seconds.

This drone came with many features not available in a typical passenger drone, one of which was fully augmented interior, and a stealth setting that made the drone reflect light around it. I'd never been more thankful for a state-of-the-art piece of machinery like this one. The drone was equipped with many tiny cameras taking in the surrounding scenery and screening that visual onto its outer surface to blend in, and at nighttime it should've been even more effective.

As soon as I triggered stealth mode, the drone slowed down, not meeting normal flight speeds. It began rising above drone airspace into altitudes higher than what would be safe. These vehicles weren't meant to function this high, which I experienced personally in the mountains earlier. They were meant to be lighter, faster, and that sacrificed durability and pressure sustainability. There weren't any oxygen tanks, and as soon as the air quality outside the drone got too thin it would automatically trigger circulated air, but that would be a temporary fix until Kelly and I produced too much carbon, and we suffocated.

The drone plateaued just below the level the system would have triggered circulated air, and I saw Kelly as pale as a ghost, and I didn't think it was possible to see that kind of complexion on her. The blood had drained from her face, and I couldn't decide whether it was due to the abrupt change in altitude, or the thought of facing Bailey.

Switching modes from D.D.A., collision sensors turned off, our drone blinked off the overlay screen in my contacts. We would no longer be visible among the rest of the drones, but we would still be in danger if any international aircraft were landing in the area, and Seattle was known to be a high trafficked hub of travel. I took a deep breath trusting that Lord Wyndall's personal drone was the best that money could by, and if it took us up here, that it was probably safe.

I was going to relax, until I saw what my subconscious was trying to will into nothing, but it wasn't nothing. Another drone was following our previous path on the overlay that I had yet to turn off from my interface. I wasn't in drone air space, normally I would have turned it off, but I didn't because deep down I knew we weren't clear. It sped straight up through the traffic, not caring about the near misses that the other automated drones had to veer out of the way to accommodate her.

One drone in an act of its anti-collision software quickly moved out of the way, only to create a cascading collision avoidance among the other passengers, and there was one too many close calls that two drones connected, and their blips on my screen flashed red as they descended.

We were in stealth mode, I knew she wouldn't be able to see us easily, but we were traveling slowly to optimize the optical illusion of being invisible. There were two scenarios: she kept her current speed and crashed into us if I couldn't avoid her through manually pulling out of the way in time, or she slowed down to search for us and we prayed she had some sort of night blindness to aid in her passing right by us. I knew we weren't invisible, that's not what stealth mode was.

When you know something was within reach, you could be blind to how close it really was, or you could be patient and notice when all you had to do was grab it. Bailey didn't seem like the impatient type. She was perfectly fine shooting suction cups on the ceiling waiting for her time to be up. She was a pilot just like me, she was trained the same.

Everything I'm thinking now, could be going through her own head. If she doesn't see the lights of a drone in the distance, will she slow down? Will she know my drone had stealth capabilities? Will she look for me, or will she pass right by?

"She saw our drone break from the pack, she knows we're up here." I explained to Kelly.

"Do you feel that?" she shivered and wrapped her arms around my shoulders. I knew what she was talking about, it was the instinct that I thought was only my own. That eerie sensation of dread that made my stomach clench. Nothing good ever came from that feeling, and when I was racing it only ever meant I needed to evade an incoming drone.

It was too dark to notice Bailey's drone visually, but I watched my overlay as the dot that represented her drone flickered now that she was no longer in drone airspace. I switched to manual, and lifted the drone higher triggering the drone to close off the external airflow. A countdown timer popped up onto my contact telling me how much time we had with circulated air, plenty of time to get to where we needed to go, if we avoided being caught.

With her arms over my shoulders, Kelly sobbed. Her face pressed into my cheek, and she strained to say, "You should be more careful about who you pick for an assist." It was then that I realized she wasn't sobbing anymore, it was a laugh, and with her arms around me I saw what her ability was firsthand. It felt like pins and needles numbing my whole body as she pulled me through the seat, not over it, or around it. She had turned me into a ghost unable to touch anything with her touch on me.

My link disconnected, and she established control of the drone plunging it down at a sickening speed. I knew then that our stealth mode couldn't keep up with the rapid images. Nausea overcame my whole body, and I tried to clamp onto anything, but with Kelly's arm still wrapped around my neck I was nothing.

All I could do was choke out, "Why?"

But she was unresponsive.

I had no other choice but to let my instincts take over, and my eyes swirled with the night around us as I growled at her, "Pull up!" She didn't stop, but her head jerked like a rusty wrench to spot me. As her grip loosened, the numbness faded, and I grabbed her with a firm yank. Staring at her I said again, "Pull up!" And she did, but not soon enough.

Kelly knew my command was the worst thing I could have done for both of us, as soon as it was done. Our drone flung straight into an oncoming drone. Without a word she reached for me again, and she was too fast. One moment I saw her, and the next she was behind me grabbing my torso. She made us both turn into nothing, and as the drone collided with the other, we transferred through the side of our drone and dropped through the top of an oncoming drone, landing solid, slamming into the inside. We gasped for air as the wind was knocked out of us on impact. Kelly had made us phase through solid objects, avoiding the collision all together, but it wasn't coincidence that there was a drone conveniently located close enough to our drone to transfer so seamlessly.

Her voice sent chills down my spine, "If you had been traveling by yourself, you probably would have got away."

I remained silent, and Kelly charged at her, but stopped as soon as she saw her eyes. As I stared up at her I wondered why I was so upset about everything. I only wanted to sit down, needed to sit down. So tired and, as my eyelids became heavy, I watched Kelly collapse onto the floor and place her head on the seat next to her.

"Don't hurt her," Kelly said before fading away.

I yawned before realizing what was happening. Quickly, I dug deep and focused on keeping that pulsing feeling behind my eyes when everything became dark, and my body heated with power. Adrenaline coursed through me, and I righted myself to sit in the backseat of the drone as she sat across from me with her pilot seat swiveled around.

Bailey smiled at me, her dark makeup haunting against the night sky and the illumination of the drone. She threw her leg over the other, showing off her platform boots, and she leaned back.

"I overheard you pick her for your assist in the forest," she said conversationally as if she hadn't tried to murder me several times already, and this was just a lovely day trip to the park, "I pretty much wrote her off

302

as a waste of time when you disappeared and had to rely on some blood tracking to find you."

"What did you say to her?" With my eyes dark I knew whatever glamour my power gave off would be similar to all those times I was with Cable. How could she resist telling me all her secrets like a typical girl's night out?

"Couldn't just tell her to kill you herself, it doesn't really work its best that way, you know? It has to be more subtle, had to be more clever than the average fixer." She was boasting about her efforts, clearly impressed with herself, and reveling in how it paid off for her. She couldn't just kill me now, she had to make sure someone knew how much she went through for this, before she finished things off.

"Or course not," I placated her.

That was a key flaw in people like her, needing to be recognized for their power, when how they used it had to remain a secret. Her ego gave me time, and if I was honest with myself, it was also my weakness as well… I had to know. The more I stared at her the more I was distracted, and a need built within me. I hung on every word, I was enthralled, and I needed to hear everything.

It was a deep human instinct to be curious, and I was the most curious of them all.

I lifted an eyebrow, and leaned in, even feeling the power in my glamour ebb and flow… weakening the longer I listened.

"She had the same need that all pilots have," she paused seeing if I would finish her sentence for her, but I didn't, "to feel the force of flying within our hands, and the more we feel that speed, the more addicted we become to that thrill of so much power at our fingertips."

I understood what she was talking about, more than most, it was control. It was appreciating the skill in truly mastering the machine. There were too many things in life that acted without your consent, did things without being asked, and took away any chance we had to feel alive... to feel human. And when I thought that, I cringed. I wasn't human. Bailey noticed my reaction but couldn't possibly have known the meaning of it. She merely laughed, clearly enjoying any disgust that would surface from her manipulations.

"I only had to tell her it was her right to pilot any drone that she entered, and when she heard my name, she had to protect you the only way she knew how... fly down into the city as fast as possible where she could hide between the buildings, or in a parking garage.

"It was brilliant really, because a descent like that with no thought other than the need I implanted makes it hard to pay attention to anything, let alone avoid obstacles. There is only the need, and the stronger the need is the more they are blinded. She must have really wanted to protect you, and there was no other thought in her mind other than to take control and dive." She just started laughing, and her eyes swirled making me dizzy. How she could so casually find the suffering Kelly must have gone through humorous turned something on inside of me.

My voice hummed sounding like a stranger even to my own ears, "Tell me what's that like to hold someone's life in your hands?"

"It was luck that you chose to have your bounty

with you when I needed to find you. I felt nothing but relief when I found you again, you were supposed to be dead, but then when everyone saw you and your healer walk out of the village, I had to take a detour to find you again. It's you who has my life in your hands.

"It's you or me," she gritted her teeth trying not to tell me anymore. "I have just enough left in me to let you fulfill your greatest dreams. To fly." At her words, the hatch of the drone opened up to the brisk night air.

"I'm already dead," I told her, "You saw it yourself."

"Then you had to walk out of the village. You could have stayed there until the races were over and disappeared. You could have stayed in the forest, let the explosion speak for itself. You could have stayed dead. I gave you two chances to leave. I walked away, stayed quiet twice," she pleaded with me, "I already promised you I'd claim her as my bounty, you don't know what you've done!" Bailey screamed at me, and her hands pulled into her hair fists clenched and her jaw tight.

Kelly stirred at the seat beside me, but otherwise remained sleeping.

"I'm already dead," I repeated to her again, "it wasn't me that walked out of that village. I'm just a ghost you're haunted by." I leaned back and asked her a simple question, "Are you satisfied with what you've done?"

Her teeth were grinding at this point, and her eyes swirling with her power twitched at my words. Her hands slid from her hair, and the heels of her hands pressed into her temples and scrapped down her face, then back up into her hair. Bailey crazed.

"I thought he was wrong about you, but he was

right all along. You can't exist, and I'm the only one that can stop you before it's too late." Bailey reached behind her waistband and pulled out a pocketknife and in one swift movement stabbed her own thigh. She screamed, and the air around us became heavy with a surge of static that prickled at my skin.

"There's a feeling you get when you're in control of a drone, and you turn off the dampeners to hear the wind move around you with a hum. Can you feel the wind, Tyler?"

And I could feel the wind, the hatch fully open to the outside, the wind flowed through the opening whipping my hair over my shoulder as the drone moved on autopilot through traffic. I could hear the buzz of other passenger drones as they passed around us utilizing their collision avoidance systems due to our slow pace. I closed my eyes and listened to the sound that boomed at the speed of them, it was magical just as she knew it would be.

"Grab hold of it, don't let go of that feeling. It is control, it's the only thing you have control over," Bailey's voice was soothing, and I felt it course through me. I knew I was in danger and I needed control even more so than ever before. I needed that control, and she offered it to me. It would be so easy, I only needed to grab it, and it was so close. I opened my eyes and was drawn to outside the hatch. It was inviting me to take control of the only thing I had control over, the wind.

I felt the wind caress me, and as much as I hated to admit it, I had a connection to it, and just as Lord Wyndall had said... I was part Numa, it was in my blood to control the wind. My body floated in the seat, letting the wind consume me, and I couldn't let it, I was the one in control. I had to be, so I forced myself to settle back into the seat.

The more I thought about control, the more I knew my eyes darkened turning into night themselves. I looked at Bailey, and felt the dizziness of staring into her eyes, of hearing her voice like a lullaby. She offered control, and I needed it.

I growled at her, "I'm nothing, I never existed, you don't need to find me anymore." And after I told her this, because I needed control, I needed her to know that I was dead, and that she didn't need to come after me. I was trying to save myself, so that I could leave and never be followed again. But that didn't change what I was going to do, what I needed to do. I had to take control of the sky.

Bailey repeated my words, "I'm nothing, I never existed," her voice was dull, lacking the musical quality it had before. The damage was already done.

I leaned over Kelly's limp body and nudged her out of the way while I placed a kiss on her forehead. She groaned, and I whispered to her, "We're free now. I'm taking control of the skies."

We were both doomed.

## Chapter Thirty-Seven

*Let Go*

Words were a tricky beast, always meaning what they say, but never meaning the same as what you hear. That's the thing with words, they could always be interpreted in the most unexpected ways.

I only meant for Bailey to think that I was dead, make her believe it with her every fiber and being that her job was complete. That she could let go, move on, and leave Kelly and me alone. Don't follow us into the night, let us start a new life.

"I am nothing, I do not exist." Simple words, their meaning so clear to me.

Until you hear them said out of someone else's mouth, and it meant so much more. I should have been panicked by the way she said them back to me, should have known the mistake I made, but I needed to feel the wind and take control of my life.

The desire to control was so deeply rooted that there was nothing I could do but meet the call. I don't know why I thought about freedom in the moment I held onto the handle above my head, leaning myself out into the crisp air. All I knew was that even aliens were imprisoned by their desires, and I was no different.

There was no such thing as control.

And I let go.

I turned around in the air. I found it was easy to move within it like it was part of me. I let it cradle my head, and my hair floated above me, cascading into the night and slithering over my face in waves.

Looking up at the drone, I fell.

It felt peaceful as I watched the drone become smaller, until a shadow emerged from its open maw and came after me. My heart panicked, and my sense of wonder disappeared. I thought I was free, that she would know I was dead, that we could move on, that she would let me live. She dove, her body descending upon me faster than I was falling as she bulleted down.

As she came closer, her eyes were dead, and the determination to kill me that was in her eyes in the Servun village was nowhere to be found. In the wind I could hear her repeat the words like a mantra, "I am nothing. I do not exist."

I reached out to her before she could pass me. I controlled the wind around me, and I moved with ease to meet her. Grabbing her arm, I pulled her to me and slapped her face with no response. She didn't react, the sting of my palm nothing to her numb cheek.

"Snap out of it!" And at the same moment I said it, I too snapped out of my stupor to realize that I was there with her, and we were both falling. I tried to slow us down by willing the wind to pick us up, to have the wind be heavier than us, but the wind moved too fast, and what parts I could control slipped past me only jerking us slightly before we broke through the flimsy hold.

"Bailey!"

I tried again, and I had a better hold on the wind, before the weight of Bailey in my hand yanked me down and we were picking up speed. The tops of the suburbs small roofs lit by streetlights below us the size of ants. We didn't have much time.

Not experienced enough, not powerful enough to hold us both up. I knew deep down that I could have saved myself if I let go. Enough in me to slow myself down enough before the ground for a survivable impact. But I couldn't let go.

It would have been easy, I had to continually adjust my grip on her as the stress made my hands clammy. I'd wipe off a hand and grab hold of her wrist again, and the crook of her armpit. Holding on, I'd send another burst of energy to solidify the wind around us, and again her weight would pop the bubble as we jerked in the air and continued our speedy descent.

I took her face in my hands and pulled her up to me. I stared into her eyes and forcefully growled, "You are! You exist!" It was cruel of me to do to her, with such a short amount of time before the end. She could have gone without knowing, without feeling it, without the panic that crossed over her as she looked from me then down at the fast-approaching ground.

Taking her arm again, I held firm and sent another burst of energy into the air. I felt myself hover for a moment before the weight jerked us down again into reality. Dazed, she then shook her head at me an understanding washing over her.

"I was right the first time." Sadness in her voice she lifted her hands to my face and stared at me with those eyes swirling like bowls of ink.

"You have to let go," she said melodically, soothingly, "I'll be fine, Tyler, you can let go." She even smiled at me to add to her illusion, she was fine…

I could let go. I had to let go. My grip lightened on her arm, and I sent another blast into the air. My grip wasn't strong enough anymore. Her wrist slipped through my fingers and I hovered for only a moment before slowing my fall.

She was farther away from me, and I was about to dive after her before the same voice filled my head, she's fine... I can let go.

I saw her lips move, and as she became smaller, and harder to see, the wind blew into my ears letting me listen to her say, "Begin message: Camy, babe, I wanted to let you know that I did it all for you. In my dresser drawer there's a necklace, I know how you hate rings. Will you wear it for me?

"I've never said this to you before, but every time I razzed you it's what I meant to say but couldn't, I love you. End message."

The wind made my eyes water and, on instinct, I pulsed the air again, sending our bodies farther apart.

"She is fine." My words trembled in my throat. "I can let go." But my chest was tight and heaving. It didn't matter that she had tried to kill me... How could Cable do something like this to someone?

I reasoned to myself that it was over now, and that when Achon revealed himself at The Last Transport that the only person that knew I was alive, would be Lord Wyndall.

There was no need to worry about Cable hurting anyone else, now that his mission was complete, now that I was gone.

Exhausted, I knew I only had one more burst of energy left in me before I would pass out. It was better that way, not seeing the end. Last time I fell into the forest I wanted to see everything, experience every last second of my time. But as I fell, I didn't want to feel anything. I was nothing, I did not exist. I was dead.

With everything I had, I pushed all of my energy outward and I suspended in the air. Floating for the longest I had ever floated. The houses were bigger now, the size of play blocks, I didn't have much time left. My eyes fluttered before a bright light shined in my face below.

Out of nowhere a drone appeared in the light, scooping me up into the open hatch. Kelly was breathing heavy, and the hatch closed the same moment my eyes did.

Chapter Thirty-Eight

*Gone*

Newsreel: Young Woman Commits Suicide Jumping from Stolen Drone.

#

The identity of the woman, and the person the drone was stolen from remained anonymous at the request of the grieving parties. Only Acatalec and I knew the truth of that story. Bailey had been manipulated and, if saving my life was suicide, then we'd have to take the time to redefine a few things. I was too blinded by the situation in the heat of the moment, but when I thought back on the events, Bailey had saved me more than once.

If it weren't for her, I'd be dead.

It sounded ridiculous, even to me, but in the forest, my drone had a parachute and plenty of time to jump before detonating. Her programming didn't have to have a countdown, the hatch of the drone didn't have to open at my command, I didn't have to punch out the glass to escape... she had given me a chance. She had done her job, while still allowing me to live.

In the Servun village, she was skilled at combat, and she had missed Achon's heart. Close range, and she had missed his heart, then left without finishing the job herself. The rockjaws were dangerous, and could have killed him, but it also gave someone the chance to save him. That someone was me, and both of us lived. She again, did her job while giving me the chance to live.

She had been serious in finishing the job that night in the sky, but in the end... she still saved me again. Bailey had forced me to let go, giving Kelly the time she needed to wake up, and use her ability to phase the entire drone underneath me, and escape my fate on the ground.

Bailey had saved my life.

Over and over again, she had saved me.

And I let her go.

It was because of her that whoever was after me thought I was dead, and right now Kelly was safe.

"Did you ever have the chance to watch the races, Aura?" Rem's mother, Lauren, asked me.

"No, I'm not a big sports fan," I replied while she flicked on a small screen in the shop.

"Oh, well it's not really a sport, dear. My daughter was in the finale. She did so good out there," she boasted, filling with maternal pride.

"Wow, she must be really talented."

"I always knew she was going to make it. Getting to the finale and finishing top three puts her in the court's good graces. I know you're just passing through, but the work that you and Peyton have been doing in the shop has been so helpful that I've been meaning to ask you..."

"Everything you've done for us, we're really grateful."

"Well, you see, I bring up the races, because well, I sent her there to find someone, and it's been months since the races ended. She hasn't been answering my calls, and I really must go to court to make sure everything is okay and see if she needs anything."

I nodded. "I've done the same thing to my own mom. I understand. I should probably call her sometime," I said with a pang of regret in my voice.

"Yes, you should," she chided, "A mother's heart can only take so much."

Sighing, I nodded at her. I'd have to figure out a safe way of letting her know I was all right, but then I hesitated, wondering if doing that would put her in danger. I didn't know if easing my guilt would be worth the chance. Rem's mom smiled at me and patted my shoulder where I was hunched over an old-school scanning screen reading programing code for errors. Helping out at the repair shop was how I earned my keep to live in the shed next to the garage with Kelly until we figured out our next situation.

"While I'm gone, I think you two would do a wonderful job watching out for the shop for me. Would you do that for an old mom like me?" She asked sweetly, and I wouldn't have considered her old at all. She appeared like she hadn't aged since thirty, and I wouldn't have pegged her for Rem's mom, if she didn't say it herself when we stumbled into her shop a few months ago.

"We'll help out anyway we can."

"Oh good, I was hoping you would say so. Not being part of court, or the regency class, we don't really get to know all the race details, so it'll be nice to see what it's all about and find out how she's doing. We didn't get to watch the full race, but I did get a recording of the final ceremony. I think you and Peyton could be good friends with my Rem one day if you stuck around. You remind me of her grit to work hard and give it your all. If nothing else, watch the recording so that you can know what she looks like to say hello to her one day. If you two ever find yourself at court in Numa, you'll have someone to show you the code, as you young people say these days."

I gave Rem's mother a courteous nod of agreement, even knowing that I had no intention of seeing Rem, court, or anyone else from Acatalec again once Kelly and I left here. She was a sweet woman, and I didn't have the heart to tell her we'd be leaving as soon as she returned. I'd come to really care for her like my own family, since coming here. Lying to her was hard on my soul, but I didn't want to drag her into my troubles if my name got around. I'd leave Rem's contacts in the shop for her to find, so that one day when she returned, she'd know that I had come, and that I was safe.

It would have been this week that I left, and I should have, but I couldn't say no to such a simple request after she'd done so much for us to get back on our feet.

Rem's mom linked me the video, and I smiled seeing Rem stand next to Achon as part of the final three pilots, only to scowl at the first-place winner Shard.

"It's unorthodox to delay a Hand Rite Ceremony," Lord Wyndall pronounced to the elite Acatalecians surrounding them, "but I've found that our winner has relayed that they have already bonded with another!" The crowd gave shocked gasps and murmured their gossip at such a discovery.

Lord Wyndall calmed the crowd with a regal hand.

"As you all know, such a ceremony may not be done twice, and it is the lands way of telling us we are fortunate to have many strong, powerful people within our regions, but there is yet another stronger than this that is destined to help our prosperity. What luck, and fortune we have that there is another pilot amongst our people that has yet to be discovered."

The crowd cheered him.

Wyndall had a way of turning the crowd in his favor with pretty words. Though, he had told his people and the court that he could not complete a Hand Rite Ceremony, that they had insisted happen with the winner of the races, he eloquently quieted their concerns, and diplomatically insured the court didn't lose face for a broken promise. I was impressed by his leadership, as much as I was impressed by the way he took charge of those cameras with a kind of mischief most would miss.

"The Regents will gather for a summit to discuss a future arrangement for the Hand Rite, and I promise you, the people, will have yourself a queen."

The crowd again murmured their surprise by his statement. What I could only assume was some sort of reporter suddenly called out to their prince.

"Have you decided your Hand Bond will too be your abett?" The crowd roared at the question, everyone in a fuss about this new revelation, and I couldn't tell if it was because they were upset or excited by the turn of events. Bailey had told me what it meant to be an abett, it was a bond more intimate than any other, more permanent than human marriage; it was a bond for life, for more than power, for love.

It was then that the Lord Prince Wyndall targeted

the closest survey drone, with those sinfully blue eyes like he was digging into the depths of my soul, and pulling at me he said, "I will find her."

My heart stilled, and I was sure every other eligible citizen in Acatalec shivered with me at the intensity of him. I remembered those words, and I remembered how he sounded when he said them to me as I lifted off in his drone. The tips of my ears heated, and the inside of my stomach fluttered. This recording was from months ago, I reminded myself. Whatever glamour was on him would be long gone from his system by now. He was his own man now, uninfluenced by my powers. He was free, and he was gone.

I was gone.

I couldn't go back.

I was so delusional from the recording that I could have sworn I heard his voice in real life, asking Rem's mother if her shop provided services as well as repairs.

"What kind of services were you looking for?" she asked the man from the front desk. She seemed nervous, but I refused to turn around. Refused to let myself believe. It wasn't possible.

In a deliciously husky voice he said, "I'm looking for a pilot."

## From the author...

You've made it to the end of book one!

I'm excited to share with you the next adventure, so don't forget to drop by my website to sign up with my newsletter: www.steviemarie.com entering your email gets you updates on my writing progress, freebies, and more. Or at the bottom of the newsletter you can choose to be updated only when a new release comes out... like book two of The Acatalec Series, *Acatalec Chosen*.

Before you go:

Did you enjoy *Kingdom of Acatalec*?

Reviews help other readers decide to take a chance on something new that they might love too.

It doesn't need to be long. Simply a few words that pop into your head can be very helpful.

None of this would be possible without, you, my fellow readers. I thank you from the bottom of my gooey heart.

Thank you for letting me share my world with you.

You are a book hero!

Chat soon,
S.M. McCoy
www.steviemarie.com

## A word about the author...

Stevie Marie is the author of young adult paranormal fantasy and the Divine Series. Born within the apex of another universe, where magic flows like leaky faucets, and forged from the fires of the Underrealm, she dug her way to Earth and reluctantly participates in human society, secretly returning to her home world to relay the stories of her monsters, and the troubled love of her people. When she isn't writing she's narrating audiobooks, crafting clothing in her sewing room, or surviving mom life in the rainy city of Seattle, Washington.

Website www.steviemarie.com
Bookbub www.bookbub.com/profile/s-m-mccoy
GoodReads www.goodreads.com/steviemccoy
Twitter www.twitter.com/authormarie
Facebook www.facebook.com/AuthorStevie

CPSIA information can be obtained
at www.ICGtesting.com
Printed in the USA
LVHW080547130922
728185LV00015B/531

9 781509 242719